FATAL FLOWERS

A DR PIPPA DURRANT MYSTERY

MIRANDA RIJKS

PROLOGUE

I listen. There's the irregular thrumming of traffic from the adjacent road and my heavy breathing. Otherwise, there is silence. I kick the body. There's no resistance, just his stomach wobbling like a heap of revolting slime. For a moment, I consider moving him. But no. That would be more trouble than it's worth. I've switched off the lights and checked that there is no CCTV.

I'm alone and I'm safe.

I don't allow myself to think about tomorrow and the what-ifs. The man is dead, and he deserved to die. His eyes are open, staring up at the night sky like milky black beads wedged in his narrow face. Unseeing now.

I've done the world a favour.

The anger is still coursing through my veins. I pick up a terracotta pot and am about to hurl it to the ground, but no. If someone is walking along the road, they might hear the smashing of brittle clay on concrete. Instead, I give the body one last kick and stride back into the building. I take my anger out on the plants instead, swiping them off the benches, grinding my heels into their heads, spraying soil all over the floor. But I'm careful. Don't want any footprints left behind. I'm not stupid. Far from it. When I'm at the door, I remove the extra-large slip-on boots that cover my trainers. Two sizes larger than my normal shoes, they are. I place them in a plastic bag and peel off my gloves. My breathing is quieter now and my heart rate back to normal.

I let the light of my torch bounce around the building. Not too much, in case anyone sees it through the glass in the ceiling.

A garden centre is a veritable arsenal of instruments of death and torture. Spades, forks and knives, chemicals, wire. Even those deep fish tanks could work a treat if you're strong and agile enough. But in the end, I chose a simple piece of garden twine. Not the jute string that frays and snaps, but the extra-strong, green and shiny polypropylene twine. It's still in my hand. I wind it up and place it in the bag with the boots and gloves. Later, I'll burn the lot. But for now, I need to go home.

1

'Where's Lily?'

Bella paces up and down the kitchen. It has all the mod cons, with a steamer oven and a Thermomix, those magical machines seen in the *Master Chef* kitchens, and a hot stone inbuilt into the black granite island. Everything sparkles, predominantly because Bella doesn't cook, but also because she has two cleaners, employed on alternate days. Bella wanted the best, and Gerry obliged. And, in return, Gerry travels the world, raking in the dosh importing plants and garden sundries, and bedding any girl who will have him.

Except not today. Gerry is at home, upstairs in his office.

'Sit down,' Annette says. 'You're making me nervous.'

'What am I going to tell the girls?' Bella ignores her mother and runs her manicured fingers through her newly dyed ash-blonde hair.

'Since when do teenage girls watch or listen to the news?' Ollie is seated next to Annette at the kitchen table. He picks at the side of his thumbnail. 'It's much more important that we keep our name out of the press.'

'Your name,' Bella says, her heels clip-clopping on the shiny marble floor. 'Thank God I married Gerry and took his name.'

Ollie thumps his forearms on the table. 'Right. This is what we're going to do. Mum, do a fire sale of the business—'

'What's a fire sale?' Bella says.

Ollie rolls his eyes. 'Sell the business at a low price just to get rid of it.' He turns his head towards Annette. 'As I was saying, sell the business pronto, or just shut the bloody place down. No one is going to want to shop there when they know a murder has taken place.'

'The voyeurs might,' Bella says.

Ollie ignores her. 'The real money, as I've been telling you for years, is in the site. I know at least two developers who would snap it up, apply for planning permission and build a load of nice executive homes. You'll make a few mil. Then you can jet off around the world or do whatever you want to do in your dotage. No hassle. Lots of fun.'

'There's a cruise I fancy. Gerry doesn't want to go, but I could take you, Mum—'

'Belt up, both of you!' Annette screams.

Bella and Ollie look up in alarm. Annette never loses her temper. The tic under her left eye that normally flickers like a gentle butterfly is violently hammering up and down.

'I have no intention of selling the garden centre, now or ever. It's your father's legacy, and it's thanks to him that you're both spoilt, rolling in money. Materialistic.'

Bella and Ollie start talking at the same time.

'That's not fair, Mum,' Ollie spits. 'I've earned a bloody fortune in the City.'

'And I married a wealthy man. The money in trust is used for the girls' schooling and the occasional holiday.'

Ollie and Bella scowl at each other. It's very rare for them to be in agreement, and they seem uncertain how to act in unity.

'The point is, I'm not going to sell, and you can't make me.' Annette enunciates each syllable slowly.

'If you refuse to sell, how are you going to manage this disaster? I've got a mate who runs a PR firm, and they do crisis management.'

Annette places her palms on the table and swivels her legs to the side. With some difficulty she heaves herself up. Bella hates it when her mum puts her large arthritic knuckles and soil-encrusted fingernails anywhere near the table, but she's learned not to say anything.

'I'm going home to take a tincture and spend some time in the potting shed. I don't want to be disturbed. If you get hold of Lily, tell her there's some cold chicken in the fridge.'

'I thought Lily was vegan,' Bella says.

'Last month,' Annette says. She looks every one of her seventy-three years.

Bella and Ollie watch their mother hobble out of the kitchen, both wondering whether the arthritis has stretched its tentacles over the whole of her body.

'Why the hell can't Lily and Stijn look after themselves? They should be making Mum supper, not the other way around. Poor Mum,' Ollie says when they hear her old Volvo spluttering to life. 'Can't be much fun finding a murdered man.' Ollie is good at empathising with his mother when she's not there.

'I've never seen a dead body. Have you?' Bella asks.

'Yes,' Ollie says without elaborating.

They both think of David, their father. He had a massive heart attack five years ago on a business trip to Holland. He returned home in a box, and the coffin was never opened. Annette's tinctures didn't do him any good.

LILY IS A QUIVERING wreck by the time she gets back to Annette's tumbledown farmhouse. The baby of the family, Lily has just turned thirty and still lives at home, even though she married Stijn eleven months ago. Bella used to call her 'the mistake'. Ollie called her 'the afterthought'. Annette had called her Dumpling until, at twenty-one, Lily screamed that she forbade her mother from calling her that ever again. David had called her 'my darling'. When David died, Lily wanted to die too.

She pours herself a brandy from David's stash, kept in a mahogany cupboard in the corner of the living room. After tipping the liquid down her throat in one go, she is still spluttering when she knocks on the door of Annette's potting shed.

'Potting shed' is a bit of a misnomer. It is an extravagant glasshouse built on bricks, held up with wrought-iron struts and electric louvred blinds that automatically open or close depending upon the heat and light, with a door painted oh-so-very-tastefully in Farrow & Ball's Cooking Apple Green. Annette calls it the 'potting shed' in memory of the semi-derelict construction that was its forefather. Everyone knew Bella and Gerry meant well when they packed her off to a spa for a long weekend. They wanted to emulate those television house and garden makeover programmes and give her the ultimate surprise. On Annette's return, she found this magnificent structure had sprouted out of the ground, replacing her very favourite place on earth. Lily had noticed her mother's expression of dismay, which she quickly replaced with a smile, and reached out to hold her hand. Lily knows her mother still misses the original version. It was all too much, happening just eight months after David died. Out with the old, in with the new.

The louvres of the shutters are closed, but Lily can see light escaping around the edges of the pale-green wood.

'Mum, can I come in?'

'Just a moment, Lily,' Annette says. Her voice sounds strangled. 'I'm coming out.'

A few seconds later the lights go off and the door opens. Annette is wearing the same black tent-like dress with its enormous pocket at the waist that she's been wearing all day. Her legs are encased in green tights, and her feet look large and ungainly in khaki rubber clogs. All three children agree that Annette has no dress sense. It wouldn't matter if she had a model figure or was grossly obese; the garments she favours are so shapeless it's irrelevant what is underneath. In fact, Annette is slender. The only parts of her that are oversized are those knuckles and the cascade of fly-away, silver-grey hair she piles on top of her head.

'It's awful, isn't it?'

'I can't believe the bastard cut off all the heads of the houseplants. Those beautiful crimsons and pinks just scattered across the floor. The *Phragmipedium Schroderae*. It makes my heart bleed.'

Lily stares at her mother. Of course it was distressing that the plants were all beheaded, but a murder is far worse than the slashing of an orchid. In fact, to make a comparison is quite ridiculous.

'Come on, love, let's go and eat something.' Annette puts her hand on the small of Lily's slender back. Lily likes to think her mother has magical energy coursing through her, because otherwise how could she get all the plants to grow to be so strong and healthy?

Annette's kitchen is nothing like Bella's. The wooden cupboard doors are stained with ancient sticky finger marks, and the surfaces are ringed with water marks from cups of tea. The oven is from the 1950s, and Annette describes her fridge as modern because she's only had it fifteen years or so. She doesn't have a dishwasher, so every evening it's Lily and Stijn who have to do the washing-up.

Annette takes some chicken leftovers out of the fridge,

whilst Lily puts two baked potatoes in the microwave, an addition that Lily provided when she moved back home.

'I don't want one,' Annette says, pointing at the microwave.

'You need to eat,' Lily says.

'Not hungry, love.'

They both watch the turntable in the microwave go around and around.

'It was awful, wasn't it, Mum?' Lily says, wiping strands of auburn hair off her forehead.

Annette nods.

'The thing is, I'm sure I recognised him from somewhere. He had a narrow face, almost as if someone's put it between two books and squeezed together. I've definitely seen him before, just can't place where.'

Annette shivers. 'I'd rather not talk about it.'

'Other than the fact he was motionless and his skin was grey, you'd never have known he had been strangled. His shirt had a high collar. I didn't even notice the ligature marks. Did you?'

'Lily, change the subject.'

'Oh, Mum, I can't. We need to talk about it. Do you think we'll have any customers?'

Annette sits at the kitchen table and buries her face in her hands. 'People love scandal. I don't suppose it'll make much difference.'

'What are you proposing? Spot the ghost in amongst the terracotta pots?'

'Don't be facile, Lily.' Annette picks up her glass of green-brown mush. She takes a small sip. 'When can we reopen?'

'The day after tomorrow, assuming they finish their forensic examinations as expected.'

Annette pales.

'What is it, Mum? You're normally so brave and practical. Has this got to you?'

'Something like that,' she mutters as she stands up. 'I'm going to bed.'

'But it's only six-thirty!'

'And I'm not as young as I used to be.'

Lily frowns at her mother's retreating back. She can't recall the last time Annette went to bed before midnight. She took to her bed for fifteen long days after David died, but then she snapped right out of it and was back to their normal mum.

Lily sends Ollie a text message.

Mum's acting weird. Lx

What do you expect? Someone was murdered at her beloved business.

It's more than that. Lx

Ollie doesn't reply.

2

PIPPA

It's the headline on BBC South news. A dead body has been discovered in a garden centre near the coast. I'm listening with half an ear, finishing off a cup of coffee, glancing through the notes of the client I'm expecting shortly.

Rocks Garden Centre was established twenty years ago by David Gower, and since his death in 2013, has been run by his wife and other members of the family. The police have not released the name of the deceased.

I close my binder, and an instant later, the phone rings.

It's Detective Sergeant Joe Swain. 'Pippa, we need your help. A dead man has been found in a garden centre.'

'I heard about it on the news.'

'It's murder and we need you. Can you meet me at the garden centre in an hour?'

'I've got a client due any moment, but when I've finished with her, I'll make my way to Worthing. I need to be back here for 6 p.m. though.'

Joe Swain persuaded me to become a consultant psychologist to Sussex police only a few weeks ago. I let him think it took several double espressos and a large piece of chocolate fudge cake to win me over. In fact, it was the fear that I had lost all my clients as a result of my involvement in an earlier murder case. I needed the work. The press headlines lauded me as 'Storrington-based psychologist Doctor Philippa Durrant aka the psycho-hunter'.

And Joe was insistent. 'We couldn't have solved that murder case without you. You have so many specialist skills with your knowledge of lie-detection techniques. It's your duty to help us!'

I sighed and agreed to help the police five days a month, flexible working depending upon their needs and my client list. Such work isn't new to me because I was a forensic psychologist years ago and am well qualified to work with the police. It's just that, these days, I am more comfortable helping private clients suffering with anxiety or stress.

Rocks Garden Centre is positioned on a major coastal road between Worthing and Brighton. From the outside, the car park appears larger than the garden centre itself. A series of dilapidated greenhouses have been knocked together, supported by rusting stanchions. Despite its decrepit appearance, Rocks is something of a legend in West Sussex. Even non-gardeners know about it, visiting for a slice of the best gooey fudge cake in the South, or some handmade soap or a house-plant in a crazily coloured container. According to my green-fingered friend Jane, true horticulturalists won't go anywhere else.

It's late afternoon on a Wednesday, a time when it would normally be busy with elderly customers gossiping over a cup of tea. But the car park is empty. Two police cars are positioned across both the entrance and exit. A blue-and-white police tape cordon is pulled across the entrance. The traffic is almost at a standstill on the main road as people rubberneck to see what's going on.

I indicate and turn into the entrance.

A uniformed policeman puts his large hands on the roof of my car and bends down level with my passenger window. 'Sorry, ma'am, but you can't come in today.'

Mungo growls.

'I'm here to meet Detective Sergeant Joe Swain.'

'And you are?'

'Philippa Durrant.'

'*The* Philippa Durrant, psycho hunter?' His eyes are wide, and he rubs his fingers through his straggly hair.

I squirm.

He unties the tape. 'Can you park at the far end of the car park? They're nearly done looking over the car park.'

There are a couple of people dressed in white paper suits walking slowly outside the entrance, their heads down, gazing at the ground.

The police constable murmurs into a crackling walkie-talkie and then I drive slowly into the car park, the car's wheels crunching over large stones and sinking into deep potholes. As I turn off the engine, a shadow passes over the driver's window. I glance up. Detective Sergeant Joe Swain is looking as dapper as always, wearing a sharply-cut navy suit, smiling with those sparkling large eyes. His dark face is lined with stubble, and I wonder if he is growing a beard. I hope not.

'I've spotted some delphiniums that have your name on them!' Joe says, grinning.

I'm impressed that he remembers my love of blue flowers.

'How can you promise me delphiniums when the place is shut?' I ask.

'Alas, I can't give them to you today. We can't walk through the garden centre, but my understanding is there will be a lot of plants available cut-price in the near future.'

'You're too mean to buy me good quality?'

He shakes his head as he smirks, then opens my car door and stands to one side.

'Wait, Mungo,' I tell my faithful black Labrador. 'I promised him a walk along the seafront,' I explain to Joe as I slip out of the car, grabbing my bag off the passenger seat. 'What's happened?'

'Vandalism and murder, by the looks of things. The body of a middle-aged man was found this morning about 9 a.m. Cause of death appears to be strangulation.'

'Ergh,' I mutter, coming to an abrupt stop, one shoe poised either side of a particularly large muddy puddle. 'You're not going to show me the body, I hope.'

Joe laughs. 'No. The body is covered up. Most of the garden centre is out of bounds as it's still a crime scene, so I'm going to take you to the offices. I want you to meet the owner and a couple of her staff.'

'Have you identified the dead man?'

Joe shakes his head. 'They all claim not to recognise him.'

'Hardly surprising, since this place is open to the public.'

'But that's the thing. According to the forensic team, the man was killed between 8 and 11 p.m. last night. The garden centre is shut then, and none of the staff are admitting to being on-site.'

'Is there CCTV and an alarm system?'

'The place was locked up at 5.40 p.m. yesterday evening and unlocked at 8.16 a.m. this morning. It's not alarmed. Unfortunately, our dead body showed up amongst the terracotta pots, and the only area covered by CCTV is the front of the store, where the tills are.'

'Very convenient,' I murmur as I follow Joe around the side of the main greenhouse.

'Officially, you're here as a psychologist to support the staff through the trauma. Unofficially, I want you to spy on them.'

I stand stock-still. It takes a moment for Joe to realise I'm not following him. He cocks his head to the left and raises his hands as if to show he was joking. I don't find it funny.

'I'm not a spy, and I'm not doing subterfuge. I have a code of ethics to follow and I refuse to breach it. Not for you or anyone.'

Joe strides towards me, his arms outstretched. I step backwards to avoid those large, warm hands grasping my shoulders.

'I'm not asking you to do anything you're not comfortable with. Just let me know if you think anything is untoward. Is that okay? And if you're up for it, you can see these new clients in the evenings. We might even be able to pay you double.' Then he mumbles, 'But probably not.'

I sigh. 'I can't be bought,' I murmur quietly. But I follow him anyway.

The office block is a large Portakabin. We pass two offices with glass windows to the right of the corridor, both empty. There is a closed door at the end. A sign reads 'Staff Room'.

Joe pauses. 'They're in shock. I'll ask some questions, and feel free to butt in.'

'But Joe, I can't do anything now. I've got to be back in Storrington to see a client at six p.m.'

'Fine. We'll introduce you, and they can book time to talk to you over the next few days.'

Before I can say anything, Joe opens the door and stands back to let me in. I am woefully unprepared for this.

I recognise the policewoman – the Family Liaison Officer.

'Janet Curran.' She extends her hand and nods at me. She knows exactly who I am. 'Let me introduce you to the team.'

I look around the small room. There is a sagging sofa and four plastic chairs. A microwave and kettle stand on a simple table adjacent to a stainless-steel sink and a small, battered fridge. The overhead fluorescent light makes my eyes water.

A young woman with pale auburn hair perches on the edge of a chair, two men – both sporting green T-shirts – sit as far away from each other as possible on the sofa, and an older woman is looking out of the window with her back to me.

'I'd like to introduce you all to Doctor Philippa Durrant.' Joe beams at me. 'She's a psychologist and is here to support you through the shock of what has happened. Pippa will arrange times to speak to you all individually and confidentially over the next few days.'

The woman at the window turns around very slowly and stares at me, but not before I notice the fleeting wrinkling at the centre of her brow, the raised upper eyelid and tense, drawn-up lower lids, followed by a brief puckering of the nose and raised cheeks. She has a tic under her eye that starts firing manically. Within half a second, she is smiling at me and extending her hand, but she can't control that tic.

The sight of me invoked fear and dismay.

3

Lily dumps her electric-blue Mini Countryman in the Shire and Horses pub car park opposite Rocks Garden Centre. She slings her canvas bag across her body and jiggles from foot to foot on the side of the road, waiting for a gap in the incessant traffic. Eventually she spots a small space between a white van and a lorry and sprints across the road. The lorry driver puts his right hand on his horn and waves his left hand in disgust. Lily turns around and gives the driver her middle finger. She can't be doing with arseholes today.

She ducks underneath the blue-and-white tape that seals off the entrance to the garden centre car park and dashes towards the front door.

'Excuse me, miss.' The young policeman holds out a hand as if to stop her. 'We're closed.'

'I know you're bloody closed. I'm the owner – well, the owner's daughter. I need to speak to your boss. The tall, black man.'

'DS Joe Swain? He's not here yet.'

'What's he doing? Having a leisurely fry-up at the greasy spoon?'

The policeman opens his mouth, then shuts it again.

'Oh, forget it!' Lily says, scowling.

'I don't think you're allowed in.' The young lad is no match for Lily when she's in one of her up moods.

'Tough,' she mutters, pushing the door open with her small backside. 'The plants aren't going to water themselves.'

She throws the policeman a sneer and then, feeling sorry for him standing there like an idiot with his fluffy facial hair and gormless gaze, she winks at him before turning away. She doesn't have to see him to know that he will be flushed scarlet. Lily does that to young men.

She stands and slowly looks around the houseplants greenhouse. It's a mess. There isn't a single flower, or even a bud, left on any plant. Many have been knocked over, and compost – which is scattered with petals, crushed flowers and shards of broken pots – has been tossed across the floor.

Lily feels her bottom lip tremble. She's like her mum in that regard. Lily loves plants. She talks to them. She feels their energy, and right now she's standing in the midst of a bloodbath.

It doesn't even smell right. Normally the atmosphere is heavy with moisture, the sweet scent of flowers mingled with earthy peat and high humidity. Lily has never been to a rainforest, but she reckons her houseplants section would be just like a tropical rainforest. She weaves through the benches, taking care not to tread on any flower heads, her nose quivering at the odour of decay.

She needs to go outside to her tool shed, but doing so she'll have to walk past the terracotta pots where the dead man had been found. Not feeling strong enough for that, she paces over to the sundries area, selects a long-handled brush, tears the cardboard packaging off and carries it back to houseplants. The rhythmic sweeping is therapeutic, even if it breaks her heart to see all her little babies destroyed.

'Shit!'

She drops the brush. If they're not letting anyone in, Sandra, the girl who runs the pet concession, won't be in. The fish and small animals won't get fed; their cages won't be cleaned. Lily loves plants, but she's not so keen on rodents and even less keen on fish. She walks over to the pet department. The hamsters are making a racket, pumping their little feet on their hamster wheels. Lily has no idea what to feed them with. She takes her mobile out of her pocket and searches for Sandra's telephone number.

She's waiting for the phone to connect when there's a cough behind her. Lily jumps and drops the phone.

'S-s-sorry, sorry...' the young policeman stutters.

'What is it?' Lily snaps. There's something about him that makes her feel superior. Perhaps it's his voice, which sounds like it hasn't quite broken. She wonders if he gets teased back at the station.

'There's a man in a lorry asking for you. We haven't let the lorry in because of...Well, anyway, it's blocking the road a bit, so you might want to come out front.'

Lily rolls her eyes as she bends down to pick up her phone. She's got a missed WhatsApp call from Stijn. Her heart does a little somersault. They have been messaging each other ever since the body was found. The last message she sent him was at 2 am, a rambling, semi-coherent diatribe about the dead man and her fears and how she wished Stijn was there to wrap her up in his strong, protective arms. That's the trouble with having a foreign husband and, worse still, one who's a truck driver. He's never around when she needs him most.

'What's his name?' Lily asks, her eyes bright with anticipation.

'Some foreign name.'

'Stijn Eikenboom?'

'Something like that.'

Lily does a little hop of joy and then races through the pet department, weaving through the sundries, leaping over the mess in houseplants and out past the tills and through the exit.

He's standing at the entrance, hands on hips, head tilted to one side, fair hair floppy, bright-blue eyes flashing, his face covered in dark-blond stubble. The articulated lorry is half pulled up on to the verge, its hazard lights flashing, traffic backing up behind it as far as the eye can see. 'Shelton Bros' is written in green across the sides.

'God, I'm happy to see you!' Lily throws herself on him.

'I'm God now, am I?' He nuzzles his face into her auburn hair. At six feet three inches, he towers over her. Lily isn't short, but she feels minuscule in Stijn's arms.

'Can I take you here?' he murmurs. 'In the back of the truck?'

Lily loves Stijn's guttural accent. She pulls back from him.

'We've had a murder at the nursery. It's awful,' Lily says.

Stijn rubs his finger over Lily's wet lips and slowly puts it in his mouth, sucking hard.

'I know. It's awful, but you are so beautiful and I'm horny.' He thrusts his bulging crotch forwards.

'Excuse me, sir, but you can't leave your lorry there.'

The young policeman materialises behind Lily. Stijn will eat him for breakfast, Lily thinks.

'I'll drive round the back then. You'll open the gates for me, won't you, baby?'

Lily blows him a kiss as he hauls himself back into the truck, sliding into the driver's seat. Lily does another jig as she races around the side of the building, running as quickly as she can past the back of the algae-encrusted glasshouses, bounding over potholes, until she reaches the trades entrance. She removes a bunch of keys from the pocket of her apron, selects a small silver key and slides it into the padlock.

'Miss, miss!' The policeman is out of breath. 'Miss, you can't let him in. No unauthorised people until the DI gives the say-so.'

Lily swings the gate open and stands to one side to let the supersized truck pass through. She grins at Stijn as he sticks his tongue out at her and jiggles it from side to side.

'No!' the policeman wails.

But there is nothing he can do. Stijn's truck is through, and Lily is running towards it.

Stijn bends down, his arms outstretched towards Lily.

'Get in,' he says, his voice husky. '*Ik ben geil*,' he murmurs to himself.

Lily knows what it means: 'I am horny.' The only phrases she knows in Dutch are related to sex. Stijn is a good teacher. They've made love many times on the narrow bed wedged behind the driver's seat in Stijn's truck.

'There are police around, and it's eight thirty in the morning and we've had a murder here,' Lily says, trying, but failing, to resist Stijn's strong pull.

'All the more reason,' Stijn says, unbuttoning his fly slowly, seductively.

'Mrs Eikenboom!'

The voice is deep. Lily starts and turns around. She stumbles with one foot on and the other foot off the truck step.

Detective Sergeant Joe Swain puts out a hand to steady her. Lily sees the flash of annoyance in Stijn's eyes and she mouths, *I'm sorry*.

'Why is this gentleman here?'

Lily struggles to stifle a snigger. If there is anyone who isn't a gentleman, it's her rough-and-ready husband.

'This is Stijn, my husband. He's dropping off a delivery. We've got a business to run. We can't turn a plant delivery away. They're living creatures, you know. Need looking after.'

Joe nods. 'Can you offload quickly please, and then leave?'

'He's family!' Lily says, her face creased with indignation.

'When you've finished offloading, sir, perhaps you could make yourself known to my colleague. We need to ask you some questions.'

'What? Why?' Lily explodes.

'We have spoken to all other employees but not to Stijn. As a matter of procedure, we need to eliminate him from our enquiries.'

'Is it because he's foreign?' Lily puts her hands on her hips and thrusts out her lower lip. 'And what about Gerry? I bet you haven't interviewed him. Gerry Shelton. He's my sister's husband.'

'It's fine, Lily. Let it go.' Stijn places his arms on top of the large steering wheel and leans forwards. Lily can't take her eyes off Stijn's open fly. 'I've got a few deliveries to do around Sussex. I'll see you later.'

Joe nods, turns around and walks back towards the garden centre.

'I'll help you offload now,' Lily says to Stijn.

'Come here. I'm so hard. I need you now.'

Lily opens her mouth as if to answer, but then she follows Stijn's eyes. The tall, black policeman has turned around and is staring at them.

'*Verdomme*,' Stijn swears in Dutch.

He does up his flies, opens the driver's door and jumps down. Lily dances around the lorry to meet him. She puts out her hand as if to cup his genitals.

'Not now.' Stijn pushes her away.

'I thought you were horny,' Lily says breathlessly.

'Not now.'

Stijn walks past her. At the back of the lorry he swings open the doors, presses a button to lower the tail lift and in no time has offloaded seven trolleys packed full of houseplants and several large containers of garden furniture, lifted out as effortlessly as if the boxes were empty. He strides back to the front of the lorry, hops up, leans inside and returns with a docket.

Handing it to Lily, he says, 'The paperwork for you.'

'But can't we?'

'Meet me at the flat in an hour.'

She nods.

4

PIPPA

A psychologist should never judge a client, not when they first meet or anytime during the client and patient relationship. Being judgmental isn't listed per se in the British Psychological Society's code of ethics, but it certainly sits outside the four ethical principles of respect, competence, responsibility and integrity. But we're all human, and despite my concerted efforts not to judge people, I still do.

They were an odd bunch, the management team at Rocks Garden Centre. The boss, Annette Gower, an ageing hippie, looked as if she should have retired a while back, but it was her reaction to me that raised suspicions. I suppose she must have recognised me from the news or else she was unhappy to be faced with a psychologist. I'll find out soon; I'm on my way to meet her now.

Her daughter, Lily, who introduced herself as deputy manageress and general dogsbody, has a perfectly symmetrical face and a beauty that doesn't seem to fit with her grubby hands and ripped jeans. The two men seated as far away from each other as physically possible on a small sofa, were employees, departmental managers. I can't even remember their names. The final person was a woman with large doughy arms and a face that reminded me of a hot-cross bun – round and marked with moles and dimples. She manages the coffee shop.

As I slow down to turn into the entrance to the garden centre, I spot them: a huddle of journalists wielding cameras and microphones. There is no way I am going anywhere near them. My face is too familiar, and the thought of the press badgering me again brings me out in a cold sweat. I put my foot on the accelerator and carry straight on. When my heart has slowed down, I call Joe.

'Sorry, Pippa. I hadn't thought that one through. Come in via the back on Sea Place Lane. It's a little-used trades entrance, and there's no one there. I'll open the gate for you.'

I swing the car around and drive back the way I came, turning right at the roundabout. I almost drive past it. The sign, 'Rock's Nursery Trade', is inconspicuous.

Joe opens the gate for me. By the time I have parked up, Joe is on the phone, pacing backwards and forwards, talking rapidly with an earnest expression on his face. I would like to smooth out the creases on his forehead, but instead I stand awkwardly to one side, waiting for him to finish his conversation.

'Thanks for doing this, Pippa.' Joe shoves his phone in his pocket. 'The SOCOs have all left. The garden centre will reopen to the public tomorrow, and we're letting the staff back in this afternoon to clear up. We've identified the body, but we're not making that public knowledge yet.'

'Who is he?'

Joe hesitates. That annoys me. He trusts me enough to request my help, yet he's wary of giving me too much information. I know he's only doing his job, but still...

'Forget it,' I say, and start walking towards the office.

He rapidly catches up with me. 'He's called Scott McDermott. Sixty-three years old, from Findon.'

'What was he doing in a garden centre?'

'That's exactly what we need to find out.'

We walk in silence. Joe holds open the door. 'Annette Gower is waiting for you. First door on the right. Come and find me when you're finished. I look forward to the feedback. You'll tell me everything, won't you?'

I snap. 'No, Joe. If I discover anything illegal, then I will share it with you, but otherwise, not.'

'Not even if you think she's lying?'

'I will take a view. But please understand, I will not break my code of ethics for you or anyone.'

He is silent. I wonder if he's regretting involving me, spending budget unwisely. But it's too late now. I'm inside, and three steps later I'm knocking on Annette Gower's door.

I have to squeeze past boxes filled with merchandise, a cluster of ailing plants and papers piled on every surface, in order to navigate the three steps to the chair facing Annette's desk. Her eyes are sunken, surrounded by purple rings, and that little flickering nerve is pinging rapidly.

'How are you feeling?' I ask as I settle down in the chair.

'I'm fine. Absolutely fine. It's my children and the staff that we need to be worried about. I really don't know why I need to be talking to you. No offence, or anything. What are you going to do to support them?'

Annette Gower is not fine. She tries very hard to convince me, and perhaps herself, and if I wasn't such a seasoned professional, I might have missed it. I note the way she avoids giving a straight answer, how she asks a question in response, how she claims to fail to understand. I look at her body language, the rocking in her chair, that tic under her eye, the smoothing down of her tunic dress.

'I'm very sorry about the tragedy that happened here.' I

show her the palms of my hands, the vulnerable parts of my wrists. Unconsciously, she mimics my body language, and her shoulders relax downwards. 'You have a beautiful garden centre. Alas, I'm no great horticulturalist myself, but all my keen gardening friends won't shop anywhere else.'

'Thanks. That's good to know.' She sinks farther into her chair. Her smile reaches the corners of both eyes, and her lips rise equally on both sides.

'How can I support you?' I ask.

'You can't.' She crosses her arms across her chest and stares beyond my shoulder, her eyes glazing over.

'I gather from DS Swain that you found the body.'

She nods.

'Did you know him, Scott McDermott?'

I hope I haven't overstepped the mark by telling her his name, but Joe was so cursory with his instructions. Nevertheless, I'm ready. And there it is. The raised eyebrows, the flat lower lip, that micro-expression of fear.

'No, I've never seen him before.' Her hands rise to her face, and she places her palms across her reddening cheeks. 'I'm sorry. I feel nauseous every time I think about him, seeing his lifeless body lying there.'

'That's quite understandable,' I say, thinking that if she was feeling nauseous, the blood would be draining from her face, and perhaps specks of perspiration would appear on her brow and upper lip. This cluster of reactions points to a lie.

Annette Gower knew the dead man.

'How do you think he got in, late at night?'

She peers at me. 'I thought you were here to support me, not to act as a police informant or an inquisitor.'

'You're right. My apologies. Tell me how I can support you.'

'To be blunt, Doctor Durrant, I don't need support from anyone except my closest family. I'm lucky to have my children living nearby, and my youngest, Lily, and her husband live with me. I'm not some old, lonely widow in need of psychological support.'

That's me put back in my box.

'Do you have children?' she asks.

'This conversation isn't about me.'

I study this woman. She is wily. She may look like an ageing hippie, but there is something sharp about her, a skin of hide that I am struggling to pierce.

Annette Gower places the palms of her hands on the edge of her desk and levers herself out of the chair. 'However well-meaning DS Swain is – and, indeed, you are – I think we're done here. I'll see you out.'

'What did your mother say?' Gerry asks.

'That she's not selling the business. Same old.'

Bella is painting her nails. She hasn't done her own nails in years, but her manicurist is on holiday, and she'd rather do it herself than chance a visit to someone she doesn't know. Someone who might have questionable hygiene. Someone who might not have scrubbed their hands between clients.

'It's nonsense. All she's doing is devaluing the place, and with a murder on the premises, who the hell is going to want to visit it now?'

Gerry paces up and down the kitchen, his hard leather shoes clacking against the marble. No one in horticulture wears suits and ties except Gerry. Sometimes he even dons a natty bow tie, in green, of course. Gerry takes his branding very seriously.

'I suppose your avaricious brother came up with some scheme for selling off the land,' Gerry mutters.

Bella looks up, the little brush in her right hand heavy with pale-pink varnish. She's still in her satin, floral dressing gown that slips off her shoulders. 'Yeah, he did actually.'

'Look, Bella.' Gerry kneels down in front of her, his knees creaking. Sometimes Bella regrets marrying a man twelve years older than her, even if his sexual appetite is thrice hers.

'Don't touch me. You'll smudge my nails.'

He ignores her. 'You need to speak to your mum. I've told her before that I'll happily take over the running of the garden centre. Vertical integration makes a lot of sense. I can speak to some potential investors and buy her out, or I can—'

'Gerry, belt up. Go and speak to her yourself. I'm not getting involved in stuff I don't understand.'

Gerry grabs the overhang of the marble work surface to steady himself as he stands up. He knocks over the little pot of nail varnish. The viscous, pale-pink varnish spreads slowly across the black marble.

'Fuck,' they both say, staring at the little puddle.

'I'll go and see her tonight.' Gerry straightens his tie and bends down to pick up his briefcase.

'You've barely got time to run your own business let alone take on another one,' Bella says, frowning.

She's trying to wipe up the nail varnish with a paper towel.

'I'll put in a manager.'

'What about Lily?' Bella asks.

'What about her?'

'Could she run it?'

Gerry roars with laughter. Spittle foams at the corners of his lips. 'That's almost as ridiculous as suggesting her lazy prick of a husband run it.'

'Why did you employ him if you don't like him?'

'I didn't think he'd become family,' Gerry mumbles. He slams the door behind him.

. . .

OLLIE GOWER DOESN'T WORK ANYMORE. That's the advantage of being employed by an American investment bank in the City of London from the age of nineteen. After stacking up a few million in bonuses, Ollie decided to retire aged thirty-one and make way for some up-and-coming youngsters.

That's the story he spun, repeated so often that he has come to believe it himself. In reality, he had to jump before he was pushed. Nowadays, Ollie spends a lot of time sailing around the Med and the Caribbean. He gets involved in the occasional deal. He used to scoop healthy dividends along the way. These days, funds are running through his fingers like sand. At least his appetite for cocaine has lessened since Fabian became a permanent feature in his life. Not that the rest of the family know about Fabian. There are many things Ollie keeps to himself.

Ollie is still in bed, languishing on silk sheets. Fabian is naked, upside down on the floor at the foot of the bed in some contortionist tantric yoga pose. As much as he loves Fabian's body, Ollie can't watch. He reaches across the bed and grabs the television remote control. He flicks through the channels until he finds the news.

'Must you?' Fabian asks. His voice sounds strange from his upside-down position. 'I need silence to finish off my routine.'

'Piss off downstairs or somewhere else altogether,' Ollie hisses. He turns the volume up on the television. 'Shit, I'm sure I know him.' Ollie sits bolt upright in bed.

Fabian is now sitting cross-legged, his hands in the prayer position.

'*Namaste*,' he murmurs.

He bounces from his cross-legged position up on to the end of the bed in one fluid movement.

'Know who?'

'That man.'

They both listen to the broadcaster. 'Scott McDermott was

found dead at Rocks Garden Centre near Worthing in West Sussex two days ago. The police have launched a murder enquiry.'

'Scott McDermott. Who was he? Doesn't look like your type.' Fabian shimmies up the bed and starts nibbling at Ollie's neck. Ollie pushes him away. His eyes are narrowed, his forehead in a frown. 'Bugger. I can't remember where I know him from, but I'm sure I recognise his face.'

The doorbell rings.

Ollie clambers out of bed, pulls on a pair of underpants and strides to the window. He tugs back the curtain an inch and peers on to the street.

'What the hell is Gerry doing here?'

He lets the curtain fall back. The doorbell chimes again.

'Go and lock yourself in the dressing room and don't come out until I tell you to,' Ollie says.

Fabian pouts but doesn't move. Ollie is hastily tugging on a T-shirt and pair of jeans.

'Go!' he screams at Fabian, before bolting out of the room and down the stairs. He glances at himself in the ornate gilt mirror in the hallway, plasters on a smile and opens the front door.

'Gerry! What a surprise! Come in, old man! What brings you to Hove? Were you passing? Got time for a coffee?'

'Sure,' Gerry says, following Ollie into the kitchen.

'Excuse the pun, but this murder must be the final nail in the coffin,' Gerry says.

Ollie sniggers but stops when he realises Gerry isn't smiling.

'Bella and I think I should buy the business off your mother so she can retire in peace.'

'You?' Ollie puts his finger on the top-of-the-range Jura coffee machine.

'Either I can buy the whole thing outright or—'

'There's just been a bloody murder there. Surely it isn't the right time to be–'

'That's the thing. It is.'

Ollie sighs and hands Gerry an espresso. There is a crash from upstairs.

'What's that?' Gerry asks.

'My cleaner.' Ollie curses under his breath. 'She's useless. Always breaking things.'

'Anyway, as I was saying, I'd like to buy the garden centre. What do you reckon?'

Ollie rubs his chin. He doesn't want to offend Gerry, but he thinks it's a ridiculous idea. He did a credit check on Gerry's business only a few months ago, and Gerry is massively over-stretched, mortgaged to the hilt. Ollie wonders how he sleeps at night, owing so much to that many people. The fancy house, the fast cars – he reckons it's all on credit, an illusion. He's never said anything to anyone because, as much as Bella annoys him, she's family, and there's no point in rocking the boat unnecessarily. But Ollie is not prepared to risk his inheritance of the garden centre on a dreamer.

'To be honest, I think we'd earn more money by shutting the place down and selling the land to a developer. It's prime real estate.'

'You might be right, but we're talking about your parents' legacy here. It's not just about money. Your dad built up that business, and I'm sure that's why your mum doesn't want to sell it. There's too much emotion involved. If I buy it, the business would stay in the family. Your mum can potter around to her heart's content, and Lily can keep her job.'

'I thought employing one person in the family was enough of a headache for you.'

'Stijn. Yes, well, he hardly counts.' Gerry takes a large sip of coffee, but it's too hot, and he grimaces as it burns his tongue.

'Anyway, why don't you think about it? Let's bring it up at supper tomorrow night.'

'Is Mum up to her regular Thursday evening supper?' Ollie had assumed she'd bail out with all the stress of the week.

'As far as I'm aware, it's still on. Bella mentioned it.'

Gerry pours the remainder of his espresso into the sink. 'Must be off now. Things to do, people to see and all that.'

Pompous prick, Ollie thinks.

'Let's see what Annette says tomorrow.' He moves towards the door.

'Actually, Gerry, give me some time to think about it. Tomorrow is too soon.'

Ollie can't see the scowl on Gerry's face, as he has his back to him. But at that exact moment Fabian pokes his head over the stair banister and sees Gerry's face contort with anger, his fingers white as they grip the handle of his briefcase.

6

'Where are you going?' Annette catches Lily trying to sneak back out.

'I've got a doctor's appointment.'

Lily is annoyed with herself for saying that. Now her mum will either be worried or wonder if there's a baby on the way. And there isn't.

'Are you all right?'

'Yes, nothing to worry about.'

Annette looks sceptical.

'I'll be back as soon as I can. A couple of hours tops.'

Lily skedaddles around the side of the greenhouses, ducking out of view of the policemen, and then sprints across the road to her car. She sees the back of Stijn's lorry disappear around the corner.

Stijn's flat is on the second floor of a small block of flats on the outskirts of Pulborough, near the station. Every year the block gets flooded. The River Arun fills up, bursts its banks and spills across the fields into the houses and apartments that have been built on the flood plain. Defences have been constructed over the past few years, but Stijn's block still gets affected.

Unsurprisingly, the bottom flats lie empty, unrentable and unsaleable. Lily wonders whether the block is safe or whether the foundations are crumbling through dampness. Perhaps one day the whole place will tumble down.

When they first got engaged, Lily suggested she move in with Stijn. He clasped her close and said, 'I'd never put anyone as precious as you in a dump like this. Let's save up for a place of our own.'

'When are you going to sell this place?' Lily had asked.

'It's worthless. There's no point in selling it. Let's keep it as our secret hideaway.'

Lily thought that was so romantic, and now they use it as their bonking pad. Lily carried on living at home, and when they got married, Stijn moved in with her and Annette. Once Lily nearly let slip about the secret flat.

'I'm going to Stijn's place,' she said to her mother.

'What?'

'I mean, where he parks up the lorry. That trading estate near Storrington. Next to Gerry's warehouse.'

She thinks she got away with the bluster.

However fast Lily drives, Stijn always gets there first. It doesn't make sense to her, as she's in a nippy car, whilst Stijn is driving an articulated lorry. He parks the lorry in the half-empty trading estate around the back of the block of flats, tucked away so no one can see the Shelton Bros lorry parked up where it shouldn't be.

She rings on Flat 5's doorbell. The buzzer sounds and the lock on the front door releases. She races up the stairs. Stijn is standing in the doorway, naked.

'What if someone sees you?' Lily gasps.

He doesn't answer but pulls her inside, kicking the front door shut behind them and making love to her right there in the hallway. He's rough this time and quick. Quicker than usual. Rougher than usual. Lily feels like crying, but she turns her head towards the wall and bites her lower lip.

'Hey you,' Stijn says, grinning at her lasciviously.

Lily blinks the tears away. Perhaps this is what it's like once a relationship has settled down. More about fulfilling carnal needs than tender love. She wouldn't know. Despite her angelic face and curvaceous body, Lily only had one boyfriend before Stijn. And he was a married man fifteen years her senior.

Lily bends down and pulls her knickers back up, adjusting her skirt and blouse. 'I need a glass of water. Do you want anything?'

Stijn is sitting on the floor, panting. 'No.'

She walks into the little kitchen, finds a clean glass and turns on the tap. 'It smells funny in the flat,' she calls out to Stijn.

'The cannabis plants,' Stijn says. 'They'll be ready for harvesting soon.'

Lily doesn't do drugs. The first time Stijn offered her a spliff, she looked at him with big eyes. He hasn't stopped teasing her since.

'I'm Dutch. Of course I smoke dope,' he said. It was another of his reasons for keeping the flat. 'I could grow my plants at your mum's, but I don't think she'd approve.'

Stijn had smirked. Lily laughed in agreement. She supposes there are a lot more dangerous things than cultivating a couple of marijuana plants.

'Come back here, Lils. I haven't finished with you yet.'

Lily puts her empty glass in the sink and walks back into the hall. The walls are scuffed and dirty.

Stijn raises a hand up towards her.

'No, Stijn, I can't. I've got to get back to the garden centre.'

'Oh come on!' he groans. 'I'm ready for more.'

'I can see that.' She smiles coyly. She still gets a little embarrassed looking at her husband in all his large, naked glory. 'But I've got to go back. Mum's waiting for me. The place is a tip, and the police are still there.'

Stijn drops Lily's hand. 'Annette's at work?'

'Yes.'

'Wow. I thought she'd be staying at home, what with all the shock. I was going to offer to come in and help you clear up, but if Annette is there, I'll steer clear.'

Lily knows Stijn isn't keen on her mother, but it still hurts when he articulates it.

'Haven't you got any deliveries to do today?'

'Of course I have,' Stijn snaps. 'I was only trying to be nice.' He stands up and throws on his clothes.

'I know, and I appreciate it. I'll see you tonight, okay?' She leans towards him to give him a kiss, but he dodges away, and Lily is left swaying mid-air.

'I'll be late tonight. Might not even make it back.'

He strides into the bathroom and locks the door behind him.

'Where are you going?' Lily asks.

She waits for his answer, but it doesn't come.

7

PIPPA

'Pippa, hold on!' Joe is striding across the car park towards me. I have my hand on the car door.

'I've finished talking to Annette Gower, your suspect.'

'Annette Gower isn't my suspect!'

'She should be.' I climb into the driver's seat.

'Wait, Pippa. What do you mean?'

'She's lying. She knew the dead man.'

'She has a solid alibi.'

'She could have an accomplice.'

'What's the motive?' Joe's smile is smug, as if he has caught me out. It annoys me.

'I don't know, Joe. It's your job to find out.' I make the tone of my voice as sarcastic as I can.

'She's a seventy-something-year-old lady with a solid alibi. She may have been lying about something—'

'She knew the dead man,' I repeat.

'So you say. What else did you discover?'

'Nothing, I'm afraid.'

Joe's phone rings and he turns his back on me. He strides towards the garden centre without looking back, and is swallowed up inside the building.

As I drive out of the tradesman's entrance, I switch on the radio. It's tuned into BBC Southern Counties.

Police have released the name of the man found deceased at Rocks Garden Centre. Scott McDermott, from Findon, West Sussex has been described by neighbours as a businessman who keeps himself to himself. Detective Sergeant Joe Swain has confirmed that this is a murder enquiry but would not be drawn on further details.

I turn the radio off again. As I head north, I wonder about Scott McDermott. I have no doubt Annette Gower knew him, but why did she deny it? Is she the murderer? With her arthritic joints and slender stature, it seems unlikely. But perhaps she set it up, paid an accomplice to do it for her. I liked that idea when I first articulated it, and the more I think about it, the more it resonates. But why kill him at Rocks Garden Centre? That doesn't make any sense.

As I approach the roundabout, having driven over Long Furlong, the stretch of road that sweeps over the top of the South Downs, I hit traffic. I hear sirens. After ten minutes of not moving, the traffic starts inching forwards. Ten minutes later and I am only just in sight of the roundabout. There is no way I will make it home in time to meet my next client.

I fumble around for her telephone number, call her, apologise profusely, and explain that I have had to deal with an emergency. I offer her a free session to make up for the inconvenience.

Eventually, I arrive at the roundabout. The traffic is backed up on the A24 northbound. There must have been an accident. Straight over is the village of Findon, somewhere I regularly drive past but never visit. I decide to make a diversion. I didn't get much information out of Annette Gower. Perhaps I can find some things out about Scott McDermott instead.

It's a sweet village with a central square and a few shops, and a mixture of elegant houses in pastiche styles. I drive around rather aimlessly, but then I spot the police cars. Two of them parked up in front of a fine Georgian house, probably mock-Georgian, I decide, but large nevertheless and well looked after, with neat borders and freshly painted garage doors. This must be Scott McDermott's home.

On a whim, I park up two streets away. I regret not having Mungo with me. A woman walking a Labrador rarely draws attention. I nip into the newsagent's. A stout woman wearing a full-length lilac raincoat and with grey hair tinged with mauve is speaking in a loud whisper.

'Shocking, isn't it? I only spoke to Mr McDermott last week, asking him if it was blue or green bins week. Green, he said. Ever so polite he was. The poor man. Never saw anyone going in or out, and it's such a big house to be living in all alone, don't you think?'

'Yes, a tragedy.' The younger woman hands over a half pint of milk and a newspaper. 'Would you like a bag for that, Mrs Jones?'

'No, brought my own, love!' She holds up a Tesco bag. 'I don't think he worked. Well, if he did, he didn't keep regular hours. What do you know?'

'Probably a lot less than you, Mrs Jones.'

She spots me listening in and winks at me. I flash a cursory smile back, pick up a bar of chocolate and make my way to the till.

'I'll be in tomorrow, and I'll let you know what the police have got to say. They rang on my doorbell this morning. Ever so exciting. But then again, poor Mr McDermott.'

'See you tomorrow, Mrs Jones.' The older woman gets the hint and shuffles out of the shop.

'Sorry about that,' she says, accepting my change. 'Are you from the press?'

'No!' I exclaim.

'It's just we've had one or two of them nosing around here in the last twenty-four hours. Enough gossip to keep the locals going for a decade.'

'Yes, it's quite shocking. Did you know him?'

'Yeah, I did actually. But I wasn't going to let on to Mrs Jones, our local blabbermouth. Bless her, she's lovely. Just a bit lonely and likes a bit of a stir.'

'We've got a couple like her in my village,' I say, popping the chocolate into my handbag. 'Rocks Garden Centre is my favourite shop in Sussex. I was only there last week.' I feel bad about lying but console myself that it's only a small lie.

'Yeah, me too. He was a keen gardener, was Mr McDermott. My son Billy is a handyman and does for quite a few of the oldies in Findon, but Mr McDermott didn't want him. Said he maintained his own garden, but he employed a landscape designer woman. As far as I know, he did his own cleaning too. A bit of a recluse. He spent money on the house, done it up fine, and he was often spotted in the garden, tidying up the borders and raking his drive. Poor chap.'

'Indeed. I hope the press aren't too intrusive.'

'No. Nothing we can't handle. Just feel sorry for his relatives – if he's got any left, that is. And for the Gowers finding a body in their shop. Such a lovely family. Was a real blow to everyone when David Gower dropped dead from a heart attack.'

'Do you think Mr McDermott knew the Gowers?' I glance around the shop and am relieved that luck is on my side and I'm the only customer.

She rolls her bottom lip. 'No idea. But with a property as

neat as his, I'm sure he'd have been a regular. He was forever pottering around in his garden.'

'Didn't he work?'

'He must have run some business or other from home, because he sent parcels every week. All over the world, they went. Me and Susie, who helps me out, used to joke that we'd pass our geography O level just from learning the names of the places Mr McDermott sent his parcels to. We'll miss him. He was a good customer here too. It's like tragedy striking twice after what happened to his daughter. I don't think he ever got over it.'

The door tinkles as someone walks in.

'Over what?' I ask.

'I've got a delivery for you. Where shall I put it?'

The man's arms are covered with intricate green tattoos that weave up under his grey T-shirt and wind their way up his neck around to the base of his skull. He wheels in a trolley full of boxes of confectionery and comes to a halt two inches from my feet.

'Sorry, love, need to deal with this,' the shop manageress says.

'Yes, of course,' I say. 'I hope things calm down around here.'

'Thanks, love. See you around.'

I WISH I knew what the shopkeeper meant when she said it was like a tragedy striking twice, that something had happened to Scott McDermott's daughter. Hearing those words was akin to being speared in the heart, bringing back memories of my beautiful Flo, my daughter who went to South Africa and never came home.

As I get back into the car and start driving, I try to think about something else, to concentrate on the road, which is now clear of traffic, but I can't. I need to find out what happened to Scott McDermott's daughter, what sort of business he was running from home. I race back up the A24, hurrying so I can get home in time to Google him before my next client arrives.

8

Gerry's business is located on a trading estate off the A27 near Arundel. He has a large warehouse and a fleet of six lorries. Although he likes to give the image that he's a high-flying, successful businessman driving a shiny Lexus and living in a new executive home, with two daughters at boarding school, the reality is he's a wheeler-dealer importing horticultural goods from across the world, predominantly plants from Holland and Italy, and sundries from China. In theory, with its wide diversification, the business should be healthy; in reality, it's subject to the fluctuations in exchange rates – rates that haven't been favourable in recent times. In fact, Shelton Bros has been accumulating worrying losses, losses that Gerry has to keep to himself. Everyone in horticulture knows everyone else. Gerry likens it to one big unhappy family.

After leaving Ollie's, Gerry climbs back into his car and slams the door. He is in a foul mood. He didn't handle the conversation with Ollie well, and decides he needs to keep the emotion out of things and focus on the hard facts and figures to convince the family that he is the man to run Rocks Garden Centre. But first he texts Mae.

Need to see you NOW

At work. Will call u later

Make an excuse. Meet me at the Premier Inn in Arundel. 30 mins

He taps his fingers on the Lexus's steering wheel, waiting for her response. After three minutes he calls her mobile. It goes straight to voicemail. He swears under his breath, then leaves a message.

'Call me.'

He starts the engine and pulls out of the parking space in front of Ollie's house. Putting his foot on the accelerator, he enjoys the powerful thrust of the car as he drives too fast down to the seafront. Gerry already has six points on his licence, so when he sees a police car in his rear mirror, he slows right down. The phone rings.

'I'll be there.'

'Good girl,' Gerry says. 'I knew you'd do the right thing.'

Turning back inland, he weaves up to the A27 and then, speeding again, he makes it to the Premier Inn in twenty-five minutes, beating his satnav's original time estimate by nine minutes. Tucking his car around the back of the ivory-coloured building, he saunters into the reception, glancing around to ensure he doesn't recognise anyone.

'A room please.'

'Yes, sir. Check-in is at twelve noon. Would you prefer a double or twin?'

'I need the room now. A double. Can't wait until noon. I'm exhausted after a long flight. I'll pay cash up front.' Too much information, he thinks, as he surreptitiously peers at the receptionist and wonders if she's judging him.

She fiddles around with the computer. He catches a glimpse of Mae, but she knows the routine, slipping into the stairwell and waiting. The anticipation is too much. He feels more like a hormonal teenager unable to control his hard-on than a fifty-five-year-old man.

'Room Seventeen, sir.'

She hands him the key card, which Gerry grabs. He sprints back towards the staircase.

Mae is lingering there, still in her uniform, biting her lip, soil under her fingernails. He pulls her towards him roughly, grinding his loins into hers.

'Not here!' she whispers loudly, trying to push him away. He races up the short flight of stairs into the corridor, only slowing down when he sees the chambermaid's cleaning trolley. The key card doesn't open the door. He tries again and again, swearing.

'Here, give it to me!'

Mae reaches for it. It opens. She walks in first, into a room that looks identical to the others they have frequented.

Gerry pounces on her from behind, pushing her onto the bed, tugging his trousers down, wrenching up her skirt.

'What's the urgency?' she asks, pushing him upwards so she can turn over onto her back. 'We're not scheduled to meet.'

'Crap morning,' he says, panting.

'So you're trying to take it out on me?'

She places the palms of her hands against his chest, briefly closing her azure eyes, unable to stop a look of disappointment from flitting across her face.

'No. It's nothing like that. Come here.'

He reaches out to pull her back towards him, his lips nuzzling her neck. He can feel his hard-on wilting, and he doesn't know why. Gerry realises that Mae won't hang around if he doesn't treat her well. He removes her clothes slowly, trying to recall the seduction routine from the porn video they watched a couple of weeks ago when they met up at the Travelodge in Spalding.

'Why's the little man not performing?' Mae asks.

'Not so much of the *little*,' Gerry says, scowling as he reaches down to help himself.

The reaction isn't quick, but with a lot of help from Mae, eventually Gerry makes love to her in the way he thinks he should; in the way he thinks Mae likes it. His bad mood is alleviated – just a little.

AN HOUR later Gerry is back at work, squirreled away in his office, pulling the blind on the internal window and opening up PowerPoint. He's not used to making his own presentations, but this is one he doesn't want to share with Kelly, his secretary, and so it takes him an inordinate amount of time to create some rather basic slides.

Early afternoon and there's a knock on his door.

'I'm busy,' he shouts.

The door opens anyway, and Stijn pops his head inside.

'I'd like a word, mate.'

'Come in and shut the bloody door,' Gerry hisses. 'And don't call me mate. I'm your boss.'

'And my brother-in-law,' Stijn says with a broad grin. 'How's Bells coping with all this drama? Oh yes, I forgot. She's a lady of leisure, so it won't affect her one drop.'

'What do you want?'

'Who said I wanted anything?' Stijn tips his head to one side and puts a finger in his mouth.

'Just spit it out, Stijn. I haven't got time for your games.'

'Today you're right. I do want something. I want a promotion.' He stands with his thumbs in his jeans pockets, his legs far apart.

'On what grounds?' Gerry pales.

'Because I'm good at what I do. I want to travel less so I can spend more time with Lily.'

'I'm not running a bloody charity! The answer is no.' Gerry

stands up, kicks his chair backwards and places his palms flat on the desk, leaning forwards. 'Get out of my office and go and do your job, otherwise I'll fire you.'

Stijn laughs. The vein on the side of Gerry's head, underneath his receding hairline, pulses visibly. He moves his mouse around and pulls up a page on the computer.

'You've got five fucking deliveries to do today. How many have you done?' Gerry shouts.

'Five,' Stijn says, grinning.

'Get the fuck out of my office!' Gerry yells.

There's a knock on the door, and Kelly pokes her head around.

'Everything all right, Mr Shelton?' She glances at Stijn, who stares at her cleavage. She blushes.

'Yes. Stijn is just leaving.' Gerry sits down and glares at the computer screen. Kelly holds the door open for Stijn, who licks his lips at her, his eyes still on her bust.

Gerry puts his head in his hands. He would do anything to be rid of Stijn. He mooted the idea with Bella only a couple of months ago.

'You have got to be joking!' she exclaimed. 'If you fire Stijn, it'll crack this family in two. You've no idea what trouble that will cause. It's out of the question, Gerry. Promise me you won't do anything stupid!

'I promise, my love,' Gerry said, crossing his fingers behind his back.

9

Ollie is shaken. Not from Gerry's visit and his proposition, which he thinks is ridiculous, but because he has remembered where he saw Scott McDermott. The faint outline of a memory came to him when he was in the shower, and now he needs to be sure.

Fabian is in the kitchen making himself a sandwich. Ollie runs downstairs, a towel around his waist.

'Can you go and do a shop, Fabian? We need food for supper, and to pick up a bottle of Silent Pool gin.'

Ollie likes the turquoise and copper bottles as much as he likes the aromatic taste of the locally produced gin. Bella gave him a gin subscription for his last birthday, and having sampled a large number of craft gins, he is now overly fond of, Silent Pool, distilled in Guildford. It's become his favourite. There are six empty bottles lined up on the dresser.

'Do I have to?' Fabian pouts.

'Yes.' Ollie hands him four fifty-pound notes.

Fabian's eyes widen. There will be at least fifty quid left over for him to pocket. Fabian shoves the notes into his trouser pocket and slowly wanders around the kitchen, putting his plate in the dishwasher, wiping down the already-clean granite worktop.

'Go now!' Ollie says a little too vehemently.

Fabian blows Ollie a kiss and disappears into the hallway. When Ollie hears the front door slam closed, he darts into the living room and takes out his stack of photo albums from the walnut-inlaid armoire. Ollie has always been tidy, and as a boy he compiled meticulous albums, labelling each photograph with names, places and dates. His favourite birthday present of all time was the Olympus camera his father gave him for his eighth birthday. A typical young boy would have destroyed a proper camera, but Ollie wasn't typical. He studied the instruction manual and quickly took on the role of official family photographer. Wherever they went, Ollie was there to snap memories.

He starts at the beginning, flicking through the pages, looking for the Brylcreemed head. He finds the photo in the third album. As he stares at the picture, the memories come back to him. The humiliation, the shame, the desperation for the earth to open up and consume him within its dark, peaty depths.

David was desperate for Ollie to be the macho son of his dreams, the boy who would play football for the county and go on to Cirencester to study agriculture or Pershore College to study horticulture. Every Saturday morning from the age of six to twelve, David dragged Ollie to football club. The coach and Ollie's teammates didn't want him there any more than Ollie wanted to be there, but David paid for the pitch to be maintained, he bought new goalposts, and Rocks Garden Centre sponsored the first and second teams in return for their logo of two intertwined leaves being embroidered on every item of clothing. Ollie's only consolation was that he was never good enough to make the first or second teams, so didn't have the added humiliation of wearing his father's business logo on his chest.

Most Saturdays, David stood on the sidelines, screeching instructions at Ollie. He tried – he really tried – to keep his eye on the ball, to get his feet to move in the right direction, to follow his dad's advice, but Ollie lacked basic coordination. Occasionally, David got distracted, chatting to another dad or, even better, meeting up with a friend. Ollie remembers the man with the greasy black hair because it was the only time in his football career that he scored a goal. Elated, he turned around, ready to bask in his dad's glory. But David wasn't watching. He was talking animatedly with a strange man, and when practice was over, rather than going straight home as normal, David, David's friend and Ollie went to a coffee shop so they could carry on talking business. And for the first time in his life, David bought Ollie a Coca-Cola.

It was such a momentous morning, Ollie had captured the glass of Coke in a photograph. The reflection of the dark, greasy-haired man was caught in the glass.

Ollie stares at the photo. Then he flips open his iPad and does a search for Scott McDermott. The only picture he can find online is the one issued by the police, the one he saw this morning on the television. He compares the two. He can't be one hundred per cent sure, due to the distortion of the image in the glass and the fact the man is twenty-five years older, with grey as opposed to black hair, but the likeness is strong.

Ollie groans. David, his deceased father, knew the murdered man, Scott McDermott.

10

PIPPA

It happened seven years ago. Mila McDermott drowned in a canal accident whilst on holiday in Holland during a visit to stay with her mother, Janneke Visser. She was seventeen. There are scant details in the single article I can find on the internet.

She lived one year less than Flo.

It still stymies me, reading about the tragedies of young lives cut short. But Mila McDermott died in an accident. There was no suggestion that anyone was culpable. At least Scott McDermott knew what happened – not that, I suppose, it made it any more bearable. I do a search for 'Janneke Visser', but it is a common Dutch name and, as I have no idea where she lives, I don't make any progress.

I wonder if Janneke and Scott were ever married, or perhaps they divorced years ago. I am about to check under births, deaths and marriages when I glance at the time. I only have twenty minutes until my next client arrives. Instead, I

Google Scott McDermott again, but Scott McDermott from Findon has no recent internet presence whatsoever. He is not listed as a company director, he hasn't applied for planning permission and he doesn't appear to have donated to any online charitable causes. I sigh and shove my laptop to one side.

This is so frustrating. My curiosity about the murdered man has ramped up significantly. Knowing he suffered a similar tragedy to mine, I wonder if we would have been friends.

VERONICA STOTT IS A RELATIVELY new client. Behind the designer labels, manicured nails and expertly-coiffed hair is a sad and lonely woman in a marriage that is unravelling fast. She places her Prada handbag on the glass side table and bursts into tears the moment she sits down.

'Take a deep breath, Veronica,' I say.

'He's back with that woman,' she says, gulping.

'Tell me about it.'

'I found a receipt.' She blows her nose on a cotton handker-chief, making a surprisingly loud raspberry snort that still surprises me, despite hearing it several times during every session. 'He didn't even try to hide the receipt, and that hurts the most. It's as if he wanted me to find it.'

'What was the receipt for?'

'A necklace, designed with a twee little heart.'

'How do you know it was for her?'

'He knows I don't like hearts, so he wouldn't buy it for me. Plus it looks like a bespoke design. Who else would he buy a necklace for?'

'Have you asked him?'

'No. I don't want to know. Or maybe I do want to know. Oh God, I'm so confused.'

She puts her face in her hands. I can see the ridge of her natural nails underneath the pale-pink artificial talons.

And then the thought hits me. I wonder who the garden designer woman was that Scott McDermott employed. Could she have worked for Rocks Garden Centre? There are just too many threads pulling me towards that place, and now even my client is talking about it. I force myself to concentrate on what Veronica is saying, to help her question her suppositions, her limiting beliefs, to help her decide what she really wants and to confront the fears she has around leaving her cad of a husband.

As soon as she leaves, I make the most of my fifteen minutes between clients.

The shop in Findon is listed in *Yellow Pages*.

'Hello. This is Philippa Durrant. I was in earlier, and we were talking about Scott McDermott.'

'Yes, love. How can I help?'

'I hope you don't mind me asking, but you mentioned that he employed a garden designer. Mr McDermott's garden is so beautiful, I was wondering if you knew who he used. I'm looking to get my garden overhauled and am finding it difficult to get recommendations.'

'Oh yes. It's Isla-Mae Carruthers. She used to live in the village and had her own business, but I think with the recession, things got tough, so she moved away. She's been working for Rocks Garden Centre for a little while. She gets a guaranteed income that way. Do you want her number? I've got it here somewhere.'

'Thank you. That would be very helpful.'

I hear shuffling and chattering voices, and then it sounds as if the phone has been dropped. Eventually she comes back on to the line and slowly reads me out Isla-Mae Carruthers's mobile number. I thank her profusely.

So Scott McDermott did have a connection to Rocks

Garden Centre, if only through Isla-Mae Carruthers. I wonder if Joe has worked that one out. I wonder if I should ring him, eat humble pie and share my findings. But I hesitate. He doesn't want me to be an amateur sleuth; he wants to use me for my interviewing and people-analysis skills.

11

Annette is a good cook. She likes to have her children around her, and when they grew up and tried to cut the apron strings, she drew them back in by establishing a Thursday dinner get-together. If they showed up, they got their washing done, a box of frozen meals and, on occasion, some additional cash to have fun with at the weekend. David called it bribery; she saw it as an effective ploy to keep her children close.

After David died, Bella suggested that perhaps it was too much work for her, keeping up the old routine, especially as Annette was having to work full-time. Bella even suggested that Thursday dinners be held at her house. But Annette was having none of it. And so Thursdays stayed the same, with everyone sitting down around the dining-room table at 7 p.m. sharp. David's place wasn't laid, but no one ever sat in his chair.

'WHAT ARE you doing here so early?' Annette stands on tiptoes to give Ollie a kiss on the cheek.

'I need to talk to you before the others get here.'

'And there I was thinking you were going to give your old mum a hand with the cooking.'

'I can if you want,' Ollie says.

Annette laughs at the reluctance in his voice. She hands him a peeler and a sack of potatoes.

'How are you doing, Mum, with the murder and the police presence?'

'It's very unpleasant. I keep on thinking how your dad would have dealt with it.'

'Did you know Scott McDermott?'

'Good heavens, no. Why would you even ask the question?'

Ollie stares at his mum's slightly hunched back. She is cutting carrots with vengeance, the knife chop-chop-chopping rapidly on the Pyrex board.

'The thing is, Mum, Dad knew him.'

She stops chopping but doesn't turn around. 'Of course he didn't.'

Ollie steps over to his mother and puts his hand on her arm. He can feel the slight trembling.

'Turn around, Mum.'

'What is it?'

'Dad did know Scott McDermott.'

'I don't know what you're talking about, Oleander.'

Annette only calls Ollie by his full name when she's unhappy or angry. Ollie wonders whether she even realises she's doing it.

'I've got something to show you.' Ollie puts down the potato peeler and removes the photograph from his calfskin wallet. 'This was Scott McDermott.'

Annette peers at the photograph. 'It's a glass of Coca-Cola!'

'Look more carefully, and you can see the man in the glass. I was about ten. I'd scored a goal for the first and only time in my football career, but Dad was talking to this man and he didn't see it. He then took me and this man for a drink. He bought me a Coke.'

'Your dad bought you a Coke?' Annette frowns.

'First and last time. And this man' – Ollie points at the face – 'this man is Scott McDermott.'

Annette shakes her head. 'Love, you're totally wrong. This man was a sleazy salesman. I can't even remember his name. He hung around for a while, wanting to persuade your dad to do a business deal. Trust me. That is not Scott McDermott.'

'But—'

'There's no but, Ollie. Can you get on with peeling those potatoes? Otherwise the meal won't be ready in time.'

'Did you know Scott McDermott?' Ollie insists.

Annette slams her fist on to the chopping board. Several pieces of raw carrot slide off onto the floor. Ollie is startled. He can't remember the last time he saw his mum lose her temper. It just isn't like her.

She turns away from him, takes a deep, audible breath and speaks more calmly.

'This murder has taken a lot out of me. I don't know why you're fixated on your dad or me knowing the man, because we don't and we didn't. It's stressful enough having the police poke into our affairs without you throwing around false accusations. Can we please change the subject?'

'Okay,' Ollie says, slipping the photo back into his wallet. He bends down and picks up the carrots, rinsing them under the tap before placing them back onto Annette's chopping board.

'Sorry, Mum,' he says, feeling ten years old all over again.

BY FIVE TO SEVEN, the chicken is roasted, and Bella and Lily are laying the table.

'Where are your husbands?' Annette shouts through from the kitchen.

'I'm not sure Stijn is going to make it,' Lily says quietly. She's glad she's not in the same room as her mum and so doesn't have to see the look of disapproval.

'Gerry should be here,' Bella says, glancing at her Cartier watch.

Annette walks into the dining room holding the roast chicken aloft.

'I'm not waiting,' she says. 'Sit down.'

Ollie carves the chicken as normal, whilst Annette places mounds of roast potatoes, carrots and beans on everyone's plates. As she's about to serve herself, Gerry bounds in.

'Sorry I'm late.'

Bella raises her neatly arched and coiffed eyebrows at him. He takes a laptop out of his briefcase and places it on the table in front of his place setting.

'What's that for?' Annette asks.

'I've got something I'd like to share with you all.'

'After we've eaten,' Annette states. She can't abide technology at the dinner table. They all know to switch off their mobiles, or even better, leave them in another room.

'Where's Stijn?' Gerry glances around as if Stijn, in his six-feet-three-inches glory, could be stowed away in a corner.

'He might not make it,' Lily mutters.

The sound of knives and forks and chewing makes them all uncomfortable, aware that no one is talking. The events of the week don't seem an appropriate topic of conversation.

The moment Lily puts the last morsel in her mouth, Gerry swaps his laptop and empty dinner plate around.

'I've got something I'd like to propose to you all.' He clears his throat and stands up.

'Not now, Gerry,' Ollie says.

'The sooner the better,' Gerry states. 'We need to clear the air and have a plan for moving forwards.'

'Moving forwards from what?' Annette asks.

'The future of Rocks Garden Centre, in particular, as a consequence of the unpleasant events of this week.' He pauses and looks around the table, his gaze lingering on Annette's face.

'I've prepared a short presentation on why I think I'm the best person to maximise the potential of the family business, and if you agree, Annette, I will seek an independent valuation and raise the funds to buy you out.'

'Buy out of what?' Stijn lopes into the dining room. 'Sorry I'm late, Ma.'

He bends down and kisses Annette's jowly cheek. She bristles. Stijn leans over and kisses Lily on the lips, lingering a little too long.

'Are you hungry, darling?' Lily asks.

'Starving.'

He pulls out the empty chair between Lily and Bella and plops down, legs spread wide. Lily jumps up, finds a clean plate and piles it up with a chicken leg and vegetables.

'Did I interrupt something?' Stijn grins at Gerry.

'Yes.' Gerry turns the laptop around so they can all see it.

'Since David died, this family has been under considerable pressure. Not least Annette, who has taken on the mantle of running Rocks Garden Centre. Despite doing a fine job, you're at a time in your life when you should be able to retire, take things easy. Bella has chosen to be a stay-at-home mum, which I fully endorse—'

'Even though the girls are at boarding school,' Ollie mutters.

Bella throws him daggers.

'Ollie has other business interests, and Lily, while she is excellent at plants, doesn't have the commercial experience. So that only leaves me.'

'What about me?' Stijn interjects.

Gerry ignores him. 'The garden centre would fit in very well with my plans for vertical integration. I've prepared some facts and figures here.' He brings up a page of graphs with wording too small to read. 'And I propose buying the business. Annette, you can either keep the property or sell the whole lot to me lock, stock and barrel.'

'No!' Annette says. She leans heavily on the table, pushes her chair back and stands up slowly.

'No to which part?' Gerry asks, his small piggy eyes wide with surprise.

'No to it all. I am not selling. To you or anyone else. So long as I am alive and compos mentis, I will not sell.'

'But Mum, that's silly. Wouldn't you like to go on a cruise?' Bella says, pouting.

'Listen to me!' Annette says. Her eyes are watering. 'The answer is no!'

'Hear, hear!' Stijn says.

'Keep out of it!' Gerry glares at Stijn.

'Gerry, I told you to hold fire,' Ollie says. 'This isn't the way—'

Lily jumps up. Her face is flushed. She rushes out of the room, but not before she lets out a little sob.

'Now look what you've done!' Stijn leans forwards and narrows his eyes at Gerry.

'Keep out of this,' Bella says. 'Gerry only wants what's best—'

'You just don't get it, do you?' Ollie shouts. 'This is about what Mum wants. Think about her for once.'

Annette is shaking. 'Get out. All of you. Just get out. I want to be left alone.'

They all stare at her. Annette is never forceful, never confrontational.

'I said get the hell out of here!' she screams.

12

Ollie can't sleep. It's 2.37 a.m. and Fabian's soft snoring is driving him insane. He throws back the duvet, pads downstairs and switches on the table lights in the living room. He pours himself a brandy, curls up in his favourite black leather and chrome Zanotta sofa, and thinks about his mum. Ollie is certain she is lying. He is sure his parents knew Scott McDermott and that his mum is covering something up. But he doesn't know what to do about it.

'Can't sleep?'

Fabian startles Ollie, and a mouthful of brandy goes down the wrong way. Ollie's coughs disintegrate into sobs.

'What's up, darling?' Fabian flings his arms around Ollie. 'I know you don't like to share stuff with me, but sometimes it's best to let it all out. You know you can trust me, don't you?'

Ollie sniffs. 'It's family things.'

'Just because I haven't spoken to my family in eight years doesn't mean I can't support you.'

'I know, Fabes.' Ollie never shares, and isn't about to now. 'I appreciate it, but go back to sleep. I'll be up soon.'

But Ollie doesn't go up soon. He falls asleep on the sofa and wakes when the sun rises. He tiptoes upstairs so as not to awaken Fabian, slips on some Lycra shorts and a T-shirt, and goes for a run along the seafront. After a quick shower in the spare shower room, he is sipping a strong cup of coffee in the kitchen when he hears the post drop through the letterbox. He has managed to get to the post before Fabian every day for the last six weeks. Ollie doesn't open the bank or credit card statements, all final demands. He just slips them into the bottom drawer of his bureau in the study and locks it carefully, keeping the key in his back trouser pocket.

And then the phone rings. He is tempted not to answer, but he doesn't want Fabian listening to any messages, so at the sixth ring he grabs the receiver.

'Yes?' he says.

'Mr Gower?'

Ollie's heart sinks.

'This is Detective Sergeant Joe Swain. We would like a quick chat with you. When would be convenient?'

Ollie gulps. 'Am I under suspicion?'

'No. Should you be?'

'Of course not. I don't go anywhere near the garden centre. Can't stand the place.'

'Why's that?'

'It was my dad's business. He and I didn't always see eye to eye.' Ollie pauses.

'Great. I can be with you at 11 a.m. if that suits.'

'Here? Um, yes. Okay.'

Ollie hangs up. He paces around the living room and then decides to move the Maserati. He doesn't need the policeman to see the fancy car outside the house. The engine roars as he starts it up, but then there's a rap on the passenger window.

'Shit, Fabian, you gave me a heart attack.'

'Where are you going, babes?'

'Just picking up some stuff.'

'I was planning on going to the gym. Would you like me to do the shop for you?'

'How long will you be out?' Ollie asks.

'Till lunchtime, I suppose.'

Ollie switches off the engine and climbs out. He chucks the car keys at Fabian.

'I can take the car?' Fabian says, his mouth wide in a gasp, clasping the keys to his chest.

'Just don't crash it,' Ollie says as he strides back to the house.

Fabian stands there for a moment, open mouthed, and then realises that he's getting to drive the Maserati for the first time in his life. He grins, does a little jump and climbs into the car.

JOE SWAIN ARRIVES on the dot of 11 a.m.

'Nice place you've got here.'

Joe takes in the shiny black front door with the ornate gold knocker, the pale oak floorboards in the hall, the large-framed modern art on the walls and the huge vase of exotic orange blooms on an antique console table. He follows Ollie into the kitchen, state of the art, super-tidy and shiny, with the exception of two cereal bowls and two mugs in the sink.

'Do you live here alone?'

Ollie nods. Joe glances at the kitchen sink.

'Would you like a coffee?' Ollie asks.

'Thank you. Black, no sugar, please.' Joe sits down. 'I gather from your mother that you have never had anything to do with the family business.'

'Yes. I can't keep a plant alive, and I'm not keen on the general public.'

Joe laughs. 'Can you tell me where you were on Monday night?'

'So, I am under suspicion?' Ollie's shoulders are hunched up.

'I never said you were. I am just trying to establish the whereabouts of everyone associated with the garden centre.'

'How are you tracking down all the customers?' Ollie's voice is taut.

'I am sure you will appreciate that, as this is an ongoing investigation, I can't discuss our processes or reasons.'

'I was here on Monday night,' Ollie says quietly.

'Can anyone vouch for that?'

'Yes. A friend of mine.'

'Could you please give me this friend's name and address?'

Ollie gulps, but he is a quick thinker. 'He's called Fabian Sherman. I don't know his address, but I can give you his telephone number.'

'Thank you, that would be helpful.'

Ollie flicks through the address book on his mobile phone and reads out a number. He's rather pleased with himself that he remembers to do that rather than reciting Fabian's number, which of course he knows off by heart. He switches on the coffee machine, which makes its normal racket, and so he doesn't hear the front door open.

'Darling, I left my wallet upstairs. Can you nip up and get it for me to save me taking off my shoes?' Fabian shouts from the corridor. And then he enters the kitchen.

'Hello. Who are you?' Joe asks.

'Fabian. And who are you?' Fabian asks, fluttering his eyelids. When he gets no immediate response, he glances from Joe to Ollie and back again.

There is a heavy silence. Ollie hands Joe a coffee in a fine white porcelain cup that wobbles on its saucer.

'I think you've just saved me a phone call, Fabian Sherman,' Joe says.

'You, mister, haven't said who you are!' Fabian whines.

'Detective Sergeant Joe Swain.'

'Ooooh, a policeman. How very exciting!'

'Fabian, can you get your own wallet? I need to speak to DS Swain in confidence.'

Fabian scowls but does as he's told. When Ollie hears Fabian's footsteps on the stairs, he strides across the kitchen and shuts the door.

'I've got something I need to tell you,' Ollie says to Joe, crossing his arms. The last thing he wants to do is drop his mother in it, but he's worried that not telling Joe Swain about Scott McDermott might be perceived as withholding evidence. And perhaps, if he tells the policeman, then in return Joe Swain might keep quiet about Fabian.

'I've seen Scott McDermott before. Well, at least I think I have.'

Ollie walks to the island unit and the silver dish where he leaves his keys, wallet and phone. Extracting the photograph of the Coke glass from his wallet, he tries to flatten out the creases before handing it to Joe.

Joe looks at it and then glances quizzically at Ollie.

'I'm ninety-nine per cent sure the person reflected in the glass is Scott McDermott. He was a friend or a business acquaintance of my dad's. I took the picture over twenty years ago.'

'I see.' Joe peers at it. 'You think your mother is lying when she says she didn't know Mr McDermott?'

Ollie lets out a moan. 'Possibly. But Mum wouldn't have anything to do with his murder. That's a joke. She's a good woman. Wouldn't harm a fly. If she knew him, it was just a coincidence.'

'Thank you for sharing that with me, Mr Gower. May I take a photograph of your photo please?'

'Yes.' Ollie hands it to him.

Joe stands up, takes a photo with his phone, then places his empty coffee cup in the sink, along with the other dirty dishes. 'I just need to have a word with your friend Fabian.'

Ollie sighs. 'I lied about that too. He's my partner and he lives here. But no one in my family knows about him and I'd like to keep it that way.'

'I'll do my best to keep your secret,' Joe says.

He walks towards the door, but Ollie jumps up and reaches it first, holding it open for him. Fabian pretends to be nonchalantly walking down the stairs, but it's obvious to both of them that he was standing on the second-to-lowest step, listening to their every word.

'Mr Sherman, could you confirm where you were on Monday night?' Joe makes sure he is standing directly in front of Ollie and blocking Fabian's view of his boyfriend.

'I was here. We cooked supper and watched *Love Island* and went to bed. I think that's right, isn't it, Ols?'

'Thank you, both of you,' Joe says, and puts his hand out to shake Ollie's. 'I will be in touch.'

'He was rather gorge.' Fabian licks his lips as the front door closes behind Joe.

'Go and get the shopping,' Ollie snaps, turning around and walking back into the kitchen. He slumps down into a chair and puts his head in his hands.

13

PIPPA

I have noticed synchronicities happening more and more in my life of late. Coincidences perhaps. Or perhaps not.

The phone rings and it's my son, George.

'Hello, darling. I was just thinking of you.'

'You're a grandmother!'

I jump up and do a little jig with excitement. 'That's wonderful! How is Marie and the baby?'

'She's fine and little Louis is well too. They're both at home asleep.'

'That's quick. When was the baby born?'

'On Monday at 5 a.m.'

'Oh,' I say. That was four days ago. I feel a stabbing in my stomach as I realise how far down I am on the list of people George wants to share his life with. 'Can we Skype so I can see Louis?'

'Another day maybe. I'll email you a photograph.'

I want to ask if I can fly out to Geneva, but instead I bite the inside of my cheek until I draw blood.

'Anyway, I just thought you'd want to know.'

'Congratulations to you both.'

'Thanks. Bye—'

'Wait, George. Please. I'm trying to track down someone on the internet and I'm struggling to find—'

'Please don't tell me you're involved in another murder case.'

'Well, actually—'

'Have you forgotten how the last one panned out? How Marie and I nearly got killed, and you too?'

'Actually, George, it was thanks to me that the murder got solved.'

He grunts. 'Right now I'm focusing on life and not death, and I think you should too.'

He hangs up.

I throw the phone on to the table and screech. Mungo looks up in alarm. I bend down and hug him, thankful that at least my beloved hound isn't judging me. He gives a little woof, wriggles out of my arms and scampers to the front door, his tail wagging wildly.

'What is it?' I ask just as the doorbell rings.

I look through the peephole but can't see anyone, so I open the door. Lying on the doorstep is a bouquet of delphiniums.

'Wait!' I shout as Joe strides up the path towards his car. He turns around and walks back towards me, a wide grin on his face.

'Delphiniums are out of season. I searched high and low, but the plants aren't available until the spring, and flowers are only available from June to August, so I'm afraid this is the next best thing. Some fake flowers.'

I pick up the bunch of long stems with their delicate blue petals, tied with raffia. It's only on very close inspection that it's apparent they're artificial.

'Thank you. That was very kind and unnecessary.'

We stand looking at each other awkwardly.

'Would you like a coffee?' I ask. 'Actually, I've discovered something about Scott McDermott.'

'I haven't got time for a coffee, but I have got time to give that dog of yours a quick cuddle.'

He follows me inside.

'Did you know that Scott McDermott was a keen gardener and was running a business from home, sending parcels all over the world? He employed a landscape gardener called Isla-Mae Carruthers, who works for Rocks Garden Centre. It stands to reason he probably knew the Gowers.'

'He did know the Gowers. I had a very interesting conversation with Ollie Gower, Annette's son. You were right, I was wrong. Annette Gower has been lying to me, and I'm going to question her again. I may also get a warrant to search her house.'

'You are?' Whilst Annette is certainly hiding something, I can't believe she's a murderer. But something holds me back from saying any more. Perhaps it's the flash of anger I saw in Joe's eyes when he said Annette had been lying to him. Perhaps it's my concern that Joe sees the world in black and white whilst I prefer to see shades of grey.

'When this is all over, can I take you out for dinner?'

'Yes, thank you.' I blush.

'Can you attend the interview with Annette Gower?'

'Yes, but ...'

Joe swivels around to face me, his eyebrows raised.

'I want you to listen to my professional opinion, even if it's contrary to yours,' I say.

He opens and closes his mouth, and then bursts out laughing. 'It seems we're both inclined to eat humble pie, but only small portions of it.' He steps towards me and gives me a brief kiss on the cheek. 'Can you make 4 p.m. tomorrow afternoon at Rocks Garden Centre?'

. . .

THE JOURNALISTS HAVE GONE, as has the blue-and-white police tape; the garden centre has reopened to the public. I am surprised the car park is so full. I had assumed that a murder might have put people off from visiting.

A coach-load of elderly passengers are dismounting from a bus and slowly snaking their way towards the entrance. Squeezing past them, I enter the garden centre and am surrounded by bountiful displays of artificial blooms in every colour of the rainbow. I notice the blue delphinium and wonder if Joe bought them here. And then there are tiers of buckets filled with real flowers, large heads of white rhododendron, roses, Calla lilies and the bobbing spheres of dahlia in burnt oranges and reds. Dazzled by the wonderful array of colours, I slow down and then enter the houseplants greenhouse, where the air is heavy with moisture, and I breathe in the earthy smell of peat.

The sound of gushing water makes me look up, even though I know there is a large waterfall built into rocks and a pond underneath heaving with koi carp so big they make me feel uncomfortable. Carrying on through the horticultural sundries department to the outdoor plants area, I note a small table with a sign behind it: 'Garden Design Services – Enquire Here'. I pause. There are piles of leaflets on the table and a large photo album. I flick through it, admiring the beautifully designed gardens.

'Can I help you, madam?'

I am startled. The woman has mesmerizing azure eyes, so bright I wonder if she is wearing coloured contact lenses. Her hair is jet black, cut into a bob, sharp, straight lines reflecting the thin line of her lips. She is wearing the Rocks Garden Centre uniform; green T-shirt and black trousers. They do nothing for her hourglass figure.

'I was just wondering about your garden design services.'

'You're talking to the right person. How can I assist?'

I glance at my watch. 'I have a meeting now, but perhaps I could catch up with you later, in about half an hour?'

'Sure, but I will have to leave on time today. I need to take my elderly mother to a doctor's appointment.'

'Of course. And you are?' I ask the question, even though I know the answer.

'Isla-Mae Carruthers. I'll see you back here in thirty minutes.'

She smiles. I study her physique, those slender wrists, and wonder: would she have the strength to strangle a man?

'Is everything all right?' she quizzes.

I snap out of my reverie. 'Yes, apologies. See you later.' I hurry away.

THERE IS a glass window in the hallway of the office block that looks into a small office, where four people are seated at computers. As I hesitate, a woman shaped like a jelly baby gets up and lifts the window.

'Can I help you?'

'I have a meeting with Annette Gower and DS Swain.'

Her face clouds slightly. 'They're in the boardroom. Second door down on the right. Please sign your name in the book.'

I glance down and see the opened visitor's book. Joe has signed his name with large, curved flourishes. I would like to study his writing, to use my graphology skills to get a better insight into his personality, but now is neither the time nor place. When I put the biro back on the table, she says, 'You can go to the boardroom. Just knock on the door.'

I give her a cursory smile. My heart is beating a little too fast. I take a couple of deep breaths and then rap on the door.

'Come in.'

The room is bright and utilitarian, with overhead fluorescent lights. Health and safety notices are attached to the side wall, and a large whiteboard is on the rear wall. There are no plants or pictures, nothing to suggest this is the office in a garden centre. Joe is seated at the far end of the long dark-wood table. He gets up and walks towards me.

'Thank you for coming, Doctor Durrant.'

I raise my eyebrows, but he doesn't respond. Annette is seated to the left of the place Joe's had vacated. Her shoulders are hunched, but her face is impassive when she glances towards me. Joe guides me to sit on his right, opposite Annette.

'Mrs Gower, you know Doctor Durrant. She is here in her capacity as a psychologist and police consultant. You indicated that you have no objections to her presence.'

Annette doesn't respond.

'Mrs Gower, did you know Scott McDermott?'

'You have asked me that repeatedly, and I have given you my answer.'

I keep my eyes peeled on her face, trying not to be distracted by the twitching nerve under her eye. The micro-expressions, the shifting in her seat and the words she chooses, all add up to a cluster of deceit.

There is a silence, and I decide to fill it. After all, Joe hasn't told me not to.

'Why have you not disclosed the fact that a member of your staff, Isla-Mae Carruthers, worked as a landscape gardener for Scott McDermott?'

'Did she?' Annette's voice is flat, unsurprised. 'How would you expect me to know who all our clients are? We have hundreds of thousands of people coming through our doors every year. I don't know them.'

'Mrs Gower, we believe you are lying.' Joe glances at me. I nod. 'Do you understand that if you knowingly withhold information from us, you are impeding this investigation and may be prosecuted?'

Annette trembles and pulls her cardigan tighter around her body, wrapping her arms around her sides.

'Yes.' Her voice is tremulous.

Joe thumps the heel of his hand on the table. It startles both Annette and me.

'It is about time you start telling us the truth. Do not lie to me! I will ask you again: did you know the deceased?'

'I might have met him. But I meet a lot of people, and it doesn't mean I know them.'

Joe stands up and leans forwards on the table menacingly. The whites of his eyes are bright, accentuating the dark pupils. 'Which bit of *do not lie to me* don't you understand?'

Annette's bottom lip quivers and her eyes water. I feel sorry for the woman. Joe is a big man, and even I am feeling intimidated by him.

'Did you know Scott McDermott?'

'Yes,' she whispers.

Joe explodes. 'You are impeding this investigation. Perverting the course of justice is a criminal offence with the potential of life imprisonment. You could spend the rest of your days in jail. Is that what you want? Do *not* lie to me!'

'She's about to tell us the truth, aren't you, Annette?' I speak in a low, calm voice, trying to take the heat out of this interview.

Annette's eyes are red-rimmed and large.

'I knew Scott McDermott, but not well. He was a regular customer, had been for years. He knew David, my husband, better than me. I never went to his house or anything.'

'Why did you withhold that information from us?' Joe lowers himself back into the chair.

'I was scared. I didn't – I don't – want anything to do with this murder.'

'You have no choice. It took place on your premises, and I

want to find out why. I have all the time in the world, so why don't we start again? When did you last meet Scott McDermott?'

'I d-didn't. I-I haven't,' she says, stuttering.

'Have you or have you not met with Scott McDermott in the past month?'

'No.' Annette is gripping herself even harder. But on this occasion, I think she is telling the truth.

'When was the last time you met Scott McDermott?'

'Last year. I don't remember when exactly. I saw him from time to time when he came here shopping.'

'My colleague here mentioned Isla-Mae Carruthers. Who is she, and what is her connection with you and with McDermott?'

I am impressed with Joe's recall ability. He didn't write her name down, and from his reaction to my earlier question, I assumed this was news to him.

'She works for me. She is a landscape gardener, and we started employing her directly about two years ago. I believe she redesigned Mr McDermott's garden.'

No hesitations or deviations or involuntary movements or unusual micro-expressions: Annette is being truthful about her relationship with Isla-Mae Carruthers.

'How often did you see McDermott in the past year?'

'I don't know.' Annette keeps her eyes down.

'Not good enough!' Joe roars.

Annette pales. She reaches for a glass of water, but her hand is trembling too much to grip it. A fine layer of perspiration dots her forehead and upper lip.

'Joe, I think we should take a break,' I suggest.

'Why?' he glowers at me.

'Mrs Gower doesn't look very well.'

'And I am not feeling very well either, because Mrs Gower here is refusing to tell us the truth. This is a murder enquiry,

Mrs Gower, and if you are involved in it in any way, now is the time to be telling us. Now.' He bangs the table again.

'I'm sorry, I feel faint.' Annette sways slightly.

I jump up, run around to her side of the table, pick up her glass of water and, lowering into my knees, hold the glass to her lips. She takes a few sips.

'I have a weak heart,' Annette mutters.

'Right,' Joe says. 'You can go now, but I want you at the police station at 9 a.m. tomorrow morning. Understood?'

I help Annette to her feet, and she leans on me as we walk out of the room.

'I'll go to my office,' she says.

'Do you need me to get a first aider to look after you?'

'No, I'll be fine. Nothing that some deep breathing can't sort out.'

When I have settled her in her chair, I walk back to the boardroom. Joe is on the phone, pacing backwards and forwards, talking animatedly. I haven't seen this harsh side of him before and I don't like it. I hesitate, but he looks up and gestures for me to wait.

'She's a lying old woman and she is involved in this murder. Do you agree?'

'Yes, but I don't think she's a murderer.'

'She's a liar, and whatever her age or her health issues, she is impeding this investigation. I will not have it!'

Joe's fury takes me aback.

'People lie for different reasons,' I say. 'She may be protecting someone or even just the memory of her dead husband.'

Joe harrumphs. 'Can you send me an email with your thoughts on this interview? Something's come up, so I'll touch base with you later or tomorrow.'

I am dismissed. I glance at my watch. I've got another ten minutes until I am due to meet Isla-Mae Carruthers. I wander back into the garden centre, intending to have a cup of coffee, but the staff are packing up the restaurant, wiping tables, removing cakes from the display counters. Instead I make my way back to the landscape gardening stand and pick up a leaflet.

'Hello, love, can I help you?'

I am impressed by how well trained and friendly the staff are. She has tight grey curls that appear to have been set with rollers, and her deeply lined face suggests she is well beyond the age of retirement.

'I'm meeting Isla-Mae Carruthers. I am looking to remodel my garden.'

'Oh dear.' She lays a hand on my arm. 'I think there must have been a mistake. Isla-Mae left about fifteen minutes ago. She didn't say anything about meeting a client. I hope you haven't come especially. It's not like Isla-Mae. She's normally so efficient. Why don't I take your name and telephone number and get her to give you a call in the morning?'

'Don't worry,' I say. 'I'll call Isla-Mae myself tomorrow.' I pick up a business card. It reads 'I-M Carruthers, Garden Designer'.

Who would have thought there could be so much intrigue in a garden centre?

14

PIPPA

When I get back to my consulting room, the answer machine is flashing. I press play.

'My name is Oleander Gower. I was wondering if I might have an appointment to come and see you. As soon as possible please.'

I return his call immediately. I know it's impetuous, but it's as if I have a point to prove, both to George and Joe. I need George to respect me, to know that I am worthy to be his mother and grandmother to his son. And Joe, I want to see him again. My rational mind is telling me to stay away from him, to concentrate on the job. But my intuition is screaming to me, *Get involved, be brave, and see where it takes you.* Hopefully to Joe, or at least Joe without the temper.

'My diary is fully booked, but I could see you this evening.'

He jumps at it.

I have a full afternoon, back-to-back clients needing support to combat anxiety, post-traumatic stress disorder and depression. I want to pour myself a large glass of red wine and curl up on the sofa to contemplate the tumultuous events of the day. I'm happy for George and Marie but upset that my son is so distant. My heart is aflutter as I think about Joe. Quite ridiculous for a fifty-something woman. On the dot of 6.30 p.m., the doorbell rings.

Oleander Gower is tall and athletic-looking with very short, honey-coloured hair as thick and wiry as a brush.

'Hello, I'm Ollie.' He extends his hand.

I gesture for him to sit in my client chair.

'Mum said she spoke to you shortly after the murder in the garden centre.'

I wonder whether he knows I was in the interview this afternoon. I decide not to volunteer that information so just nod, opening my palms and smiling to encourage him to carry on speaking.

'That detective, Joe Swain, is treating Mum like a common criminal. She didn't do it. There's no way she was involved even if she did know the man.'

'The man?'

'Scott McDermott. And it's all my fault.' He rubs his knuckles into his eyes.

'What's all your fault, Ollie?'

'I told Joe Swain that Dad knew McDermott, and by default he's assumed Mum knew him. I need you to persuade Swain that my mother is innocent. It's ridiculous that she's being treated like this.'

'DS Swain is not going to arrest anyone without evidence. I'm sure he knows what he's doing. Shouldn't you be talking to him rather than to me?'

Ollie slumps farther into the chair. He looks like a sad, lost little boy in a man's body.

'Tell me what you know.' I am ready for him, my end-of-day tiredness suddenly dissipated.

'I don't know anything other than Mum is acting weirdly,

and if I'd got involved in the business after Dad died, our family wouldn't be falling apart.'

'Did the rest of your family want you to get involved?'

His laugh is bitter. 'No. Mum did everything she could to keep me away. It's only Lily she's let in. Silly Lily. She can grow plants, but she's useless at business.'

'How did that make you feel?'

'Rejected again. Nothing I do is good enough. I wasn't up to scratch for Dad, and I'm not good enough for Mum.'

'How true is that?'

'It's totally true,' he says angrily. 'And now my jerk of a brother-in-law wants to muscle in. At least Mum isn't having that.'

Ollie's mobile rings. He takes it out of his trouser pocket and answers it.

'Mum. What's up?'

I can't hear what she's saying, but I can observe Ollie's face, which goes as pale as chalk.

He stands up. 'I'll call a solicitor. Yes, Peter Reading. I'll come too. Stay strong, Mum.'

He glowers at me. 'The bastard has arrested Mum! He's arrested a seventy-three-year-old widow! It's a travesty. I've got to go, got to call our lawyer.'

15

'What are you doing here?' Ollie snarls at Gerry.

They are standing in Annette's kitchen, dirty dishes piled high in the sink.

'We heard Annette has been arrested, so Bella asked me to come over and check what was happening.'

'My dear sister couldn't come by herself?'

'Bella is otherwise disposed,' Gerry says.

Ollie turns to Annette, who appears to have shrunk by several inches, her shoulders curling forwards and the tic under her eye flickering manically.

'Go to bed, Mum. I'll bring you a hot chocolate.'

'A brandy,' she mutters.

'And a brandy.'

The two men watch Annette struggle out of the room.

'I thought she was arrested,' Gerry says, frowning.

'She got confused. She was taken in for questioning, and apparently the policeman said he was considering arresting her. She was in there for four hours. Four bloody hours questioning a woman who should be retired. It's disgusting. I've told Peter Reading, our solicitor, to file a complaint.'

'That's why she needs to take a back seat in the business. She's too old for all of this.' Gerry flexes his fingers back and forwards. They make an unpleasant cracking sound.

'For God's sake, Gerry, now is not the time.'

'No, Gerry, it's not. Have a heart, mate!' Stijn lopes into the room and slinks on to a kitchen chair.

'Butt out, Stijn,' Gerry spits.

'Ollie, don't you think it's about time I had a promotion?' Stijn says, smirking.

'Shut the fuck up!' Gerry towers menacingly over Stijn, but they both know that he wouldn't last five seconds in a fight. The Dutchman is wiry and fit, as well as being nearly fifteen years younger.

'No need to lose your temper, Gerry,' Stijn drawls.

'I'm your boss. You should show some respect.'

'I give respect where respect is earned.' He tilts his head to one side.

Gerry takes a step backwards but puts his hands on his hips. 'I could fire you tomorrow. Right now, in fact!'

Stijn stands up, and Gerry takes another step backwards. 'Go ahead! Lily and I are talking about me joining the garden centre. There's plenty I can do there to help out.'

'Cut it out, both of you!' Ollie yells.

'What's going on?' Lily wanders into the kitchen, ethereal-like in a long, thin powder-blue cardigan that splays out behind her.

'I was just telling Gerry about our little chat about me joining the garden centre. He's not in a very good mood is our Gerry!'

Lily snakes her hand around Stijn's waist. 'Let's go to bed, shall we?' She leans up and gives him a kiss on his neck.

'Now, there's an offer I can't refuse!' He makes big eyes at Gerry and lets Lily lead him out of the room.

'What is it between you and Stijn?' Ollie asks.

'Can't stand the man,' Gerry mutters.

'He works for you and you introduced him to this family.'

'I know, and I regret it every day. He's not good enough for Lily.'

Ollie lets out a puff of air and turns his back on Gerry. He's got a headache and bigger concerns than any rivalry between Stijn and Gerry.

16

PIPPA

It's been a long, emotional week, and I'm just relieved that it's the weekend. I awoke at 7 a.m., as I do every morning, fed Mungo and let him out, then made myself a cup of tea and headed back to bed to read the papers on my iPad. I must have dozed off, because I awake to the ringing of the telephone.

'It's Annette Gower speaking. I need to see you.'

'Okay,' I say, rubbing my eyes.

'Can I come to you? I'd rather not be seen with you at the garden centre?'

'Yes, I suppose so. When were you thinking?' I will have to go downstairs to hunt for my diary.

'As soon as possible. I looked you up in the telephone directory. I'm in Storrington now.'

'I don't normally consult at the weekends—'

'This isn't for a consultation. It's urgent.'

I HAVE no idea what she wants to tell me, but I intuit that it is important, and if it can help the case, then I need to assist. I wonder if I can charge Joe overtime. Hurriedly I throw on a blouse and a pair of jeans and slip my bare feet into flat shoes. I grab a jumper, dab my face with concealer, line my eyes with kohl and then run down the stairs.

Thirty minutes later, Annette is settling into my client chair in my office. Her face has taken on the pallor of her grey hair. The rings around her eyes are a deep purple, and her skin is more wrinkled than I remember. Without a doubt, the events of the week have affected her deeply. Her dark-grey dress and long, black, shapeless heavy-knit cardigan dwarf her.

I hand her a glass of water and sit down opposite her.

'I thought you had been arrested,' I say.

'No. Apparently I wasn't. It was very confusing and extremely unpleasant. That policeman...' Her voice trails off. Her right leg is jiggling under her voluminous skirt and the tic under her eye is flickering.

'I'm here because I don't know who else to turn to, and, frankly, I'm scared.' She lifts the glass to her lips, but her hand is shaking too much, so she puts it back down on to the table.

'Why don't you speak to DS Swain?'

'You are joking!' she exclaims. 'He as good as accused me of being a murderer. He interviewed me for four hours yesterday. I don't trust the man. You're a consultant to the police, aren't you? I need you to tell him.'

I can't help but raise my eyebrows. 'Tell him what?' I lean back into my chair.

'I think I will be the next to be murdered.'

'Wow! Why do you say that?' I feel a little frisson of excitement. I know it's wrong to feel that, but I enjoy being the confidant, the pseudo-detective.

'After my husband died, I found out he had another business, a nursery, growing plants for medicinal uses.'

'Like cannabis?' I ask.

'Oh no. Nothing like that!' She flushes and straightens her skirt. I clock the cluster of movements, the fleeting expression of fear, the verbal and nonverbal disconnect. She's hiding something.

'I've been trying to extricate myself from the business, as it's a headache I can do without, but there are people who want to maintain the status quo.' She wriggles in her chair as if she is shifting away from the truth. 'I think Scott McDermott had something to do with the business, and now I've been threatened.'

'Threatened?' So this has got something to do with the murder.

'I've received a warning. Several warnings.' She clasps and unclasps her hands, and her face is contorted with fear. I suppress the urge to reach out and touch her.

'I receive single stems of flowers twice a day. It started with balsamine. You'd probably know it as impatiens.'

I look at her blankly.

'They're ordinary bedding plants sold everywhere. Even the supermarkets. And then I got a yellow carnation, followed by an ornamental cabbage and *Lotus corniculatus*, commonly known as birdsfoot.'

I interrupt her. 'I'm sorry, but I don't understand.'

'Have you heard of floriography, the language of flowers?'

'No.'

She sighs. 'It's the meaning attributed to flowers. It's been around for millennia. In the Victorian era, coded messages would be sent with bouquets of flowers.'

'To clarify, what you're saying is that many flowers were attributed with meanings?'

'Exactly. Impatiens, as the name suggests, is impatience. Yellow carnation suggests disappointment. The cabbage relates to profit and money, and birdsfoot is revenge.'

'Forgive me for suggesting this, but could you be imparting meaning where there isn't any?'

Tears well up in Annette's eyes and she bites her lower lip.

'Believe me, I've tried to think that for the last few days, but now I can't. Yesterday I received a single-stem orange lily. It signifies hatred.'

'But your daughter is called Lily!'

'We named our daughter after the white lily. Purity.'

'And you don't think that these flowers could be meant for Lily?'

She shakes her head. 'They have been left in the places I go to. On my desk at work. Under the window wipers of my car. The doorstep of my house. No, it's totally clear that they're meant for me.'

I am stumped for words. I have never come across anything quite so bizarre. I am also wary of believing Annette. Why wouldn't someone threatening her leave real messages, written in words? It's as if she can read the doubt in my mind, despite my trying to keep a neutral expression.

'You just think I'm an old, stupid hippie, don't you?'

'No, of course not. Please carry on.'

'Yesterday a lobelia was left outside my office door. It signifies malevolence. Last night I got *Lotus corniculatus*, more commonly known as birdsfoot trefoil. It means revenge. And when I let the cat out, I found a marigold on the doorstep. Pain and grief. As if that wasn't bad enough, this morning the postman delivered a black rose with a sprig of cypress. And some of these plants aren't even in season. Whoever sent them has gone out of their way to source them.'

I raise my eyebrows.

'A black rose and cypress means death. They both mean death.'

I lean forwards and reach for her hand. The skin is rough,

and she has soil caked underneath her fingernails. 'I can see why you're scared, but we must tell DS Swain about this.'

She pulls her hand away and shakes her head vigorously. 'No. He won't understand... he won't understand about the flowers. He has it in his stupid head that I am guilty of a crime. I need you to help me. Please.'

'But I don't know what to do! I'm a psychologist, not a policewoman.'

'I need to go away,' she says. 'Run away. Go into hiding. But I can't. If that Joe Swain thinks I've done a runner, he'll come after me. He won't understand. And then the children might get into trouble.' She starts trembling. 'Maybe they'll go after my children. Lily is so naïve and married to that sleaze of a Dutchman. She could have done much better. At least Gerry provides for Bella, but he's greedy, always wanting more, and he's really not as clever as he thinks he is. The girls, they are so vulnerable. Even Ollie could be targeted. David protected us all, and now I have to, but I simply don't know how. I need you to persuade the police to give us protection.'

'This other business – does DS Swain know about it?'

'Good heavens no! And I beg you not to tell him.' She leans forwards and grabs my hands.

'But why?' I ask.

She flinches and drops my hands. 'It's skimming the edge of the law.'

'Can you explain?'

She shakes her head. 'It's better you don't know.'

'If it's illegal activity, then you need to tell us. I'm sure the police will look kindly upon you.'

Annette grabs the arms of the chair and hauls herself up. Her face is grey and the tic under her eye is hammering.

'I should never have said anything. Just ask the police to look out for my children. That's all. I'm sorry I disturbed you.'

17

Gerry is at Gatwick Airport, off on a little buying trip to Italy. If Bella has noticed that his foreign trips inevitably fall on a Friday or a Monday and eat into the weekend, she hasn't said anything. Perhaps she wants him out of the house as much as he wants to be gone. He tries to keep these jaunts to term times only because he likes to be home when the girls are back from school. Exeats, half-terms and school holidays are clearly marked in his diary. It's just as well that their posh girls' boarding school announces term dates on the school's website.

He is standing outside WH Smith, pacing back and forth. She's late, and Gerry does not want to miss the flight. He's booked them into a new luxury hotel in Verona, and they've got tickets for the opera tomorrow night. Bella prefers Take That to *Turandot*. Such a philistine. Not that they can go to the Arena di Verona; it's the wrong time of year. But this performance in a small theatre will be more intimate, and the cast is good. Gerry is new to opera, but from the way he speaks, one would think he is an aficionado.

'Boo!' she says, grabbing him by the arm and leaning in to

give him a little kiss on the neck. Her dark hair is swept up underneath a blue fedora, accentuating her azure eyes.

'Not here,' he hisses, stepping away from her. She pouts. 'Come on, we'll miss the flight if we don't hurry.'

Gerry likes to splash out on Mae. She's not like Bella, who takes his wealth for granted. Mae appreciates him and his gestures. When he buys her gifts, she is so thankful, treating him to all sorts of special tricks in bed, taking him to heights of pleasure far beyond anything he has ever experienced before. Even better than the girl in Bangkok.

That first buying trip, when they went to Florence, Mae clapped her hands and danced around like a little child. She was in awe of the architecture, the sensuous food, the exquisite plants, and she threw her head back and laughed with uninhibited joy as she tried to mimic the cadences of Italian. When he took her to the opera – her idea, her passion – Gerry was more entranced by her reactions to the music than watching and listening to what was happening on stage. Tears flowed down her cheeks, her hands were clasped to her chest, her body swayed with the melodies.

And now opera is Gerry's thing too.

'Mustn't have too much pasta this weekend.' Mae pats Gerry's protruding stomach as they settle into their seats at the front of the plane.

Gerry scowls. He doesn't like to be reminded that he's old enough to be Mae's father and at least three times her girth.

When the airplane is cruising and they each have a glass of bubbly, Gerry leans back into his seat and lets out a loud sigh. 'What a bloody awful week.'

'Let me make it better,' Mae says, licking his earlobe and blowing her hot breath into the hairy canal of his left ear.

He shivers. 'Thank you, love.' He squeezes her hand.

· · ·

TUTTI AGRICOLA IS LOCATED thirty miles south of Verona. They grow and export outdoor ornamental plants, fabulous specimens of camellia and hydrangeas, verdant and lush in straight rows as far as the eye can see. Although Shelton Bros imports plants, Gerry is no horticulturalist. He relies on Pete, his Kew Gardens-trained plant buyer, when it comes to all things growing, but he doesn't like to pass up on a trip to Italy, especially if it means he can play away with Mae.

Gerry and Mae are standing in an immaculate yard with a neat modern building constructed from glass and brick behind them and fine-combed shingle underfoot. On all three sides there are flat fields with rows and rows of plants in pots, lined up in perfectly straight lines, disappearing into the distance. Mae puts on her sunglasses and peers at the sheer enormity of the growing operation, at how each row is comprised of plants of identical shape and height. Gerry turns as he hears footsteps coming towards him and grins at the Italian owner. He has met Alessandro Romano several times before and is grateful that he speaks fluent English.

'It is my pleasure.' Signor Romano pumps Gerry's hand. He nods deeply towards Mae. 'Madame.'

Mae is impressed by the smart Italian with his slicked-back black hair and navy jacket with gold buttons.

'You know the history of *Camellia japonica*?' He directs the question to Gerry.

Mae replies. 'Yes. Native to Japan and China, it was imported into Europe in the mid-eighteenth century and became as popular as the tulips one hundred and fifty years earlier. At one time the camellia was the symbol flower of Italy due to its red, white and green foliage, was it not?'

Alessandro's eyes nearly pop out of his head. 'Madam is so knowledgeable,' he says, laughing.

'Have you suffered any problems with *Aphis Toxoptera aurantii*?' Mae asks.

Gerry shuffles to one side. He hasn't got a clue what she's talking about.

'No, we have good aphid control. Our plants are nearly one hundred per cent disease resistant.' He breaks off a leaf from a mature plant and shows her the underside. 'The climate here suits the camellia very well.'

Alessandro Romano turns towards Gerry. 'Who is this lady? She has much plant knowledge. Does she work for you?'

Gerry isn't sure how to answer the question and fumbles over his words.

Mae comes to the rescue. 'I'm a horticultural consultant.'

When Alessandro has his back to them, Mae pinches Gerry's backside so hard he bites his tongue and draws blood to stop himself from squealing.

Things haven't exactly gone to plan. Gerry thought Mae would slip into the background whilst he steered the conversation. Now he is worried that Alessandro will mention her when he next speaks to Pete. And Gerry does not want anyone at work knowing about Mae.

LATE AFTERNOON and they are back in the hotel room, an ornately decorated boudoir with long brocade curtains and a glass chandelier, befitting an Italian palazzo. They are slick with sweat and panting after a vigorous love-making session which was highly satisfying for Gerry and deeply unsatisfying for Mae.

'How are the plans progressing for your big takeover?' Mae asks, guiding Gerry's hand to encourage him to finish her off. She's learned that there's nothing Gerry likes to talk about more than his business aspirations. And she's learned that stroking his ego is as important, if not more so, than stroking his disappointingly small penis.

'Disaster,' he says, removing his hand and rolling sideways

out of bed. 'Bloody disaster. The old cow won't even discuss it. Said she has no intention of retiring.'

'We'll have to come up with a way of persuading her then, won't we? Shall we strategise, big boy?'

Gerry swings his legs back on to the bed and dives on top of Mae. She has to stop herself from crying out as his bulk compresses her breasts and pushes the air out of her chest.

'Strategise,' he murmurs as he lowers his head farther and farther down her body.

18

'Stay,' Stijn says, making a lunge for Lily as she slips out of bed.

'I can't,' she says, sighing. 'Have to go to work.'

'I hate that you work weekends,' Stijn says. He pouts. 'I want to be with you.'

'Come along too.'

Lily wraps a blue and white kikoi around her torso, a traditional cotton sarong she bought when she travelled around Africa. She walks out of the room, gently closing the door behind her.

When Stijn hears the taps opening in the bathroom and the heavy clunking of the ancient boiler, he thinks about Lily's suggestion.

'Yes, I will. I'll go with her to the garden centre,' he mutters to himself, jumping out of bed.

He paces out of the room, not bothering to cover himself up, uncaring if Annette sees him in all his naked glory. She has run into him a couple of times in the corridor between their rooms. The first time, she rushed back to her bedroom, her cheeks aflame, slamming the door behind her. The second time, she ignored him and implored Lily to get Stijn to put on underpants before exiting the bedroom. Stijn had no intention of complying. But this morning, Annette's bedroom door is closed, and other than the noise from Lily's shower, the house is silent.

He tugs at the bathroom door handle. To his surprise, it's locked. He hammers on the door.

'Let me in, Lils!'

He bangs again, louder this time, and shakes the door. The shower stops and Lily opens it.

'What is it?' There is alarm in her eyes.

'Jump back in,' he growls.

'But I've finished.' She flips her long, wet hair back over her shoulders.

'No, you haven't!'

Stijn grasps her wrist. Lily slips and squeals, bashing her shin against the edge of the shower cubicle. She's learned not to resist Stijn.

'I'm coming with you today.' He breathes hot, foul, morning breath into her ear. 'But first I'm coming with you now.'

He turns the shower back on and pulls her inside, pushing her up against the wet, slippery tiled wall. Lily complies just to get it over and done with.

THEY ARE in Lily's Mini Countryman, driving to the garden centre. Stijn is sitting in the passenger seat and hums all the way, tapping his fingers on the window to provide a beat. He's in a good mood.

'There's nothing for you to do,' Lily insists, hoping she can change his mind and send him homewards.

'I want to learn about the garden centre. I'm bored working for that jerk Gerry. Don't like to be away from you so much.

One of these days, when you take over the business, you and me will be working together.'

Lily is silent. It terrifies her that she might be responsible for fifty staff and the day-to-day running of the garden centre. She loves her plants and sharing her passion for them with the public, but the day-to-day running, the money side of things, the staffing issues – they all fill her with dread.

Opening the garden centre up in the mornings is Lily's job, a duty she was happy to take on after her dad died. Like Annette, she's awake with the dawn chorus. But it hasn't been the same since the murder. Now she finds herself holding her breath as she walks through the greenhouses, just in case she makes another discovery. For that reason, she's glad Stijn is with her.

'I'll go and tidy up,' Stijn says after they've dumped Lily's bag in her office.

Lily wonders what Stijn thinks he is going to tidy up. If his flat and their bedroom are anything to go by, he doesn't know the meaning of the word *tidy*. Relishing his surprisingly good mood, she gives him a quick kiss on the cheek and hurries back through the outside plant section towards the houseplants. It's Lily's favourite time of day: early in the morning, when she's the first person in, watering the houseplants in silence with just the splashing and tinkling sounds of the waterfall providing a meditative backdrop.

STIJN WATCHES LILY FLIT through the raised beds of shrubs and bedding plants. She walks quickly and lightly like a nymph, he thinks. When she's out of sight, he rifles in her handbag and finds her large bunch of keys. He shoves them into his trouser pocket, shielding the bulge with his hand, and walks quickly out of the office block and around the back of the building, where there are two greenhouses.

This area is strictly out of bounds for the public. There's a warehouse and a medium-sized dilapidated greenhouse with broken panes of glass and rusted steels. Few plants are kept there. When the plants are delivered from growers, they arrive on metal Danish trolleys and are wheeled straight into the garden centre, where they are given the once-over and watered as necessary. As David used to say, 'The quicker the stock goes onto the shop floor, the quicker the punters come back for more. Keep the stock hidden away, and you won't see a raise in your pay.' He said it so often the staff still repeat it, but never in front of Annette.

At the back of the greenhouse is a smaller, newer addition: Annette's special area, her no-go zone. It's fenced in with seven-foot panels and barbed wire on the top. In the dark winter months, bright light streams from the roof of the small glasshouse.

'What's with the high-security zone?' Stijn asked Lily a few weeks before they got married.

'It's Mum's propagating glasshouse. She's into genetics and trying to grow new plant types, hybrids and the like.'

'But why the secrecy?'

'She doesn't want anyone to nick her ideas. I think it's where she likes to go when everything's getting too much. She was in there loads after Dad died.'

A few days later, Lily said, 'Do you want to see inside Mum's greenhouse? She's gone to the doctor's, so we can go and have a look.'

'Sure.'

There wasn't much to see. Just batches of green plants in different stages of growth, and a bench with plants growing under ultraviolet lights.

Lily pointed at a plant. 'What colour is it?'

Stijn stared at the strange mud-coloured leaves. 'Brown.'

Lily lifted a plant up and removed it from the light. 'See, it's really green. That's what the LED lights do.'

'Wow,' Stijn had said, but he was more interested in looking at the notebook Annette had left at the end of the bench. When Lily turned her back, he flicked it open, trying to decipher Annette's tiny, sharp, scrawling letters.

'Put it down!' Lily chastised when she saw what he was doing.

'Why?'

'It's private. Come on!'

She had dragged him by the sleeve then, out of the greenhouse.

And now Stijn intends to have another snoop around. He hurries around the back, passing the loading bay and the locked warehouse, along the side of the greenhouses, and stands in front of the gate in the tall wooden-fenced wall. It takes a while of fumbling through Lily's keys before he finds the right one. He constantly looks over his shoulder to make sure no one is watching. And then he's in.

He flicks the light switch near the door frame, and then a high-pitched noise pierces his skull.

'Fuck!' he says, frantically looking around for the alarm panel.

He was sure Lily didn't switch off an alarm when they came in previously. After five seconds or so, he decides he's better off scarpering. There are many systems that he can disarm, but he needs his kit and a bit of time, and he's totally unprepared.

Stijn mutters more expletives as he switches off the light and locks up after himself. Then he races back through the loading bay, up the steps into the office and runs straight into Lily.

'What the...?' Her blue eyes are large.

'Okay,' Stijn says, panting and holding her keys aloft. 'I

admit I wanted to snoop. I went into your mum's greenhouse, but I didn't realise there was an alarm.'

'An alarm?' Lily pales.

'Anyway, I set it off.'

She puts a hand over her mouth.

'I'm sorry, Lils. I know I shouldn't have done it. You'll forgive me, won't you?'

He gives her his cheeky grin and sticks his index finger in his mouth. For once that look doesn't do the trick.

'How could you do that?' Lily speaks quietly, the look of disappointment on her face worse than any anger.

'I'm sorry, really I'm sorry. What shall we tell Ma?'

'The truth,' she says, turning away from him.

Stijn shakes his head vigorously. 'No, we can't do that. You know she doesn't approve of me.'

'She certainly won't now,' Lily mutters.

Stijn grasps her shoulders. 'That's my point. She has enough shit going on in her life without me upsetting her. You need to cover for me. Tell her you set the alarm off or that there was a malfunction or something.'

Lily doesn't say anything.

'Come on, Lily!'

'Okay,' she relents. 'I'll tell her it was a mistake. That I thought I saw someone going in, but I was mistaken and set off the alarm.'

Stijn pulls her to him and jams his mouth over hers. Lily tries to pull away and pushes the palms of her hands against his chest.

'I need to work.'

'Do you think the alarm is connected to a monitoring station or the police?' Stijn asks, releasing Lily suddenly.

She pales again. The phone in her office rings. She picks it up.

'Hi, Lily, it's Tess on reception here. Mrs Gower is on the phone for you.' Lily blinks rapidly.

'What was Stijn doing in my greenhouse?'

'What, Mum?'

'Stijn. Your husband. He was in my greenhouse. He just set the alarm off.'

'Um, it was a mistake, Mum.'

'Of course it was a bloody mistake. He shouldn't have been there.'

Stijn is gesticulating at Lily, but this befuddles her, and she's tongue-tied.

Stijn grabs the phone. 'Ma, I'm really sorry. Lily thought she saw someone go into your greenhouse. She got scared and gave me her keys so I could go and have a look. We didn't realise you had an alarm.'

There is silence on the other end of the phone and then a click.

'What did she say?' Lily asks.

Stijn shakes his head in bemusement. 'Nothing. She said nothing.'

19

Normally Lily is awake before the alarm, bright, breezy and ready to get on with the day. But this morning there is nothing more she would like than a Sunday morning sleep-in.

Stijn is lying on his back, snoring gently. She slips out of bed and tiptoes to the bathroom. Annette's door is closed, as it was most of yesterday. She came into the garden centre via the back entrance, disappeared into her special greenhouse, silenced the alarm, and then Lily didn't see her again. She wasn't sure if Annette stayed there all day or returned home.

The garden centre was busy. The staff were putting out Christmas decorations, which Lily thought was ridiculous as it was only September. But as quickly as they were put out on display, they were bought. Cute little trinkets of angels and Santa Claus in gaudy reds and greens. Lily loves the glass and metallic baubles, particularly the pale pinks with silver sparkles and the ghostly pale greens and the baubles that have an iridescent sheen like soapy bubbles.

At some point, Stijn disappeared. He didn't say goodbye.

When she left the garden centre in the evening, her car was still there in the staff car park where they had left it in the morning.

Back at home, Annette had appeared in the kitchen to make herself a cup of herbal tea around 8 p.m.

'Mum, I'm sorry about the alarm—'

Annette waved her hand. 'I don't want to talk about it.'

Lily heard her shuffle upstairs and close her bedroom door. Stijn wasn't home either, but that was normal for a Saturday night. In the first few months, Lily had been upset that Stijn regularly went out without her, but now she's relieved. The last thing she feels like after a long day on her feet at work is a drunken night down at the pub, especially when she has to work the next day.

STIJN IS STILL ASLEEP when Lily has finished in the bathroom. She decides not to wake him, creeps downstairs and grabs an apple and a banana for breakfast. She stumbles as she trips over three black roses on the front doorstep.

'What the hell?' Lily says as she reaches down to pick them up and pricks the palm of her hand on the thorns. Two droplets of blood come to the surface. She licks off the blood and winces at the taste.

The roses are almost black. Lily finds them vulgar. Why would anyone want to turn roses blue or black when nature produces such a dazzling spectrum of colours without assistance from inky water? Real black roses are a very dark red and quite hard to come by, so there is no doubt these have been artificially assisted. There's no note attached to them, so she lays them on the sideboard just inside the front door and, shivering, hurries to her car.

The staff car park is empty except for one silver car. As Lily drives nearer, she realises with a start that it is Annette's silver Volvo. Did she come to the garden centre very early, tiptoeing around the house so as not to awaken them, or did someone give her a lift home last night? Lily debates calling Ollie but, glancing at her watch, reckons he would be very annoyed to be disturbed at 8.30 a.m. on a Sunday morning.

Pulling her anorak hood over her head, Lily hurries through the drizzle. At the front door, she takes out her keys, turns the alarm off and runs through her normal morning checklist. She hasn't got long until the rest of the staff arrive, so she paces through the garden centre, keeps underneath the covered walkway outside and then darts across to the office block. She shoves her key into the door, but it doesn't turn. Trying the handle, she is startled that the office is open. She is sure she locked up last night.

'Mum,' Lily calls out.

There's no answer. With her heart thumping, she walks down the short corridor. The light in Annette's office spills into the hallway. Her door is open, and the office looks as if a bulldozer has been through it. Papers are scattered across the floor. The drawers of her filing cabinet have been forced open and hang dejectedly, their contents spilling out. The few plants Annette was tending on the windowsill have been thrown on top of the papers, as if the soil is the topping to an obscene salad.

'Oh no!' Lily freezes, taking in the tableau of destruction, and then fear courses through her, causing her to tremble from head to toe.

'Mummy,' she whispers.

'Morning!' Tess, the receptionist, says, approaching Lily from behind.

Lily jumps and turns around to face Tess, her hand in front of her mouth, her eyes wide.

'Are you all right?' Tess steps forwards.

'There's been a break-in,' Lily murmurs.

'Goodness! Shall I call the police?'

Lily doesn't answer.

'Lily, would you like me to call the police?' Tess repeats.

'Um, yes. Thank you.'

Lily turns. She knows she needs to go to Annette's private greenhouse. She knows no one else can do this, because she is the only person other than her mother who has the key. But Lily is terrified. The most terrified she has ever been.

She walks slowly, unseeing, as if her body is being guided by an invisible compass rather than her eyes. The gate is shut. For a moment she is able to still her manically beating heart, but then she puts her key in the padlock and realises it is unlocked. Swallowing nausea, she pushes the gate open and slowly walks inside. The lights are on. She stands at the entrance.

'Mum. Mummy!' she says.

There is no answer. She steps forwards and looks around. It's been a while since she's been in here, but from her cursory glance, she can't see anything amiss. The plants are neatly lined up on the benches, the LED lights are on, the air is still. And Annette is not there.

Letting out a loud stream of breath, Lily rummages in her pocket for her mobile and calls home. It rings out. She calls Stijn's mobile.

'Yes.' Stijn speaks as if his mouth is full of stones.

'Is Mum at home?'

'What?'

'Is Mum at home?'

'I dunno.'

'Can you go and check?'

'You've woken me up. It's Sunday morning.' Stijn's Dutch accent is very noticeable.

'I know it's Sunday morning. There's been a break-in, and I need to know if Mum is at home. If she's all right.'

'Why wouldn't she be?' Stijn asks.

Lily can hear the rustle of the duvet, and Stijn's grunt as he hauls himself out of the soft bed.

'I've got a bad feeling.'

'Oh, Lils. My little Lils. It'll be fine. I will go and check.'

'I'll wait on the phone.'

'No. Give me five minutes. I need to put some clothes on. Don't want to be giving Ma the fright of her life seeing me starkers. I'll call you back, Lily.'

Lily paces up and down outside, no longer noticing the drizzle, which is rapidly turning into heavier rain.

'Come on,' she murmurs to herself repeatedly. 'Come on.'

When five minutes becomes ten, she calls Stijn back. His mobile goes to voicemail. She tries the home telephone.

'Yes?' he answers breathlessly.

'Is Mum there?'

'No. I've looked everywhere. She's not in the house or the garden, and her car isn't in the drive.'

'Her car is here,' Lily says.

'Then she's probably in the garden centre somewhere. Have you looked?'

Lily lets out a little squeal. 'I'm so stupid!'

'My silly Lily,' Stijn mocks.

'Don't call me that,' Lily snaps.

'Why not? Ollie does.'

'Ollie's allowed to. He's my brother.'

'And I'm your husband.'

Stijn hangs up.

20

'Shall I answer it, darling?' Fabian asks, yawning.

It's gone 9 a.m., but they have only had about four hours sleep after attending a particularly raucous party in Brighton.

Ollie groans. *I'm too old for that much booze, drugs and debauchery*, he thinks as he tries to prise his eyes open and focus on the greying light. *How does Fabian get by on so little sleep? Perhaps it's his youth.*

'The phone. It keeps on ringing. Shall I answer it?' Fabian is leaning over Ollie as if to reach for the phone.

'No.' He shoves Fabian away and pulls himself up in bed. The room spins. He picks up the phone. 'Yup?'

'Ollie, it's me. Lily. Mum has disappeared.'

Ollie laughs. 'What do you mean?'

'She's gone. Her car is parked outside the garden centre. Her office has been vandalised and she's disappeared. She's not at work or at home, and she's not answering her mobile.'

'Mum never answers her mobile. It's always off.'

'I don't know what to do.' Lily sounds as if she's close to tears.

'Perhaps she's visiting a friend or walked to the shops. I know a lot has happened recently, Lily, but you are being rather histrionic.'

'I've got a bad feeling, Ollie. Don't mock me.'

'Call me back when you find her.' Ollie puts the phone down.

'Who was that?'

'Lily. My sister.'

'When are you going to introduce me to your family?' Fabian whines. 'We've been an item for thirteen months and twenty-four days.'

Ollie doesn't answer. He stumbles out of bed and staggers to the bathroom. The alcohol and drugs have befuddled his mind, and the more he thinks about Lily's concerns, the sicker he feels. Annette has been acting very strangely.

Ollie takes an ice-cold shower, drinks water from the cold tap and swallows a couple of paracetamol and ibuprofen. He grabs one of Fabian's protein bars from the larder and hurries to the car. On his way out of Hove, he calls Pippa, leaving a message.

'Sorry to disturb you on a Sunday morning, but any chance you could meet me at the garden centre? It's kind of urgent. Mum has disappeared.'

21

PIPPA

I wake up late. Mungo is ravenous and desperate to go out. The rain has vanished, and the day is bright, crisp and autumnal. I call my brother, Rob, knowing he will already have been to the gym and drunk a gallon or so of the fresh juice smoothies he gets delivered daily, even on Sundays.

'Do you fancy a walk along the beach?'

'Sorry, Pips. I'm meeting a friend for lunch. Next weekend, perhaps. Are you planning on going out to Geneva to meet your new grandchild?'

'No. I haven't been invited.'

'You don't need to wait for an invitation. Just go! George and Marie will be much too busy wrapped up in the minutiae of new-babydom to extend an invitation.'

'Has George said anything to you?' I am still smarting from the fact that my son reached out and confided in his uncle, seeking his help with a new job whilst he stayed away from me.

'No, but I've got to go to Geneva for a meeting in a fortnight or so, and George seemed pleased at the prospect of me meeting baby Louis. Perhaps you should come along?'

'Perhaps,' I mumble.

It's an hour or so later – after I've had a shower, eaten a leisurely breakfast and read the newspaper – that I see I have a missed call and a message on my mobile. Ollie Gower's mother is missing. It was only yesterday that Annette Gower told me she felt threatened, that she thought she should disappear to protect herself. Is that what she has done? Disappeared? I am not sure what to do. Should I comply with Ollie's request and go to the garden centre? After Annette left yesterday, I sent Joe a long text message outlining Annette's fears. His response was curt. *Thanks!*

I can't decide whether I should get further involved. The Gowers are not my clients, and it's Sunday. I debate sending Ollie a message, telling him that I am otherwise engaged, out of the country perhaps.

After vacillating for too long, I call Joe Swain. He answers on the first ring.

'Morning, Joe. Sorry to disturb you, but I got a message from Ollie Gower that his mother is missing. As I told you in my text, she came to see me yesterday.'

'Actually, I'm on my way to the garden centre now,' Joe says. 'They've had a break-in. Do you fancy joining me?'

I smile. I can't help it. 'Yes, all right.' I try to say it nonchalantly, but I am anything but laid-back around DS Swain.

CARS ARE QUEUING to get into Rocks Garden Centre's car park. I wonder if there is a special event taking place, but nothing is advertised on the large banners at the entrance. Eventually I make my way in, trying to be patient with the elderly drivers, who park at the speed of snails. I find an empty space at the far end of the car park.

'You've got to stay,' I tell Mungo, who looks at me with large, mournful eyes and then collapses down on to the back seat with a loud huff, his black nose between his paws, his eyes half closed. I know perfectly well that this is his *I'm really annoyed with you* look. Silently I promise to give him a walk along the seafront when I'm finished. I find it ironic that, in a country where we are supposedly so dog friendly, most shops do not allow dogs inside.

I dodge the potholes and lousy drivers and make my way into the garden centre. I am amazed at how busy it is. All six of the tills are operational, with queues seven or eight customers long. And it's only noon. The Gowers clearly have a very successful business.

'Doctor Durrant!'

Ollie materialises from behind a large wooden wheelbarrow brimming with apples, pumpkins and autumnal fresh produce. It isn't until I'm standing right next to it that I realise the fruit and vegetables are artificial.

'I'm so glad you came,' Ollie says. 'I didn't get a message from you, so I wasn't sure if you'd be here.'

I feel awkward now, unsure if I should mention my conversation with Joe, and rather hoping that Joe doesn't see me talking to Ollie.

'Have you found her?'

Ollie shakes his head.

'I'm curious as to why you want to talk to me. Isn't this a police matter?'

'I don't trust those policemen. They subjected my mother to unnecessary stress. Besides, if an adult goes missing, they don't start investigating or taking it seriously for twenty-four hours.'

'Unless you have reason to believe their safety might be compromised.'

Ollie pales and steps closer to me. I feel hemmed in

between his tall, slender-but-strong body and the overflowing wheelbarrow. 'Do you think she's in danger?'

'No. No, I'm just saying that.'

He narrows his eyes at me. 'That policeman is here anyway. Mum's office was broken in to, so Lily called the police. Waste of bloody time.' He steps away from me, his trainers making a squeaking sound on the shiny concrete floor. 'I'd offer you a discount,' Ollie says, 'but my parents have a strict policy. No discounts for F and F's.'

I frown.

'Friends and family. No specials for anyone except staff. And I'm not staff, so I get zilch.' His laugh is forced and bitter.

'Keep me posted,' I say to Ollie. 'If you want to see me in a professional capacity, you know where I am.'

He nods and strides away towards the tills. As I watch him go, his shoulders slightly hunched and his walk a strange combination of loping and athletic striding, I wonder why he was so keen to meet me here. I wonder if he changed his mind about opening up to me because of something I said, or something that happened before I arrived.

My phone pings with an incoming text.

In the coffee shop. Jx

Gently I bite my lip to stop smiling. Joe has signed his text message with an *x*. Is that especially for me, or does he normally sign off like that?

What was, only a week ago, a department full of garden furniture has been transformed into a Christmas wonderland. Customers of all ages are browsing the benches stuffed full of Christmas decorations, oohing and aahing as if they are toddlers in a sweetie shop. It is only the end of September; it seems ridiculous to me that people are buying Christmas paraphernalia three months early.

I loathe Christmas. I never used to, but now I am alone and there are no young, excited faces in my life, it only serves to accentuate my loneliness. Perhaps that will change now I am a grandmother. A couple of years ago I ran a workshop for people who needed to work through emotional problems brought to the fore by Christmas. It was oversubscribed, and the local newspaper ran a feature on it. Whilst it may have helped my clients, it did nothing for me. I won't be running the workshop again.

Christmas songs are playing through the loudspeakers, those dreadful tunes with their ear-worm melodies. I feel for the staff, who will have to listen to 'Let It Snow' and 'A Holly Jolly Christmas' many thousands of times between now and the twenty-fifth of December.

The sound of tinkling glass takes me by surprise.

'Oh no, look what you've done, Florence!'

A young mother looks in dismay at the shattered glass bauble lying at her daughter's feet. The child can't be more than five or six years old. Her bottom lip is trembling, her pale eyes overflowing with fat tears. She's called Florence. It feels as if those little shards of glass are stabbing me in the chest. I stride away quickly.

The coffee shop is full of people. It smells temptingly of freshly ground coffee, but 'coffee shop' is a misnomer. They serve full meals here, and I notice many trays stacked high with Sunday roasts. It looks as if all the seventy or so tables are occupied, and the queue snaking around the food counters is long. I hesitate. Should I queue and get myself a coffee or search for Joe first? I see him then, standing up at the back of the room, waving at me. It would be hard to miss him. He is the only smartly dressed, tall, dark-skinned man in the restaurant. I hurry towards him, weaving between the tables.

'I got you an Americano and a piece of carrot cake. I hope that's what you like,' he says.

'Thank you,' I say, smiling. Just because I polished off most of the vegan carrot cake he bought me last time we were in a coffee shop doesn't mean I particularly like it. I'm more of a 'full-fat cream and a kilo of sugar in my chocolate fudge cake' kind of woman, as evidenced by the rolls of flab around my stomach, but now isn't the time to tell him that. I'm just impressed he remembered the carrot cake.

'How are you?' he asks coyly.

'Fine, thanks. And you?' Today I am in the company of the charming, debonair DS Swain, not the brutish interviewer. I shuffle in my chair.

'All is not what it seems with the Gower family,' Joe says, taking a sip of espresso. 'I think they're a bunch of compulsive liars.'

'That's a bit harsh.'

Joe harrumphs.

'Annette came to see me because she was scared,' I say.

Joe puts his coffee cup down a little too forcefully. Steaming black coffee slurps on to the saucer.

'Yes, I saw your message. Why didn't she come to see me?'

'Because she's terrified of you. I gather you carried on interviewing her after I left.'

'That is my job. What is she scared of?'

'I don't know, but she's been receiving flowers.'

Joe throws his head back with laughter. 'This is a garden centre!'

'Flowers with meanings. It's called floriography.'

'Oh for heaven's sake. That woman makes me despair. Next she'll be telling us that her tea leaves have led her to the murderer.'

'Joe, she wasn't lying. She was genuinely terrified.'

He leans forwards. 'So why didn't she come and see me?'

'As I said, she's scared of you. I told you in my text that she's worried something is going to happen to her children.'

Joe harrumphs. 'We'll keep an eye on them, but police resources need to be focused on finding the murderer.

According to Lily, her daughter, Annette's office was vandalised. It's a mess in there, but Lily can't tell us if anything is missing. To be blunt, I think this is a red herring. We need to focus on who killed Scott McDermott and why. I've got Scenes of Crime Officers dusting for fingerprints just to be sure this isn't linked to the murder.'

'Did you speak to Isla-Mae Carruthers about her connection with Scott McDermott?' I ask.

'Yes. She designed his garden but hasn't seen him in a few years. She had a solid alibi for Monday night. Tell me, did Annette Gower explain what she was so scared of?'

'Joe, she was scared someone might kill her. I told you that in my text.' I lean forwards, feeling a ball of anger in my gut. Is Joe taking Annette's fears seriously enough?

Joe leans back and rubs the edge of his neatly cut index fingernail against his thumb.

'We'll issue a missing person's report on Annette Gower. And I think it's time we re-interviewed every member of the Gower family. I'd like you to be part of that. We need to uncover this family's secrets.'

22

PIPPA

Joe gives me a quick peck on the cheek before leaving to join his officer, who is taking prints in Annette's office.

'I'll contact you about arranging interview times,' he says.

Meanwhile I decide to look for Isla-Mae Carruthers. Despite what Joe said, I want to find out how well she knew Scott McDermott.

She is standing at her desk, deep in conversation with an elderly couple, flipping through an A3 binder. I move behind a display unit laden with gardening gloves in an extraordinary array of hues and designs. Deciding it is more important to hear what she is saying than to observe her, I edge as near as I can and shuffle behind a large stand of seeds. I pretend to study the back of a packet of marigold seeds. When I remember that Annette told me marigolds mean pain and grief, I almost drop it.

'I'm sorry about that,' I hear Isla-Mae say. 'Yes, I was in Italy. A business trip. All rather last-minute, so I'm a bit behind, but I promise to have your drawings ready for you by the end of next week. If we can agree the designs quickly, I might be able to get the hard landscaping underway before the first frost.'

I can't hear the response of the customer, who has an unusually quiet voice.

'Excuse me.' I am startled and drop the packet of seeds. He has thinning grey hair and leans heavily on a stick. 'Can I just get to those?' He points at the display I'm standing in front of.

'Of course.' I move aside, and as I do so, Isla-Mae looks up. Her eyes meet mine and I am sure they widen with recognition. Damn, I'm going to have to go and talk to her now.

I hover, waiting for the couple to finish their conversation. It seems to me that she becomes increasingly animated and focuses all of her attention on them so as to avoid looking at me. Curious behaviour. Eventually they leave, and she pointedly pushes back her sleeve and looks at her watch.

'I'm so sorry, but I'm going to have to go,' she says, her blue eyes skittish. It is most curious that she is eager to avoid me.

'I turned up at the time we agreed on Friday, but you had already left,' I say.

'Yes, I'm sorry. Something came up. Perhaps we could rearrange.' She picks up a large diary and flicks through the pages. 'What is it you're after?' Her eyes avoid mine.

'I'd like to discuss having my garden redesigned. That is what you do, isn't it?'

'Yes. Yes, of course. Would a week on Thursday suit you?'

'Haven't you got an earlier appointment?'

Her sleek black bob catches the fluorescent light, making her hair appear almost blue as she shakes her head. 'I'm sorry but I'm very busy at the moment.'

I decide to go for the jugular.

'You've come very highly recommended. By Scott McDermott, actually. Bless his soul. He was a dear friend.'

Two red blotches appear high on her cheeks; her pupils

dilate; she lets the pages flip shut in her diary. Her breath catches in her throat, and for the first few syllables, her voice sounds strangulated.

'Yes. Terrible, isn't it? Yes, he was a client, but obviously I can't discuss my clients.'

I slant my head to one side. What a surprising statement. It's not as if she's a plastic surgeon, keeping the nips and tucks of her clientele secret, or even a hairdresser privy to customers' dreams or disappointments. I wonder why she has handed me a cluster of body language, micro-expressions and linguistic giveaways, all suggesting she is lying, or at the very least desperate to keep something hidden from me.

'If you get a cancellation before a week on Thursday, please can you call me.' I fumble in my handbag and produce a business card. It reads 'Dr Philippa Durrant, PhD, CPsychol, FBPsS, Psychologist'.

'You're a psychologist?' My business card trembles ever so slightly between her thumb and forefinger. 'Lots of letters after your name!' She smiles, but the creases around her eyes are not uniform. It is a fake smile.

'Yes. I specialise in lie detection,' I say, quickly turning on my heels and walking away from her. I don't need to see her face to know the expression that will be written across it.

THE SATISFACTION I get from making Isla-Mae feel ruffled is short-lived. By the time I reach the car and receive an ecstatic welcome from Mungo, I wonder if I have played a bad hand. She won't want to talk to me now I've scared her.

'Oh, Mungo,' I groan as I start the car.

I drive down to the seafront. The beach is deserted, probably because the early-morning promise of a fine day was hollow and now the sky is pewter, hanging low, threatening. A gusty wind has picked up, and I pull my navy anorak close around me and walk briskly to stop the shivering.

Mungo isn't bothered by the inclement weather. As quickly as I can throw his Frisbee along the pebbly foreshore, he leaps to catch it and deposits it back at my feet. The simple delight of my dog and the hypnotic roar of the waves tug me farther and farther along the rocky beach. I say it out loud, and it brings smarting tears to my eyes.

'I am lonely!'

The words catch on the wind and quickly fade into nothingness. I slow my breath. It shouldn't be like this. I shouldn't be alone on a September Sunday. I should be with my family. But I don't have a family any more. My husband is married to another woman. My son is a young father, in love, living in Switzerland. My daughter. I stifle a sob. My daughter is dead. At least, everyone else presumes she is. And my brother is happily dating other men. I am an orphan, as our parents are dead. All I have is Mungo.

Fifty-three years old and all alone. I need to start dating. I know I do, but I've been putting it off, concentrating on work, anything to avoid both rejection and getting my heart broken all over again.

Joe's dark, square-jawed face pops into my mind. Is the attraction mutual? I thought so, but nothing has happened. And now, if he wants us to work together, it can't. Perhaps I have read him all wrong. Perhaps all he wants is a professional relationship.

By the time Mungo and I reach home, the rain is torrential, clattering on the roof of my car so loudly I can't hear the music on the radio. We make a dash for it. Surprisingly for a Labrador, he hates the wet weather.

I give him his supper, and then I slump onto the sofa. Feeling a heavy lethargy, I switch on the television. I need some distraction, so I sign into Netflix. After an hour or so lost in a poorly acted American romcom, the details of which I won't remember tomorrow, Mungo appears and nuzzles my leg.

'Do you want to go out, boy?' I ask, pressing 'Pause' on the remote control and wearily getting up from the sofa.

I walk to the back door, unlock it and hold it open for Mungo. He sticks his nose outside and glances up at the incessant rain. It is dark now. After hesitating for a couple of moments, Mungo disappears into the inky, sopping-wet night. I close the door and walk to the fridge, pour myself a large glass of white wine and am about to go back into the living room when I hear Mungo barking. That's strange. Mungo rarely barks when he's in the garden. I open the back door again and peer outside, but can't see anything.

'What is it, Mungo?'

His barking becomes louder. There is an insistent tone to it, an edge that, in the eight years I've owned my dog, I haven't heard before.

'Mungo!'

The barking becomes more frantic. I wonder if he's caught a rabbit. He often chases them but has never actually caught one. But if he has, he wouldn't be barking, would he? I hope no one is in the garden or creeping around in the neighbours' houses or gardens.

'Come here, Mungo!' I shout.

He ignores me and carries on barking. Feeling a flutter of nerves, I leave the back door open and walk back to the downstairs cupboard to find my anorak and wellington boots. When I am togged up for the wet weather, I collect my torch from the small utility room and walk outside.

The rain becomes louder, more torrential, as if in sync with Mungo's frenetic barking.

'What is it?' I say, hurrying towards him.

And then I stop and let out a strangulated scream.

As the eldest of the three siblings, Bella takes it upon herself to call a family meeting. They haven't had an official family meeting since David died. In his day, they were regular occurrences. It didn't matter where in the world Bella, Ollie or Lily were, they were expected to attend.

When Ollie was in his training year with the bank, he was sent on a three-month secondment to Hong Kong. He received an email from David stating that they would be having a family meeting at 7 p.m. the next day. As he was nearly twelve hours' flight time away from home and abroad for work, Ollie ignored the request.

Upon his return five weeks later, exhausted from jet lag, excessive partying and brain-numbing hard work, Ollie put the key in the front door to his Clapham one-bedroom flat. It didn't turn. After tugging and pushing and kicking the door, he assumed the lock had somehow got jammed. Whilst he was waiting for the emergency locksmith, he sat at the top of the communal stairs and opened his post. His heart sank when he found the envelope with his father's messy scrawl on the front. He pulled out the letter. It read, *Dear Oleander, I have terminated the lease on your flat. When I call you home for a meeting, I expect you to be there. Your father.* In that moment, Ollie decided he would never be financially or emotionally dependent upon anyone ever again. He returned to work the next morning and requested a pay rise. He got it.

'WE SHOULD HOLD the meeting at Mum's house,' Ollie suggests to Bella. He's in the car, nearly home.

'Sorry, no can do. I've been hard at work all weekend, and I simply can't get in the car right now.'

Ollie wonders what Bella's idea of hard work is, but now isn't the time to start an argument.

'What about Gerry? Can't he drive? It makes sense to be at Mum's in case she comes home.'

'Gerry's not here.'

Ollie assumes the truth is Bella has been working her way through the drinks cupboard and she isn't in a fit state to drive. Sighing, he turns the car around and heads towards Arundel.

THEY ARE SITTING in Bella's kitchen, perched on black leather stools at her island unit. Ollie is annoyed Stijn is there. It feels like he is an imposter; it should just be the three of them. The Gower siblings.

'What did the police say?' Ollie asks Lily.

'Not a lot. They dusted Mum's office for fingerprints, had a nose around and left. That detective Swain said he'd be setting up times to interview all of us again.'

'Why?' Stijn frowns.

No one answers.

'Did the police go through Ma's private greenhouse?' Stijn asks.

'No.' Lily's shoulders sink. 'Where could she be? Where could Mum have gone?'

'Without her car, she must have gotten a lift from someone,' Ollie says.

'Are you sure she's not at the garden centre?' Bella tops up her glass but doesn't offer any more wine to the others.

'Lils and I searched the place top to bottom. She's not there.'

'We need to ring her friends,' Bella suggests.

'Does she have any?' Ollie can't recall his mum ever talking about friends. She doesn't play bridge or golf or tennis or go to art classes. Just gardening. A solitary activity.

The front door slams. They all jump.

'What are you doing here?' Gerry appears, wheeling a small suitcase.

'Mum is missing. I called a family meeting,' Bella says, taking another gulp of wine. Her teeth are coated in tannin. 'Good trip?'

'Yes. Thanks.'

It's Lily who notices that Bella and Gerry don't kiss each other.

'Where've you been?' Stijn asks.

Gerry ignores the question, removes his jacket, drops it on a chair, paces towards the fridge and takes out a can of lager.

'I asked you where you've been,' Stijn reiterates.

'Not that I need to answer that, but I've been on a business trip, to Italy.'

'At the weekend?' Ollie asks.

'Yup. The grower wanted to show me around, so we had our meetings on Friday, and I had a lovely tour yesterday. I got back early this morning. Been in the office today.'

'I wonder why you didn't take your lovely wife with you,' Stijn says.

'Because—'

'Come on, everyone. Let's focus on the issue at hand: trying to find Mum,' Ollie interrupts.

'Have you rung around the hospitals?' Gerry asks.

'Oh!' Lily puts a hand over her mouth.

Stijn squeezes her shoulder.

'No. Would you like to do that, Gerry?' Ollie suggests.

He nods, picks up the house phone and, holding his beer with the other hand, disappears out of the kitchen.

'Lily, why don't you go home and search the house? Find Mum's diary and telephone book and see if you can work out her movements over the last couple of weeks. Ring around her contacts,' Ollie says.

'It's such an imposition.' Lily stifles a sob. 'Mum hates me going through her stuff.'

'If Ma was here, we wouldn't have to do it, would we?' Stijn puts his arm around Lily.

'I'm sure we're all worrying about nothing. She's probably just taken herself off for a spa weekend to get over all the stress of that dead man. That's what I would do,' Bella says.

'Bella, you really have no idea!' Ollie slams his hand on the granite counter. 'Mum never goes away. Never!'

'And she always rings me to ask for the daily takings if I'm not with her,' Lily says. 'Especially on a Sunday, a busy Sunday like today.' She glances at her watch. 'And she hasn't called. She's been behaving oddly ever since this murder.'

'Actually, she's been super-stressed for the last few months,' Ollie says. 'Perhaps you don't notice because you live with her.' He smiles at Lily.

'I think she knows something about Scott McDermott she isn't telling us about.' Bella's words slur ever so slightly.

'You're pissed,' Stijn snaps.

Gerry strides into the room. 'No record of Annette at any of the local hospitals. I've rung Worthing, Brighton, Chichester, Haywards Heath and Redhill. Suggest you all go home and have a good night's sleep, and in the very unlikely event Annette doesn't surface tomorrow, I'll file an official missing person's police report.'

'The police already know. I'm speaking to DS Swain tomorrow regardless,' Ollie says. 'I'm going home. Lily, call me if there's any news.'

'YOU'RE VERY QUIET,' Stijn says on the drive home. 'Try not to worry.'

Lily's worrying has turned into mental plotting as to how to keep Stijn away from searching her mother's two most private places: her bedroom and the greenhouse in the garden. Annette never used to lock her bedroom door. She only started when Stijn moved in with them.

The house is in darkness and the back door locked. Stijn goes in first, flicking all the lights on.

'Would you mind searching the living room?' Lily turns her back to Stijn so her face doesn't give anything away. 'It's the place she's most likely to have hidden things. In the antique dresser or Dad's old bureau.' She doesn't see Stijn's scowl.

Lily hurries upstairs, pausing for a moment to listen out for Stijn, making sure he hasn't followed her. She opens the airing cupboard in the hall, pulls out a pile of old blankets and places them on the carpet. A small grey safe is fixed to the back wall. Lily turns the dial six times, whispering the numbers out loud – 020967 – the date of her parents' wedding. The safe door swings open.

Annette told Lily the safe code after David died. It was a time of introspection, when Annette wondered whether she would also have a short life.

'In case anything happens to me, you need to know where I keep my jewellery, passport and birth certificates. Mine and your father's wills are filed at Peter Reading's office. As the family solicitor, he's an executor.'

'I don't need to know, Mum!' Lily had cried, putting her hands over her ears. 'Please don't tell me!'

But Annette did, and once Lily has heard or seen something, she can't forget it.

Lily pulls out a pile of papers, two jewellery boxes and a bunch of keys. She then closes the safe door and hurriedly shoves the blankets back into the cupboard. Sweeping up the papers, boxes and keys, she is about to study the keys to work out which one will open Annette's bedroom when Stijn shouts upstairs.

'Found anything yet?'

'No.'

She hears his footsteps in the downstairs hall and, worried he might come upstairs, rushes into the bathroom and locks herself in.

'You all right?' Stijn shouts.

'Yes. Just a bit of an upset tummy. I'll be as quick as I can.'

Lily flicks through the papers. She finds her own birth certificate, Annette's birth certificate and Annette and David's marriage certificate. There are a few share and national savings certificates. And then she sees an envelope.

Open in the event of my death.

The words are written in Annette's cursive handwriting. She turns the envelope over. It is sealed shut. Lily's hand shakes, and her throat feels constricted.

Stijn knocks on the bathroom door, and Lily drops the envelope.

'Sure you're okay?' he asks.

'Yes. Nothing to worry about.'

'How are you going to get in your mum's bedroom? She keeps the door locked.'

Lily wonders how Stijn knows the door is locked. He must have tried it at some point or seen Annette lock it behind her.

'I've got the key,' she says.

'Thought I'd go and look in the greenhouse. Have you got the key to that as well?'

'Um, no. Actually, it'd be better if I did the greenhouse, as I know plants and will be able to tell if anything is out of place. If you've finished in the living room, perhaps look through the drawers in the kitchen. Mum keeps her telephone book in the drawer next to the back door.'

Stijn doesn't say anything. Lily waits until she hears his footsteps recede. She then lifts the cork lid of the ancient bathroom seat and pulls out all the old bags of cotton wool and sanitary towels and children's hairbrushes and shoves the two jewellery boxes, the certificates and the envelopes inside. Then she piles everything back in on top of the valuables. She puts the small bunch of keys into her jeans pocket, flushes the loo, then runs the taps.

When she's back out on the landing, she quickly takes out the bunch of keys and tries them in the lock of her mother's bedroom. The fourth key opens the door. When she's inside, she switches on the overhead light and locks the door behind her. A moment or two later it strikes her that she might find Annette dead on the floor or collapsed in the bath.

'Got to. Got to,' she repeats to herself under her breath.

She walks around the bed and pushes open the door to the en suite bathroom. She lets out a long breath when she finds both rooms empty. Lily starts by opening the drawer in Annette's bedside table. She pulls out a packet of sleeping pills, three vials of liquid in small, dark amber homeopathic bottles, David's wedding ring and a handful of jewellery. Lily opens the drawer in her father's bedside table. It is empty.

Six black dresses and three shirts hang in Annette's wardrobe. Lily is shocked that she has so few clothes. The chest of drawers is full, but there doesn't appear to be anything except sweaters and underwear. She pauses for a moment, guilt searing through her. Lily isn't even sure why she's rummaging through her mother's things. She collapses onto the bed, laying her head back on the soft pillow, inhaling the scent of Annette's rose and geranium perfume. Tears smart her eyes. Lily knows Annette would never go away without telling her. Automatically searching for a tissue, she puts her hand under the pillow, which is where Lily always keeps a handkerchief, and her fingers coil around a small notebook. Sitting up too quickly, Lily feels dizzy as she flicks through the pages. There are lots of numbers and strange hieroglyphics. And plant names. Unusual ones Lily has never heard of. She flicks to the back of the book. It is set out like an old-fashioned cash book, with debits on the left and credits on the right. Under the descriptions are a list of numbers. None of it makes any sense, until suddenly—

'Lily, there's nothing of interest downstairs. I'm coming up,' Stijn shouts.

Hurriedly Lily stuffs the notebook into the front waistband of her jeans and pulls her jumper down over it to hide the small bulge. She straightens the bedspread and plumps up the pillow, switches the light off and shuts the door behind her. As she turns, she comes face-to-face with Stijn.

'Perhaps I should have a look,' he says, placing his palms flat on the door either side of Lily's head, hemming her in, pushing his groin up against hers.

24

PIPPA

Mungo is dancing around the garden, barking frantically, running from left to right and back again. And it's obvious why. My garden has been completely and utterly destroyed. Or at least, the flower beds have. They are decimated. Dug up. The plants are scattered over the lawn; mounds of soil have tumbled everywhere. I direct the torchlight from one side to the other. It's a small garden, but I have taken care of my borders, and this year, for the first time, I spent some considerable sums buying and planting perennials. Only last week I dug in a load of tulip and allium bulbs.

'Shush,' I say, trying to calm Mungo down.

The rain is relentless, and the grass is soggy and squelches as I walk across it. And then my torchlight beam falls on something orange. I hesitate. My breath catches and my knees tremble. I can't see what it is without walking closer to it, and I'm scared.

'Mungo, come.'

My well-behaved dog appears at my side and stays close to my ankles as I move nearer. And then, when I am almost on top of it, I give out a sigh. It's a flowering plant with orange petals and bright-green leaves. I don't have orange flowers in my garden, at least not any like this. It looks like a common bedding plant, and one that I'm not particularly fond of. I can't even remember its name. It is very strange.

I wonder for a moment if a fox has got into the garden and dug up my plants, but the mess seems too calculated, too thorough. Quickly I remove my phone from my pocket and take a photograph of it, then stuff the phone back into my jacket to stop it getting wet.

'Is anyone there?' I say, feebly at first.

I repeat myself, louder this time. The outside light comes on next door. Mungo is silent now, so I assume no one is in the garden. I stand still. The rain is drenching me, soaking the hood of my jacket, and my hair is sticking to my forehead.

'Come on, let's go back inside.'

Mungo follows me eagerly.

I shake off my wet clothes and hang them on a peg in the utility room. My heart is thumping. I can't rid myself of the terrifying thought that someone is in the house. If they got in the garden, a garden that's only accessible through my wooden side gate, have they also broken into the house? But if someone is in the house, they will have been there the full two hours I've been home. Mungo is acting normally inside, but he is only a dog, and perhaps on this occasion he's wrong.

I steel myself and walk into every room of the house, firstly back into the living room, then through into my consulting room, checking the tiny foyer that links it to the outside, and finally I return the way I came and go back into the kitchen. The external doors and windows are all locked; my possessions appear untouched. With my heart hammering in my chest and my breath coming quickly, I tiptoe upstairs, encouraging Mungo to come with me, switching on all the lights everywhere I go.

My bedroom is the first room on the left. I push open the door and switch on the light before walking in. I swing open the built-in wardrobes and peek under the bed. Nothing. The bathroom is exactly as I left it. Mungo looks at me, his head to one side.

'I know I'm being silly, but...' I say, scratching him behind the ears.

The rose floral curtains in the spare room that I have never managed to get around to changing are partially closed, as I last left them. The shower room smells slightly of damp. There is no one lurking in my house. Everything is as I left it.

I pour myself another glass of wine, reckoning I deserve it this evening, but my attention isn't on the television, and after five minutes or so I switch it off.

The orange plant unsettles me. I remember what Annette told me about floriography, but first I need to identify the flower. I recall seeing an advert for an app that assists in the identification of plants. After a few minutes of searching, I download it and input my photograph. *Begonia 'Orange Rubra'*. According to the Royal Horticultural Society's website, it is hardy and dislikes waterlogging or direct sunlight. I do a search for 'floriography' and let out a little moan. *Beware*. The meaning of begonias is 'beware'. Is this a message, or am I giving significance to the work of a fox or a badger?

Should I call Joe, or will he think I'm an idiot? I vacillate. It's Sunday evening and I really don't want to disturb him. I debate calling 101, the non-urgent police telephone number, but as I practise saying it aloud, that someone has vandalised my garden and may have left me a message in the form of a flower,

I realise how very ridiculous it sounds. The police have important things to worry about. Instead I telephone my brother, Rob.

'My garden has been vandalised.'

He bursts out laughing. 'Didn't think there was much to vandalise!' he says, snorting.

'It's not funny. I'm scared.'

I explain what I found and what Annette told me about floriography.

'It sounds to me as if someone preferred your plants to theirs and did a swap with their leftovers. Although whoever it is has got bloody awful taste. Your garden is always a mess.'

'Just because I can't afford to employ a gardener.'

'Okay, I take it back. But honestly, Pips, I don't think you've got anything to worry about. Stop letting your imagination run riot, and don't listen to an old hippy woman. Do you want me to come over? I could catch a train to London from Pulborough rather than Brighton in the morning.'

I smile. That's Rob all over. My loving brother, the only person who would drop everything to make sure I'm all right.

'Thanks, darling, but I'll be fine. Let's speak tomorrow evening when you're back from work.'

SLEEP IS FRACTURED. At 1.30 a.m. I awake with a start. I am sure I heard Mungo bark. I switch on my bedside lamp, sit up and put my hand over my chest to try to slow my racing heart. My ears twitch, but I don't hear Mungo again, and the house is silent. I turn the light off and, using my phone to illuminate the bedroom, I tiptoe out of bed and pull the curtains back just a smidgeon to peer outside, but the night is black and the window is splashed with raindrops. I can't see anything.

I suppose I sleep eventually, but when the alarm goes off, I wake with a pounding headache and sore limbs. Holding my breath, I pull back the curtains to survey the damage of my garden. It looks worse in daylight, and it is quite obvious that this was the work of a human with a spade and not a wild animal. The orange begonia lies, sodden, in the middle of the lawn, even though the rain has stopped and fluffy white clouds are speeding across the bright-blue sky.

I have a full roster of clients and need to concentrate, so I make myself a strong coffee and swallow a couple of paracetamol. I don't want Mungo to further disturb the garden, so after his breakfast, rather than letting him out in the back, which is what I usually do, I put on his lead and walk him up my garden path, along the road and into the field with the public footpath. Back at home, at 9 a.m., I call Joe.

'Something strange has happened.' I wonder if I'm playing it down, but I don't want Joe to think I'm being histrionic. 'My garden has been vandalised, and someone left me a begonia plant. It signifies "beware".'

There is silence on the other end of the phone.

'Are you still there?' I ask.

'Yes. Sorry. Just thinking. I'll come over and take a look. Do you think this has anything to do with the murder of Scott McDermott?'

'I don't see how it can do, but the begonia plant is odd. Could you come at the end of the day? I've got clients until 5 p.m.'

'Sure. I'll see you later.'

Five minutes later, the telephone rings again.

'Hello?' I say. There is silence. 'Hello! Who is there?'

'Doctor Durrant, it's Annette Gow–'

'Annette, are you there?'

But she has hung up. I stare at my phone and then dial 1471 to call her back. But her phone goes straight to voicemail with a standard message. I can't even tell if I'm calling her phone.

I telephone Joe but this time get his voicemail.

'I just received a call from Annette, but she cut the line straight after saying her name. I just wanted to let you know. I think you need to follow it up.'

My voice fades away and I hang up. There is something very strange going on and I have no idea what to do.

25

While Annette's children view her disappearance as a catastrophe, her sons-in-law see it as an opportunity.

Unfortunately for Stijn, it's an opportunity he can't capitalise upon as quickly as he would have liked. He has to deliver a lorry full of pots and planters to a gigantic distribution centre in Swindon; then it's on to Stratford-upon-Avon to collect trolleys full of young plants, returning back to Shelton Bros in Sussex to offload the plants.

'Wouldn't it be better to take the plants straight to the garden centres rather than back to our warehouse?' Stijn suggests during their early-Monday-morning logistics meeting, held in Gerry's oversized boardroom.

Gerry rolls his eyes. 'Thanks, Stijn, but you're employed as a driver, not a manager.'

By the time Stijn is back in the lorry, he is incandescent with rage.

'Pompeuze idioot,' he mutters under his breath.

Stijn pulls out on to the A27 too quickly and only just misses a black Porsche Cayenne driving too fast in the slow lane. How he wishes he could quit this crap job where he has to bow to his bastard brother-in-law. Surely the time is nearly upon them when he can take his rightful place at Rocks Garden Centre and get his hands on the interesting business. Stijn always knew the plan was long-term, a plan that would need resilience and, above all, patience, but right now his patience is being tested to the limit.

He switches on Radio 1 and turns up the music so loud, the heavy beat drums out the red-hot thoughts in his head.

MONDAY MORNINGS ARE ALWAYS hectic at Shelton Bros. Gerry overseas the logistics meeting, then he has a one-to-one with the sales manager, ensuring they're on target and there aren't any issues with their major clients. Mid-morning, he meets Pete, the head buyer, and they are joined by the shiny-bald-headed, bushy-bearded company accountant, who brings them up to date on currency issues and any other budgetary concerns. All the while, Gerry sits at the head of the boardroom table while his members of staff come and go. But this morning Gerry can't concentrate.

'I need to stop you there.' Gerry holds up the palm of his hand to Pete.

The accountant strokes his beard.

Gerry leans back in his chair, and a slow smile creeps across his face. 'I've been working on an expansion plan.'

'But we're losing money,' the accountant says.

Gerry ignores him and turns to Pete. 'Your role may be about to increase considerably. Do you fancy getting into retail?'

As Pete opens his mouth and attempts to speak, Gerry interrupts him. 'Don't answer that. We're going for vertical integration. I am going to buy one of the largest garden centres in the South of England and it is a sure-fire way of getting Shelton

Bro's back into the black.' He pats his chest. 'You are looking at Mr Kingpin of horticulture!'

Pete blinks rapidly.

'How are you going to raise the money? We're already overextended on our bank loan,' the accountant says, frowning.

'Don't worry about that. It's in the family, moving from one pocket to the other. We'll get it for a steal. Just leave it to me!' Gerry has it all worked out. Ollie will want to sell to him, most probably at any price, and Lily will do whatever her siblings tell her. If he can get Rocks Garden Centre, the cost savings to both businesses will be enormous. He'll whip up a business plan, present it to his bank manager, and is in no doubt that he'll be offered a loan to cover the purchase costs.

The buyer and the accountant glance at each other. Gerry stands up, then leans forwards on to his desk. 'Now, keep schtum about this. Not a word to anyone, understand? We need to keep our competitive advantage.'

Gerry straightens up and pulls his fingers across his lips, gesticulating the zipping up of his mouth. He turns away from the two men, puts his suit jacket on, straightens his green bow tie and picks up his briefcase.

'You can go now,' he says.

Gerry grins the whole way to Rocks Garden Centre. He plugs his phone into the audio system of the car and plays 'O Fortuna' from Carl Orff's *Carmina Burana* at full blast, singing along – or rather, shouting tunelessly – at the top of his voice.

'Can you tell Lily Gower I'm here?' Gerry says to the heavily pierced young cashier.

He stands legs planted far apart, his briefcase on the floor in between them. *I'll fire the cashier when I'm in charge*, Gerry thinks. *Piercings and OAP customers don't belong together.*

'Do you have an appointment?'

'Nope. And I don't need one. She'll want to see me.'

'And you are?'

'Gerry Shelton. The name's Gerry Shelton, and don't forget it.' He points his index and middle fingers at her in the form of a gun.

The girl scuttles off to make the phone call. But Gerry doesn't wait. He strides through the garden centre, his chest puffed out, his chin jutting forwards. *All this will very soon be mine*, he thinks.

Mae is at her little table, seated, her glossy black hair falling forwards as her delicate fingers make a pencil dance across a sheet of A3. Gerry creeps up on her and bends down to blow on her neck.

Startled, she drops the pencil and sits up straight. 'God, Gerry! What are you doing here?'

'Shush!' He puts a finger across his lips and glances around to make sure they haven't been overheard or seen. He inhales her delectable perfume, the scent of gardenias. 'Meet me at the Premier Inn in an hour.'

'I can't. I've got to finish this drawing, and I've got new clients coming at 11 a.m. and noon. I'll get into trouble with Mrs Gower.'

'I don't think Mrs Gower is going to be bothering you today.' Gerry grins and licks his lips. 'Your new boss is giving you instructions. Premier Inn in an hour!'

'What do you mean?' Mae asks, but Gerry has picked up his briefcase and is walking away.

He expected her to be in the office studying staff rosters or looking over the weekend figures or signing cheques for the purchase of new stock, but no. Lily is outside watering plants.

'What are you doing out here?'

'Hello, Gerry. Any news on Mum?'

'No. But why are you out here?'

'What do you mean?' There is nothing Lily likes more than caring for the plants, and today of all days, it's the one thing that brings her a sense of calm.

'Give that hose to someone else, and let's go and have a chat in the office.'

Lily switches the hosepipe off and curls it up under a bench. She follows Gerry into the office, her fear for her mother freezing her mind. He walks straight into Annette's office.

'This is Mum's room,' Lily says.

'You're right. Thoughtless of me. Let's go into the boardroom.'

The Gowers' boardroom is nothing like his own. It is shabby, cobbled together with old office chairs pushed up against a scratched and stained long table. He sits at the head. Lily sits to his left.

'We need to talk about the future of Rocks Garden Centre. Obviously you don't have the skills and experience to run this place, so I'm offering my services. It would be a shame to see it fall into someone else's hands, this being a family business and all.'

'But—' Lily's phone trills. She grabs it. 'Ollie?'

'Hi, Lils. Good news. I just got a call from the bastard policeman. Mum rang that psychologist this morning. She's all right.'

'Oh, thank goodness!' Lily can't stop the tears from flowing. She stands up and starts walking towards the door. 'Where is she?'

'We don't know. But the good news is, Mum's okay. I'll drive over to the house to see if she's home and then I'll come to see you.'

'Okay,' Lily says. 'See you later.'

'Who was that?' Gerry asks.

Lily twizzles around, her watery blue eyes smiling. 'Ollie. Mum's fine. It was all a worry about nothing.'

Lily dances out of the room, so she doesn't see the snarl on Gerry's lips, the narrowing of his eyes and the disappointment that settles upon his shoulders, slumping his limbs.

And later, when Mae doesn't turn up at the Premier Inn, Gerry is so furious he slams his fist into the wall behind the bed and leaves a big dent in the paint and plaster, marked with reddish-brown blood from the scraping of skin all along his knuckles.

26

PIPPA

After a long day with back-to-back clients, I stand up and stretch. I didn't even have time for lunch. I am exhausted. Yawning, I collect the empty glasses of water from my consulting room and walk through the house to the kitchen. Mungo jumps up to greet me, nuzzling my leg.

'I know you're hungry.'

I walk into the utility room, open the large plastic container of dog food and my heart sinks. I've run out of dog food. Damn. I had meant to pick some up, but with so much going on, it totally slipped my mind.

Mungo looks at me with his large, trusting eyes, licking his lips.

'You're in luck for now,' I tell him, as he follows me back into the kitchen. I open a tin of tuna and a little leftover rice from yesterday and put it into his bowl. But it's not enough for my big dog. I'm going to have to go out.

The local Tesco Express is open until 10 p.m. I need fresh air, so I put on my coat, attach Mungo's lead to his collar and we amble off down the road towards the shops. It's the time of evening when all is quiet. Most people are inside their houses, home from work and school, eating their evening meals or getting ready to go out again. As we cut through the field behind my house, Mungo starts pulling on the lead.

'Heel!' I say, but unusually for him, Mungo ignores my command. 'What is it?' I ask, as he drags me forwards. I feel the first flickering of nerves. It's not fully dark yet, but the light is low and the shadows are long.

Mungo starts barking, faster, higher-pitched than normal. The *woof-woof* becomes rapid-fire, increasing in intensity. My heartbeat is pounding in my ears. And then I see what Mungo sees. Someone on the far side of the field, a figure on the pavement.

We run.

There is no mistaking who it is.

And this time my scream isn't strangulated.

Annette Gower is lying on the side of the road, her legs crumpled underneath her, her face a pale-grey white. The same shapeless linen dress I have seen her in before puddles around her body and, despite the cold weather, she isn't wearing a coat. Her fingers are clutching a single rose with the darkest and deepest red petals I have ever seen. A flower that would be beautiful in any other circumstances.

'Annette, what's happened?' I ask, my heart pounding hard. I lift up her hand to feel for a pulse. It is barely there.

She is trying to say something. 'Coon,' she murmurs. 'Coon.'

'What? Stay with me Annette! Stay with me.'

But as I hold her hand, she takes a final rattling breath and I can feel life seep from her bones.

'Wake up, Annette!' I screech. I press my fingers to her neck but I can't feel a pulse. I roll her over, put my hand in front of her mouth, but I know I am too late.

'Oh my God!' I mutter over and over again. Her lips are mottled and blue, her eyes open and glassy.

'What's happened?' A man is walking along the other side of the pavement, a Tesco bag swinging from his fingers. When he sees us, he comes running over.

'We need an ambulance, and police!' I screech. 'Quickly!'

He rushes across the road towards me. 'You're trembling, love,' he says, as I stand up. He crouches down to look at Annette. 'Poor woman. She must have had a heart attack.'

I shake my head. 'I know her,' I whisper. 'It's not a heart attack. It's murder.'

This kindly stranger with his mop of white hair looks at me as if I'm deranged. He takes a step backwards as Mungo starts whining. With shaking hands, I extract my phone from my pocket.

'Joe,' I say. 'You need to get here now.'

Twenty minutes later and there are blue flashing lights all around us. An ambulance crew is attending to Annette, but I know it's hopeless. There is no doubt whatsoever in my mind that Annette is dead.

When Joe arrives, the whole area gets cordoned off.

'Come and sit in my car,' Joe says. I am still trembling and freezing cold, my arms wrapped tightly around my torso, Mungo is waiting patiently at my feet, not in the slightest bit bothered by the frenetic activity all around us.

Joe opens the rear door of the car and Mungo jumps in, whilst I get into the passenger side. Joe leans over and squeezes my hand; his grip is firm and warming, his scent aromatic and earthy.

'I'm going to look after you, Pippa,' he says. And I know then that my feelings are reciprocated. 'One of my colleagues will take your statement and then I want you to go and stay with a friend. Let me know where you are going.'

I nod.

'My first aid skills weren't good enough,' I say. 'I should have been able to save her!'

'Pippa, that is nonsense. Thank goodness you were there, able to hold her hand as she passed away.'

More people arrive. Two crime scene investigators, covered from head to toe in disposable white clothing, walk slowly along the pavement, taking photographs and videos. As the light fades, they set up external lamps. A doctor examines Annette, and from his demeanour and body language, I can tell this is a formality. He is confirming she is dead. A tent is erected over Annette's body. I am glad. I don't want to see any more.

Someone knocks at Joe's car window. He winds down his window.

'Can I take a statement from Doctor Durrant?' she asks.

'Of course.' Joe makes as if to get out of the car, but the tiny woman with flyaway black hair opens the rear door and climbs in next to Mungo. She introduces herself as Sumana Patel, the scenes of crime officer.

'I am curious as to why you told my colleagues Mrs Gower's death was murder and not a result of natural causes,' she says.

I sit up straight. 'Wasn't it?'

'Prima facie it appears that she had a heart attack. The autopsy will confirm that.'

'Then why all the police officers, the crime tape, the tent?' I ask, waving my hands at the activity, noticing now the little crowds of people milling at either end of the street.

'Because Detective Sergeant Swain has explained the deceased's connection with the murder of Scott McDermott, and, of course, the rose placed on her body. We are considering all eventualities.'

I tell her everything I know about the Gower family, about the mess I found my garden in yesterday. And then she says, you're that psychologist; the one who was in the news, who helped the police. And I nod and Joe interrupts and says, 'Pippa

Durrant played an instrumental role in helping the police identify the murderer. She acts as a consultant to us.'

Sumana Patel raises her black, arched eyebrows and shuts
her notebook. 'I'll leave the rest of the questioning of Doctor
Durrant to you, Sergeant, whilst I get a progress update from
the rest of the team.'

When Sumana has left, Joe turns towards me. 'I'm going to
take you home now, but I don't want you staying there alone. Is
there anyone who can be with you or anywhere else you can go
for the night?'

Can I stay with you? I want to ask, but I don't.

'I'll stay with Rob, my brother.'

'I don't think there's any danger to you, but I would rather
you weren't alone.'

'It's happening all over again, isn't it?' I sigh.

'No, Pippa. There is nothing to suggest you are in danger or
that this is anything more than an unfortunate set of circumstances.'

'You don't really believe that, do you?' I lean forwards, my
elbows on my knees.

'Let's not jump to any conclusions.'

Poor Annette, I think. Poor Ollie. Poor Lily. What a mess.

27

F abian answers the door. It isn't the first time he's
answered the door to the police, so he knows straight
away who they are, even though the faces and the
clothes are different and now he is grown up and should be
able to cope with it better.

Twelve years ago, when Fabian was thirteen years old, he
opened the door to his home, a council flat on the fifteenth
floor of a high-rise block in an estate in Roehampton. He had
been attempting to complete his homework, an essay on
Napoleon, whilst eating the pizza his mum had left him for his
tea. He collapsed, screaming, when they told him his mother
had been killed crossing the road, hurrying home to be
with him.

Fabian became an orphan on that March Tuesday afternoon. He had never had a father, never bothered to look for
him. It was a one-night stand, his mum had told him. 'I didn't
regret it because I got you,' she said. Fabian has been hanging
on to those words for the whole of his life.

How things have changed. Now Fabian lives in an exclusive
terraced house in Hove with the man he hopes will become his

husband. Before long, they might have a house full of little Fabians and little Ollies. And their children will know who both their fathers are and the names of their surrogate mothers.

Fabian stares at the policeman and woman.

'Ollie?' he gasps, clutching his heart.

'Is Mr Oleander Gower at home?' the woman asks.

'Oh dear God! It's not Ollie, then?' He lets out a loud whistle.

'Come in. Please come in. So rude of me!'

He stands back and sweeps his arm to indicate they should enter. When they are standing inside the hallway, looking around at the beautiful paintings and artfully designed flower arrangement, Fabian says, 'How can we help you? I'm afraid Ollie isn't at home.'

'And you are?' the man asks.

'Fabian Sherman. Ollie's partner. Soon to be husband,' he adds, smiling coyly.

They introduce themselves, showing their police badges.

'When will Mr Gower be home?'

'In an hour or so,' Fabian says, although in reality he has no idea when Ollie might return from the gym or wherever he is. 'Can I get you something to drink?'

'No, thank you. We'll wait outside for Mr Gower to return.'

'Oh, please don't. Ollie and I share everything.' He gets a sixth sense then, that jab of intuition he cultivates with his daily practice of yoga and meditation and aura gazing.

'It's Annette, isn't it? Ollie's mum.'

'Why do you say that, sir?' The policeman runs his fingers over his neat ginger moustache.

'Because she went missing this weekend. The poor darling.' Fabian bends over at the waist, theatrical as ever. 'Annette was such a wonderful woman. No prejudice. Accepted me into the family as if I was one of her own. Such a tragedy.'

The rotund policewoman hands Fabian a business card. 'Please will you get Mr Gower to call us when he returns.'

Fabian wills the tears to come to his eyes. He sniffs and wipes his eyes with the back of a hand.

Letting the police out of the front door, he peers discreetly from behind the heavy brocade living-room curtains as they walk down the steps and get into the saloon car that is parked on the other side of the road. He watches as the woman speaks on the phone and then they drive away. And when the rear lights of the car have disappeared out of sight, Fabian wonders what he should do.

WHEN HIS COLLEAGUES report to Joe that Oleander Gower is not at home, Joe decides to call Ollie. He doesn't like breaking bad news over the telephone, and in general it's contrary to protocol, but speed is of the essence here.

Ollie is indeed at the gym, just showered and with his sports bag over his shoulder, pacing back to the car. For Ollie, the timing is good, if anything about the tragedy can be defined as good. He sobs and screams in private within the plush confines of the Maserati.

Ollie does not return home that night.

After thirty minutes or so, he pulls himself together and drives to his parents' house – Lily's house now, he presumes. He knows he should probably tell Bella first, her being the eldest, but it is Lily who will be the most affected, the one whose heart will be shattered.

The lights are on, but Lily's car is not in the drive. Ollie gulps in the night air, wondering what he will find. On the one hand, he is desperate for Lily not to be there; on the other hand, how much better if it is him who breaks the news. He leans against the car, knowing he is about to break his sister's heart. If only he didn't have to go in.

He is startled by the front door swinging open, light flooding the driveway and Lily standing there holding a tea towel.

'Ollie, what are you doing here?'

He has no choice. Ollie walks as slowly as he can. He places his hand on Lily's arm.

'What is it?' Her face pales to match his own.

'I'm sorry, Lils. It's bad news. Mum has been found dead.'

'But that's not true. She was there yesterday. You told me, at the psychologist's house!'

'That was yesterday. Today she was found dead.'

'No!'

Lily swivels away from him, dropping the tea towel, and as if she is folding in on herself, she collapses onto the floor.

'Tell me it's not true!' she whispers.

Ollie bends down into his knees and places his arm around her trembling shoulders.

'I'm sorry, Lils. Is Stijn here?'

She doesn't answer.

TWO HOURS later and they are all there in Annette's kitchen: Gerry and Bella, Lily and Stijn, Ollie and DS Joe Swain with the Family Liaison Officer, Janet Curran.

'How did she die?' Bella asks.

It is strange what grief does to people. In day-to-day life, Bella appears to be the least engaged of the three Gower siblings, the spoiled airhead and consequently the sibling one might expect to most fall apart in the face of a tragedy. But Bella seems the least emotional and the most practical. Perhaps, as the eldest, she has been silently preparing to take on the role as head of the family for the past forty-one years.

'On the face of it, a heart attack. But there are very suspicious circumstances and, I'm afraid, until the autopsy and forensics tell us otherwise, we are treating it as murder,' Joe explains.

Lily gasps and clings to the back of a chair. Stijn pulls her into a tight hug and strokes her hair, whispering into her ear.

Joe looks at them all and wishes Pippa was with him. She would know. She would know whether the tears are real or not, and what lies behind the inscrutable faces.

28

PIPPA

Joe accompanies me to Tesco Express to pick up some dog food and then drops me back at home. Hurriedly, I pack my car with enough clothes and toiletries for a couple of days. I would much rather stay at home, but I accept Joe's concern and Rob always welcomes me with open arms. Mungo is sitting on the rear seat, clipped in, but with enough lead so that he can nuzzle his nose into my arm.

Joe explains that his team will be examining my garden to check for evidence and to establish whether its destruction is related to the two murders. I have worked so hard to zip my privacy back up after the last media intrusion, when the police and media wrongly used my photograph when identifying Leanne Smith, the murdered lottery winner. And now it seems as if that privacy is being ripped apart and my innermost secrets are about to be exposed all over again.

Sensing my hesitation to leave, Joe says, 'We are putting an embargo on press reporting as much as we can. I don't envisage the need for my team to enter your house tomorrow. It's the garden we will be focusing on.'

'Oh, Mungo! What is going on?' I moan to my dog as I watch Joe's car disappear around the corner.

He sticks his nose in my armpit as I start up my car.

My imagination won't switch off. Was Annette on her way to see me when she died, or is it a coincidence that she collapsed on a pavement in Storrington? How long was she lying there and how come no one found her earlier? Joe evaded my questions, telling me all would be revealed as part of the investigation.

I am on the winding A283, which skirts the quaint little town of Steyning. It is dark, and I am driving slower than normal. Headlights appear behind me. Normally I would ignore them and not feel pressurised to put my foot on the accelerator, but these lights are blinding. I angle my rear-view mirror, and now the lights are so close I can't see them, but they light up the road to the sides of my car. I drive a little faster. The car behind me does the same. My abdominals clench and I blink fast. Is it a coincidence that I have an impatient driver behind me, or is someone following me, purposefully trying to scare me or even force the car off the road?

I drive even faster. There is a tight bend approaching and I brake only just in time, feeling the wheels of my trusty car slip ever so slightly. My heart is pounding. I'm trying to keep my eyes on the road in front of me but can't stop myself from glancing into the rear and side mirrors.

And then we are at the roundabout. I try to see the make and model of the car behind me, but it's too close, and the darkness impedes my vision. I don't indicate as I go around the roundabout or as I merge on to the A27 Shoreham Bypass. I slow down on the dual carriageway, silently begging the car on my tail to overtake me so that I can throw an obscene gesture at the impatient driver.

But it doesn't. The car slows down too, staying close behind. I want to call Joe, to ask for help, but I daren't take my concentration off my driving to make a phone call. I wish I had a snazzy new car where I could press a button and speak my commands.

I turn off the A27 onto Dyke Road Avenue without indicating. The car behind does the same. The terror creates a pounding in my ears. I slow down to turn right into Woodland Drive and have to wait as cars are coming in the opposite direction. The car behind me indicates to the right, still following. I wait until I see a small gap between passing cars and whizz across, but the car on my tail is so close it does the same. The vehicle going the opposite way hoots loudly. I nearly jump out of my seat. I don't know what to do now. If I lead my pursuer to Rob's house, maybe I'll be the next person killed. But I don't know my way around the streets of Hove, and so I swing to the left on my normal route, onto Goldstone Crescent, and to my amazement the lights that have been following me for the past twenty minutes continue on down Woodland Drive. It's a black Mercedes; I can't see the driver.

I pull over and give Mungo a cuddle. Taking several deep breaths, I close my eyes and try to still the adrenaline that is pumping through my body. How easy it is to imagine the worst.

Rob's large modern house is lit up, throwing blue light against the white walls. It reminds me of the police lights I have just left behind, and I don't like it. I park in the driveway, underneath one of several imported palm trees. Sensing my car, the drive lights up. I'm glad. I don't fancy dark corners.

'Hi, sis!'

Rob is wearing charcoal-grey suit trousers, and the sleeves of his white shirt are rolled up. He bends down to greet Mungo, who bounds up towards him.

'Are you all right?' He peers at me.

'No, not really.'

He hugs me. I don't tell him about the scary drive. He picks up my suitcase and I follow him into the house. The bedrooms are downstairs, backing onto the garden. The living rooms are upstairs with views to the park.

'You can sleep in here. My cleaning lady keeps this room ready for unexpected guests.'

He opens the door to the large guest bedroom, with its sumptuous en suite marble bathroom with rainfall shower and Jacuzzi bath. The super-king-size bed is made up with luxury hotel-quality bedlinen and piled high with cushions in pale greys and lemon yellows. The carpet is a thick-pile slate grey, the type one's toes sink deep into as if you are standing on a silken cloud. A flat-screen television hangs on the wall, twice the size of my living room TV at home.

Despite the lavish room and the grandiose dimensions, I wish Rob had put me in the single room farther down the hall, next door to the master suite. I would feel so much safer if I was sleeping in the room next to his, cocooned and safe with a window facing onto the inaccessible courtyard rather than a wide window facing on to the garden.

'Thanks, Rob,' I say, sinking onto the edge of the bed.

'I'm going to pour you a glass of wine, and we can eat when you're ready. Supper just arrived. I assume you haven't eaten tonight?'

'No, I haven't.'

I wonder what delicacies Rob has had delivered. He doesn't cook. I have no idea if he even knows how to. His ridiculously inflated banker's salary allows him a stunning modern kitchen fitted with all the latest gizmos that he never uses, and plenty of cash to buy in three-star, restaurant-standard food on a daily basis, made by a Cordon Bleu-trained chef and delivered piping hot.

After an exquisite gourmet chicken chasseur followed by

treacle tart – it never ceases to amaze me how Rob manages to stay thin – I cancel all the clients I'm due to see tomorrow, lying to them that I have an unpleasant dose of gastric flu. I hate cancelling clients, hate letting them down. Some I email, others I text. I don't want to call them at 10 p.m.

We are still sitting at the kitchen table when Rob brings me a brandy. 'It'll help you sleep.' I don't tell him that alcohol is the worst thing for sleep, and drink it quickly.

'I'm turning in now. Got an early start,' Rob says.

'How early?'

'I'm out of here at 5 a.m.'

I yawn just at the thought of it. I have often wondered why Rob chooses to live in Hove and commute into London. He wastes nearly three hours a day travelling.

'Help yourself to everything. The cleaning lady comes at ten. Just leave your empty dishes in the sink.'

He gives me a kiss on the cheek and pads towards his bedroom.

I can't sleep. Mungo is upstairs at the other end of the house. I wish he could be with me in here, but I know my fastidious brother would find a dog in a bedroom abhorrent. Whenever I shut my eyes, I see Annette's waxen face. Shortly after 2 a.m., I sit bolt upright with a start. I am sure I heard something, that a beam of light flashed on my face. I fumble for the bedside lamp and switch it on. I strain to hear anything, but the night is silent.

I pick up my Kindle and read for an hour or so, and then I must have dozed off, because I wake again at 5 a.m. with the slamming of a door. I leap out of bed and race to the window. A couple of moments later, Rob's car reverses out of the garage.

After another couple of hours of light, unsatisfactory sleep, I get up and let Mungo out onto Rob's manicured lawn. I don't suppose he'll be impressed by dog excrement, but I am too weary to do anything about it. Shortly after 8 a.m., Joe calls.

'Just checking you're all right.' His voice is comforting.

'Any news yet?'

'No, it's too early. However, I want to interview the family members. Would you accompany me?'

I hesitate.

'How about I promise you a bunch of delphinium, tea, and chocolate cake *and* dinner when the case ends? And you'll be paid for your time,' he adds.

'How can I refuse all of that?' I laugh, feeling levity for the first time in the past twelve hours. 'You might struggle to find live delphinium in late September, though, and I think I've got enough artificial ones.'

'Fair enough. I'll fulfil that promise next May.'

I smile. Joe reckons he'll still be in my life next May.

'Can you be at the Gowers' house for 11 a.m.?'

'No problem.'

Joe reels off the address.

I TAKE a shower and get dressed, cursing that I threw my clothes in the suitcase last night without giving much thought as to what goes with what. I have to make do with a cream blouse, ugly old brown woollen trousers and a burgundy cardigan, which only just goes with the trousers.

'Come on, Mungo. Let's have a quick walk in the park.'

I attach his collar to the lead, grab the house keys Rob left me, swipe the alarm fob over the panel and lock the door.

As we're walking past my car, I see it.

'Oh God!'

Under the windscreen wipers of my car is a single-stemmed dark-red rose, almost black in colour. It looks like the twin to the rose on Annette's body.

'We need to talk.' Stijn lifts a lock of hair from Lily's forehead.

'Stijn, my mother has just died! Been killed!' Lily sobs.

'I know, *mijn liefje*. I know. But things will be different now.'

Lily pushes Stijn away, and for once he doesn't resist.

'We need to talk about the notebook,' he says quietly.

Lily's back stiffens.

When Stijn pushed Lily up against the wall yesterday during their search for Annette, he had felt the hardback book wedged into her jeans.

'What is this?' he asked, pulling away, trying to tug it out of Lily's waistband.

'Nothing,' she said, darting under his arms.

'Lily, you have to tell me,' Stijn had said in a tone of voice she had never heard him use before.

Lily froze. Stijn had been rough in the past, but he had never hurt her.

'You mustn't keep things from me, Lils. We're a team, me and you.'

'I'm not keeping things from you. This is Mum's diary, and I just think it would be wrong if you read it. You know how private she is. She writes about how she misses Dad.'

Stijn narrowed his eyes. 'I suppose she's written how she loathes me, how I'm not good enough for you.'

'No, Mum doesn't think that. Besides, I haven't read much of it. I don't want to; it's just it might give me some clues as to where she's gone.' Breathing out and relaxing a little bit, Lily turned away from Stijn, speaking over her shoulder. 'Of course we're a team. I would never hide anything from you.'

When she was downstairs, she searched for a place to hide the little book, somewhere Stijn would never think to look. She pulled out volumes seven and eight of her father's *Encyclopaedia Britannica* and slid the notebook behind them.

And now Stijn is asking about it all over again.

'I told you, it's only Mum's diary.'

'You must hide it. We don't want the police finding it.'

'I know, Stijn,' Lily says, making her voice sound as sarcastic – insouciant even – as possible. He lets it go for now, but Lily hopes there won't be trouble ahead.

Gerry and Bella and the police have left. Ollie is staying over.

'I'll need to be here in the morning, so best if I stay. I'll make up my old room.'

Lily is glad Ollie is sleeping over. It will be like the olden days when they were kids, except now they are orphans and they are the grown-ups. Stijn was less impressed. He scowled and left the room.

Now Lily and Stijn are in bed. She can't stop crying. Stijn holds her tenderly and strokes her back, wiping away her tears. He produces a sleeping pill and one of Annette's herbal remedies for insomnia. Thank goodness for Stijn, Lily thinks as she eventually drifts off to sleep.

. . .

THE DOORBELL RINGS at 7 a.m. Lily is already up, sitting alone in the kitchen drinking a mug of herbal tea. She is trying not to cry, but it's very difficult. She runs to the door, thinking about Stijn and Ollie. No need for them to be woken up.

A young man is standing there. His dark hair falls in gentle waves to his collar and stubble lines his jaw. He's only a couple of inches taller than her, slender in build and has an elfin face. He is wearing a black leather jacket and tight skinny jeans that makes his legs look like pipe cleaners.

'Is Ollie here?'

'Yes.' Lily frowns. 'How can I help you?'

'I'm Fabian.'

Lily looks at him blankly.

'Fabian?' he repeats and then, sighing and crossing his arms, says, 'Ollie's partner.'

'I thought Ollie was retired. I didn't know he's set up a new business.'

'Not business partner!' Fabian says, huffing. 'Partner in life. Lover. Cohabiter.'

Lily frowns.

'I assume you're Lily?'

She nods.

'I'm your brother's lover. The person he has homosexual sex with most nights. The person who has been sharing his house for ten months. The person who gives a shit about him.'

Lily turns away and buries her face in her hands. She recalls Stijn telling her Ollie was gay shortly after they started dating. Lily had been vehement, denying it, saying that whilst she had nothing against gays, if Ollie had been, she would have known about it. Could she have got her brother so very wrong? And why has he hidden something like that from her, of all people?

Realising she's being rude, she turns around to look at this young man. 'You'd better come in. Our mum has died.'

Fabian gasps. 'Oh no!' he exclaims, his voice high-pitched and stereotypically gay.

How boring, how predictable, Lily thinks.

Fabian follows her into the kitchen. He is disappointed. The house is old-fashioned, crumbling, almost down at heel. Nothing like Ollie's house.

'What happened?' he asks.

'They think she was killed.' Lily's voice quivers.

'That's terrible!' Fabian exclaims. 'You poor darlings. Where is Ollie? Can I go to him?'

'I think it would be better if you wait down here.' Lily isn't at all sure she believes this man.

Fabian grunts. He doesn't have to wait long. A couple of minutes later, they hear the sound of the toilet flushing upstairs, and heavy footsteps descend.

'What the hell are you doing here?' Ollie's face reddens with fury.

'Sixth sense something terrible has happened,' Fabian says, walking towards Ollie. 'How are you, darling?'

Ollie takes a step backwards. 'You need to go, Fabian. Go home.'

'Darling, I know you're in shock, but really you shouldn't be pushing me away.'

Ollie's face darkens. 'Go.' His voice is deep.

'Come on, I only want to comfort you. Besides, as you've got the Maserati, I had to take a cab to get here. Seems a waste of money to take another one home.'

Ollie turns and walks out of the kitchen.

'I'm sorry,' Lily says. 'He's suffering. We all are.'

'I know when I'm not wanted.'

Fabian huffs and strides out of the house.

LILY GOES UPSTAIRS and sits on the end of the bed.

'Ollie is gay,' she says to Stijn, who is propped up in bed, reading a book in Dutch.

'Of course he is.'

'How do you know?'

'Gaydar.'

'How does a straight man have gaydar?'

'Because I swing both ways!'

Lily stares at him, her eyes wide with horror.

'Only kidding, silly Lily. Come here.' He pats the side of the bed.

But Lily doesn't move.

HALF AN HOUR later and the three of them are seated at the kitchen table eating breakfast.

'Why didn't you tell us?' Lily asks Ollie.

'My love life is no one's business.'

'It's not all right to keep such big secrets from your siblings,' Stijn says.

'Shut up!' Ollie snaps.

'What's he like, this Fabian?' Stijn does an exaggerated mincing movement with his hand.

'Shut the fuck up, Stijn!' Ollie shouts.

And then the house phone rings.

Lily answers it. She listens and nods and says yes, then hangs up.

'Who was it?' Ollie asks.

'The policeman. He wants to interview us here at 11 a.m. The psychologist woman is coming too.'

'Why the hell did you agree to that?' Stijn asks. 'You know what the police are like. They'll twist everything, make Annette's death appear to be your fault.'

Lily buries her face in her hands.

After Ollie has rung Bella and told her that she and Gerry

will be required at the house for 11 a.m., Ollie goes upstairs and locks himself in the bathroom. His dislike of Stijn has just gone up a notch.

Meanwhile, in the kitchen, Stijn holds Lily's hands.

'You must be very careful what you tell the police, okay?'

She nods.

'Tell them nothing. *Niets*, zero, zilch.'

She pales and nods again.

30

PIPPA

I back away from the car as if the rose is contaminated with nuclear waste; as if it has made my car poisonous and the air around it toxic. Mungo is tugging on his lead, pulling me forwards, staring at me with a confused expression.

'Sorry, boy, but we can't go for a walk. Not now.'

I glance around. Is there anyone here? Am I being watched?

I call Rob, because I know his number off by heart.

'Was there a rose attached to my windscreen when you left for work this morning?'

'Got a new lover?'

'It's not funny, Rob.'

'I didn't notice anything, but then I'm not sure I even looked at your car. It was still dusk when I left home. I've got a meeting in ten minutes, but I could come home this afternoon if you'd like.'

'It's kind of you, but I'm going to meet Joe.'

'Hunky policeman?'

'Ha ha. I'm helping him interview the Gower family. The remaining ones.' I pause. 'Rob, I'm scared.'

'I don't think you should do this interview. If you seriously think this rose is a warning sign, then just back off. What does the note say?'

'What note?'

'Isn't there a note attached to the rose?'

I turn around and look at the car. I don't want to get too close to the rose, and I certainly don't want to touch it, but I suppose Rob is right. I need to look to see if there's a note.

'Call me back in an hour,' Rob says. 'I'll be out of the meeting then. And if it's urgent, ring my secretary. She'll pull me out of the meeting.'

'Thanks, Rob, but I'll be fine.'

I approach the rose with caution. Leaning over the bonnet of my car, I look for a note, but there isn't one. There is just the rose with beautiful, near-black velvet petals and a stem of sharp thorns.

To the dismay of Mungo, I hurry back inside the house, ensuring I lock and bolt the front door behind me.

I call Joe.

'Someone has left a black rose on my car. I think I'm being threatened.'

He is too professional to gasp or jump to conclusions, but the long pause before he says anything speaks volumes.

'I want you to pack up your things, get in your car and drive over to the garden centre. I'll be waiting for you in the car park, and you can come with me to the Gowers' house.'

'But—'

'No buts, Pippa. I need your help to solve this case, and I will be personally responsible for keeping you safe now. Use some rubber gloves to lift the rose off your windscreen, and put it in a clean plastic bag if you've got one.'

'Where will I stay if I leave Rob's?'

'In a safe house.'

Wow. I didn't expect Joe to use police resources to put me up in a safe house. It makes me even more uneasy. Does he know something I don't? Am I really in that much danger?

Hurriedly, I shove my clothes back into my case and lug it and Mungo's bed and bowls back to the car. He jumps on to the back seat, and I give him a quick hug; my faithful hound, who has been deprived of a walk and still loves me.

I find a pair of unopened washing-up gloves under the kitchen sink – not surprising because, as well as not cooking, Rob doesn't wash up – and a roll of large zipper sandwich bags. After putting the gloves on, I lift the windscreen wiper up and grab the rose, carefully avoiding the thorns, and bung it as quickly as I can into the clean sandwich bag. The stem sticks out of the end, so I put another bag over that and secure them with a rubber band.

I put my evidence on the floor in the passenger side of the car. I would rather it is in the boot, but I don't want my suitcase to squash it when I drive around corners.

And then we're off. I'm suspicious of every car now, of everyone who so much as throws a glance my way. It's as if I'm expecting someone to give chase, but, unlike last night, there are no suspicious cars tailing me, and before long I'm pulling up into Rocks Garden Centre's car park.

Joe is leaning against his car, arms crossed, a pensive look on his handsome face. When he realises it's me pulling up alongside him, he smiles broadly, his large white teeth gleaming. His cheeks are smooth, all stubble having been neatly shaven off.

'Let's put everything into my car.'

'Everything?'

'Yes. I'll take you to the safe house later.'

'But what about my car?'

'You'll give me the key, and I'll put it somewhere safe. We might want to examine it.'

'I don't want to be without my car.'

'It'll be for a day at most. Don't worry, I won't leave you stranded somewhere.'

He grins, and I begin to relax.

'How do I know you won't nick my car?' I ask, my tongue poking the side of my cheek.

'Because as lovely as she is' – he pats the dirty roof – 'I'd rather take Ollie Gower's Maserati or Gerry Shelton's Lexus. No offence to you or your motor!'

'Fair enough.'

When we're back on the main road, I ask Joe, 'Where is this safe house?'

'You'll see later.'

'Information on a need-to-know basis?' I jest.

He doesn't answer. 'Right. To business,' he says, his eyes on the road ahead. 'I want to interview each member of the Gower family. My hunch is, they know things they're not letting on, and I'd like you to assess who you think is lying.'

'Can we video the interviews?'

'No. If we suspect anyone further, then we'll bring them into the station.'

'Am I in danger?'

'Honestly, Pippa' – he glances at me – 'I don't know. But I'd rather be safe than sorry.'

THE GOWERS' family home is a ramshackle farmhouse on the edge of the village, backing on to fields. It's not what I expected. I suppose I had assumed that a family running such a successful business as Rocks Garden Centre would live in a large modern house, or one of the beautiful period homes in the village.

The house is approached by a long track full of potholes and weeds running along the middle of the road. A low-hanging roof constructed of dark terracotta tiles with small windows underneath gives the house an oppressive feel, as if it has long hair with eyes peeking out. Whilst the house seems to be in a state of decay, the garden is anything but. There are beautiful tree specimens, acers with leaves turning burnished gold and crimson red, neatly maintained flowerbeds with late-blooming dahlias in coppers and oranges, and I catch a glimpse of rows of vegetables growing in wooden raised beds.

Outside the house are a number of cars, including Ollie's fancy Maserati. My heart quickens as we stand at the front door, with its dark-green peeling paint. I am about to enter a house of grief. To protect myself, I picture myself inside an impenetrable glass bubble.

Joe puts his finger on the doorbell. Ollie lets us in. Bella and Lily are seated at a circular wooden kitchen table, which is stained with rings and dents.

Joe introduces me to Stijn, Lily's Dutch husband. He smiles broadly, but the smile doesn't reach his bright-blue eyes. Ollie pulls out two chairs for Joe and me.

'Please accept our deepest condolences for the loss of your mother,' Joe says.

They nod. Lily wipes her sore, red eyes.

'Have you found out why she died?' Ollie asks.

'Was your mother diabetic?' Joe directs the question at Ollie.

Bella answers. 'No. Why?'

'Forgive me for asking, but was your mother a drug user?'

Ollie laughs a hard, sarcastic laugh. 'For fuck's sake. We're talking about our seventy-three-year-old mother, a pillar of society. She may have had hippy tendencies, but she didn't do drugs. None of us do.'

Ollie avoids my gaze. He is lying.

'Why are you asking?' Stijn asks. I glance at Stijn, who has asked the most sensible question.

'We found needle marks on her arm, as if she has recently received two or three injections. We understand her family doctor had not seen her recently.'

'Mother didn't like doctors. She never went,' Bella says. 'She liked to treat herself with her homeopathic medicines. Fat lot of good it did us when we had mumps and chickenpox. Do you remember, Ollie?'

Ollie ignores her.

'You haven't answered the question. How did Mum die?' Bella asks.

'Until we have received the autopsy report, we won't know. I'm sorry, but this process is never quick. Do you sell roses at the garden centre?'

'Of course we do. It's a bloody garden centre!' Ollie says.

'There's a particular variety.'

Joe takes his phone out of his pocket and brings up a photo of a black rose. He lays it on the table. They peer at it.

I'm finding this difficult. There are too many of them for me to accurately assess micro-expressions and analyse speech variants, to work out if there are clusters of linguistic anomalies, facial expressions and body-language giveaways. My process works well if I can study one person at a time, but here I can't concentrate.

'What do you think, Lily? You're the flower expert,' Bella says.

I glance at Lily just in time to see an involuntary shiver and a look of recognition.

'It's tinted. Real black roses don't exist, only dark red. That one has been dipped in ink.'

'Do you sell black roses?' Joe asks.

'No. We sell single cut blooms in dark red, and rose bushes and trees. Black Beauty is the darkest red, but you won't find any at this time of year. The bare roots aren't available until November.' Lily stands up suddenly. 'I'm sorry, I'm not feeling very well. I need to lie down.'

Stijn paces over to Lily and holds her arm. 'I'll go with you to make sure you're all right,' he says.

Ollie narrows his eyes at them as they leave the room.

'Where is your husband, Mrs Shelton?' Joe asks Bella.

'At work, of course. He can't take the day off. He told me he'll be popping in to the garden centre later to check everything's going okay.'

'That won't be necessary!' Ollie spits.

'Someone has to look after the place,' Bella snarls at Ollie. 'Silly Lily can't do it, and anyway, she's taken to her bed.'

'We'll discuss this later!' Ollie crosses his arms.

'Was there anyone in your mother's life who might have wished her harm?' Joe asks.

'No. She is a kind, loving woman who runs a successful business. Her staff all love her. Loved her.' Ollie's voice fades away.

'Are you suggesting Mum's death might be murder?' Bella asks. 'And are you suggesting it might have something to do with the death of Scott McDermott?'

Her face is hard to read. That's what Botox does.

'Regrettably I am beginning to believe the two deaths might be related. If I may, I would like permission for two of my officers to have a look at your mother's belongings, in particular to try to establish where she was over the past seventy-two hours.'

'It's Lily and Stijn who live here. You'll have to ask them, but I would have thought the answer is yes. Wouldn't you, Ollie?' Bella says.

Ollie's features tighten.

'When she is feeling better, perhaps you could ask your sister to give me a call.' Joe directs the request at Bella, who is definitely the most open of the siblings.

Joe stands up, and I follow suit. As he looks around the kitchen, his eyes settle on a row of little brown glass bottles.

'What are those?' He points to them.

'Mum's remedies. She makes her own.'

'Where does she do that?'

'The potting shed. Out there.' Bella waves her hand towards the garden.

I can't help but notice her array of sparkling rings and her perfectly manicured, pale-pink nails.

'Could we have a look?'

'I don't think Mum would like it—' Ollie mutters.

'Regrettably your mother isn't with us, and I would like to find out who killed her.'

'So you think she was killed?' Bella interrupts.

'That appears to be the most probable scenario.'

For the first time Bella loses composure. 'Why would anyone hurt Mum?'

Ollie stares at the floor.

'Do whatever you have to do to find out what happened,' Bella says, sniffing.

'I will have a couple of officers over here in the next hour,' Joe says.

JOE and I walk outside in silence. There is an impressive glasshouse structure in the rear garden. Unlike the main house, it is immaculate, sparkling, new-looking. We peer through the glass. There are benches full of plants, each with a neat label in its pot.

Joe tries the door, but it is locked.

'Is it normal to lock your greenhouse or potting shed, or whatever this place is called?' Joe asks.

I shrug. 'I've no idea.'

Joe strides around the outside trying to peer in but eventually he gives up. 'I'll get Mia to ask Lily for the key. Perhaps she can explain what her mother got up to in in this fancy glasshouse.'

We walk back to the car. When we're inside, I turn to Joe.

'You need to interview Lily and Stijn. There was a reason Lily disappeared upstairs and her husband followed her.'

'What was the reason?'

'I don't know!' I throw my hands up. 'That's for you to find out. But they're hiding something. And so is Ollie. Bella was the only one I don't have any suspicions about, but that could be to do with the Botox. But it's your call, of course.'

We're both silent for a few minutes.

'Where are we going?' I ask. I feel uncomfortable not knowing what's happening.

'To the garden centre, and then I'm taking you home.'

'To my home?' I feel relieved at the prospect.

'No, to mine.'

31

G erry is in a fine mood. It looks as if his plan will work after all, now that Annette has been found dead. Bella is all for his expansion plans, and Lily will be grateful for his help. All he needs to do is persuade Ollie he is the right person to run the business, and get rid of that know-it-all Dutchman. He'll be easy enough to palm off with the promise of a bigger salary. So it's Ollie he needs to concentrate on. But, best of all, he'll be Mae's boss, and they will be able to be together every day.

Yesterday he was livid with Mae, but today he's more sanguine. Of course, she couldn't take off in the middle of the day when she was reporting to Annette. But now things will be different. Gerry decides he'll ask for a couple hundred thousand pounds more for the loan he'll need to raise in order to buy Rocks Garden Centre, and he'll purchase a little love nest for him and Mae. She'll like that. Besides, what's a couple hundred thou on a couple of million?

He sings along to 'Musetta's Waltz' in the car, his heart soaring with the music. He parks the Lexus up near the front door in the car park, in a disabled bay. He'll soon be parking at the front anyway. He can see it now, 'Managing Director, G. Shelton', a sign to match the one at Shelton Bros. But here everyone will walk past it, will notice it. At the trading estate, no one could care less.

Gerry pats the breast pocket of his jacket. The little box is there. He strides through the garden centre, whistling quietly. Mae is at her desk, her shiny black hair covering her face as she draws. He stops for a moment to stare at her. His heart swells, and he knows how lucky he is. Bella back at home making sure all is well with the girls, managing their beautiful home, and stunning Mae on the side, making him feel like an Adonis. Gerry's not stupid. He knows he isn't any great looker, and with the passing years and expanding waistline, even his figure is going to pot. But the old codger in his underpants is a fine one, and that's all that matters. And if Mae thinks he's a big boy, then he must be. He's never asked because he doesn't want to know, but with those tricks of hers, he's sure Mae has been around the block a few times.

'Hello, gorgeous!' he whispers, making her jump.

'What are you doing here?' she says, scowling.

'Come to sweep you off your feet! I've got something for you.'

Mae glances around. 'Not now, Gerry. Not here!'

'Haven't you heard the news?'

'What news?'

'That your esteemed boss, Mrs Annette Gower, sadly passed away yesterday.'

'What!' Mae's eyes widen and her hand covers her mouth.

'I think you and me should go and have a coffee, don't you?'

'Not here. We'll be seen.'

'How about at my house? Bella will be at her mother's house all day, so the coast is clear.'

Mae shakes her head. As much as she would like to see

Gerry's house and stain Bella's sheets, she knows it's a bad idea.

'Let's go to another hotel. What about Bellingham Manor?'

Gerry's eyes nearly pop out. Bellingham Manor is *the* most expensive hotel in Sussex and quite possibly in the South of England. He took Bella there for dinner on their tenth wedding anniversary. It was a seven-course gourmet treat, setting him back the price of a week's holiday. He won't make the mistake of buying champagne in that establishment again.

'You keep on telling me I'm worth it!' Mae says, pouting.

'And indeed you are. Lunchtime?'

GERRY IS STANDING in the wood-panelled reception area, where the scent of furniture polish mingles with the perfume of lilies. The staff are speaking in hushed voices, and classical piano music tinkles in the background. He wonders whether he should wait for Mae to arrive before paying for the room. It's one thing losing fifty quid when she didn't turn up at the Premier Inn, but quite another losing nearly a grand for an hour's shag. Just as he steps up to the reception desk and removes his Amex card from his calfskin wallet, Mae sidles up beside him.

'Hello, darling. I'm so excited about our stay here.'

'Could I take your name please, sir?' the receptionist says, smiling demurely.

'It's Mr and Mrs Gerry Shelton,' Mae says, grinning.

They follow the porter to the room.

'You're a brazen little minx,' Gerry whispers in her ear whilst squeezing her backside.

The room is stunning, with views across manicured gardens to the English Channel beyond. The walls are lined with pale-salmon silk paper, and ornate, heavy brocade curtains frame the bay window. The centrepiece is the king-sized four-poster bed with antique mahogany carved posts and a silk swag at the head.

'Does sir have any luggage?' the young porter asks, clasping his hands deferentially.

'It's in the car. We'll collect it later.' Gerry hands the young man a five-pound note.

As soon as he is gone, Mae turns to face Gerry and starts peeling off her blouse.

'So, Mr Shelton. What are your plans?'

'A hostile takeover and then I will be your boss.'

Mae puts a hand out, her palm flat on his chest. 'What if Ms Isla-Mae doesn't want you to be her boss? What if she wants to be your boss?'

'That, my darling, can't happen. Only here in the bedroom, and most certainly not in the boardroom.' He laughs at his own joke.

Then Gerry sits down on the end of the bed and takes his shoes off. By the time he has turned around, she is lying on the bed, propped up on her elbow, naked except for her black lacy bra.

He totally forgets the little box in his jacket pocket.

32

PIPPA

We are in Joe's car and I feel ambushed. No, I don't. I feel excited. And then I change my mind again. What is Joe doing? Surely this isn't normal protocol.

'What about the safe house?'

'My house is a safe house. I will not let anything happen to you. Besides, no one will know you are there.'

'But—'

'No buts, Pippa. I have a spare room and a fully stocked fridge. And it's the best offer you'll get. Unfortunately police budget doesn't extend to safe houses for witnesses threatened with black roses.'

Joe is making me angry. I don't like to be manipulated. And why is he assuming that I don't have any other friends or relatives I could go and stay with? I stare straight ahead. Maybe he notices my jutting jaw and scowling face.

'Please don't be angry with me, Pippa. I feel like I got you into this mess, and I want to get you out of it. Unscathed. And

I'll be honest with you, I like you. This isn't the way I had envisaged getting to know you, and it might feel as if I'm taking you captive, but I'm not. I just want to look after you.'

'What will your wife think?'

I've been wanting to ask that question for so long. *Have you got a wife, Joe? Or a live-in lover, or even just a girlfriend?* But that's not the type of question one asks a professional colleague. And now it's just slipped out.

'I don't have a wife. I'm divorced.'

I sigh. How can I be angry with a man who is honest with his feelings? But still... It's as if he can read my thoughts.

'And don't worry, there won't be any inappropriate behaviour!'

I turn to look out of the passenger window. I don't want Joe to see my blushing cheeks.

He drops me back at my car, and then I follow him northwards, up the A24 towards Horsham.

JOE'S HOME isn't the modern, functional house I had expected. It is a small converted barn on the outskirts of Christ's Hospital, near the famous school where pupils don long black gowns and bright-yellow socks. It is long and thin and single storey, the exterior clad in silvery wooden boards. Whilst it's near the hamlet, it also seems quite isolated, surrounded by trees on one side and rolling fields on the other.

'This is charming,' I say. 'How long have you lived here?'

'Coming up for eight years. That's when Jane left me. She couldn't cope with the long hours of a policeman. It's an occupational hazard.'

I follow him into the house with Mungo at my heels. As soon as I walk in, I feel it, I notice it. A female presence. Immediately, my hopes are dashed. I pray it doesn't show on my face. Just because I can read other people's faces doesn't mean I can conceal my own feelings. There's a woman's jacket on the coat stand, a hairbrush on the kitchen table and half-made sweater in fluffy angora yarn still attached to knitting needles dumped on the sofa.

We walk down a long corridor.

'This is your bedroom.'

It's small, functional and tidy. In fact, it looks as if it's rarely used, with a neatly made-up bed, white walls and a simple mirror hanging next to the window. The view is delightful, over fields and hedgerow. I follow him back to the corridor.

'And this is the bathroom.'

There is a wicker basket full of make-up and a bottle of scented bath oil on the edge of the bath. We walk back to the kitchen.

'Would you like a coffee?'

'Yes, please.'

He uses a small Nespresso machine and then his phone rings. Joe looks at me as he's listening to the person on the other end of the phone, but it's as if he's looking right through me. He puts his phone on the kitchen table and passes me a cup of coffee.

'That was the forensic pathologist. He's done some initial toxicology tests, and it appears that Annette might have been killed as a result of ricin poisoning.'

'Ricin?' I exclaim. 'I thought ricin was only used in murders in novels and by Russian agents. Wasn't Alexander Litvinenko poisoned by ricin?'

'Yes. I can't say that we get many ricin deaths in Sussex.'

'As Annette was into plants and making her own homeopathic remedies, could she have accidentally – or even on purpose – killed herself?'

'Possibly, but unlikely. We think she was injected with it. She had restraint marks on her wrists as well.'

'That's horrible,' I mutter. 'Who would do such a thing?'

'That is what we need to find out. We have a team examining your garden, the streets in Storrington and doing door-to-door enquiries to find out if anyone saw or heard anything suspicious.'

I flinch.

'We have another team at Rocks Garden Centre and one at the Gowers' home. The DI is chucking resources at this case. And now I need to go to the station. Lily and Stijn are being brought in for questioning. Stay here, make yourself comfortable. Use the Wi-Fi. The password is on the back of the router.'

'No.'

He looks at me with surprise.

'I want to be part of the interview with Lily and Stijn. I will be able to help you.'

'I'm sorry, Pippa, but that won't be possible. We'll record the interviews, so you will be able to view them later. There's food in the fridge. Help yourself. I expect I'll be back late, but I'll call you. And Pippa. Please don't go out. I don't want anyone following you. As much as I like flowers, I don't wish to find any more.'

'Won't your girlfriend mind me being here?'

'What?' His forehead creases. And then his face breaks into a grin.

'Oh, you mean this!' He picks up the hairbrush. I can see jet-black hair tangled in its bristles.

'This belongs to my daughter, Holly. She stayed with me last week, but she's gone back to university now. She has a tendency to leave essential belongings behind.'

'So it's not you that's knitting the pink fluffy jumper?'

'No, it's certainly not!' Joe laughs. 'Incidentally, have you cancelled your clients?'

'For today, yes.'

'I think it would be prudent to cancel all of this week's.'

'Won't I be home until the weekend?' I ask with dismay.

'Possibly, but I can't say for certain.'

'And I assume it'll get into the press that I am involved in this case.'

'I don't see any reason why that should happen. We will do our best to keep it out of the media.'

'I hope you do a better job than last time.'

Joe nods and leaves.

I FEEL BAD. It wasn't Joe's fault that my photograph got into the press; it wasn't Joe's fault that my business temporarily dried up as a result of my association with the murdered lottery winner. And now I feel awkward, wandering around this stranger's house. I settle Mungo into his basket and set up my laptop, but I can't concentrate. I think back to that last conversation with Annette. There is something nudging at the periphery of my mind, something I am sure is relevant.

I get up, make myself a cup of tea and walk Mungo around the garden. It is the sound of a pigeon that triggers my recollection. The *coo-cooing* noise. Annette's final words were *Coon, Coon.* Is that a name? I assumed that it was nonsensical, the final mutterings of a dead woman. But what if she was articulating properly and was trying to tell me something? I pace around for a few minutes and then I decide I need to tell Joe. Now.

fter Joe and Pippa leave, Ollie is seething. He paces up and down the kitchen.

'Sit down!' Bella says.

'I can't.'

'Right, well, I'm going home. Got things to do.' Bella picks up her Mulberry bag, throws a cashmere scarf around her neck and clip-clops out of the kitchen.

A few moments later, Stijn comes downstairs.

'Are you staying, mate?' Stijn asks Ollie.

'Haven't decided.'

'It would be good if you could. Lils is in a bad way, but I've got to go to work.'

'What, Gerry isn't even giving you a day's compassionate leave?' Ollie spits.

'Yeah. Bastard boss.' Stijn is glad he and Ollie agree on something.

WHEN THE TEAM of police arrive, three men and a woman, only

Ollie and Lily are in the house. Ollie realises he didn't even tell Stijn they were coming.

'Have you got a warrant?' Ollie asks, hands on his hips.

'Of course.'

The policeman produces the document. Ollie glances at it. He's never seen one before but assumes it's the genuine article. If they want to search his mother's house and waste their time, it's fine by him. He goes upstairs to warn Lily.

She is curled up foetus-like on her bed, clutching a pillow to her chest. Her cheeks are stained with tears.

'Lily.' Ollie sits on the side of the bed. 'Lily, you need to get up. The police are here.'

'Why?' She doesn't move.

'They've got a warrant to search the house. You'd better come down.'

She bursts out crying. 'Why are they searching the house? I thought they're meant to be looking for the person who murdered Mum. They're not going to find him here.'

'I think they're looking for clues as to whether Mum was hiding anything. People she knew, places she went to.'

Lily's sobs become hiccups. She sits up and wipes her cheeks with the palms of her hands. She follows Ollie downstairs.

There is a young woman in the hallway, about the same age as Lily but twice her size.

'You won't touch her plants, will you?' Lily asks. 'Because she's got some valuable specimens in the greenhouse. They're all catalogued.'

'We'll put everything back the way we found it,' the policewoman reassures.

The senior officer walks in, a tall, weaselly-looking man with a prominent Adam's apple.

'Are you Lily Eikenboom?'

Lily nods. She still gets a thrill when people call her by her married name.

'We would like to request your presence at the police station.'

'What!' Lily and Ollie exclaim at the same time.

'Why?' Ollie asks.

'Detective Sergeant Swain has requested you attend an interview.'

'But why? What has my sister done?' Ollie asks. 'She's the person suffering a loss here. She's not a suspect!'

'I can't say, sir. I'm just following instructions.'

'I'm going to call that shit Joe Swain,' Ollie says under his breath. 'If he does to you what he did to Mum, I'm going to report him.'

'It's probably because I live here, and I work with Mum. I am around her the most.'

'I'm coming with you.'

Lily becomes almost hysterical. 'No, Ollie. You need to stay here. Make sure they don't touch Mum's plants or any of her personal stuff. I couldn't bear that. Please, Ollie. I'll be all right. You stay here.'

Ollie shrugs.

'Miss, do you know where Mr Stigyeh Eyecanboom is—?'

If circumstances were different, Ollie would have laughed about the mess the man made of the pronunciation of Stijn's name. 'It's Stijn, pronounced Stain. He's at work, isn't he, Lils?'

She nods.

'Miss, would you like to accompany my colleague?' He gestures towards a woman dressed in grey trousers and a navy jumper.

'Can I just use the bathroom first?'

'Of course.'

Lily hurries upstairs, grabs her handbag and mobile phone and rushes into the bathroom. She calls Stijn, but he doesn't answer. She then removes the two boxes and envelope that she took from her mother's bedroom and hid in the bathroom seat, and shoves them deep into her bag. She prays that the police don't find Annette's notebook, the one she hid behind the *Encyclopaedia Britannica*, because there is nothing she can do about it now. Nothing at all.

34

PIPPA

I telephone Joe, but his phone goes straight to voicemail. I try the police station but am told DS Swain is otherwise engaged. That's not good enough. I know Joe told me to stay put all day, but I can't. My gut tells me I have some essential information, and I need to pass it on as quickly as possible.

'Come on, Mungo. We're going to Crawley.'

When we're on the A24 bypassing Horsham, it crosses my mind that Joe may not even be at the police station. He could be anywhere, in fact. I hesitate for a moment and then decide that if he isn't there, I will ask to speak to his deputy and pass on the information that way.

The traffic is light, and twenty-five minutes later I am parking up near the police station.

'You've got to stay,' I tell my forlorn-looking dog as I shut the car door. I walk across the car park into the police station.

'I have an appointment with DS Swain,' I say to the man at the reception desk.

'And you are?'

'Philippa Durrant. I'm a consultant to DS Swain.'

He nods and picks up the phone. 'A Ms Durrant for Joe,' he says.

I don't correct him. He puts the phone down and speaks to me.

'He's in a meeting. Apparently, there's nothing in the diary to say you have an appointment with him.'

'Perhaps not,' I bluster. 'It's urgent, though. I have some vital information for him.'

The man picks up the phone again. I hope I'm not pulling Joe away from some important meeting just to give him a word that may be of no significance. But then again, as I'm here, if he's interviewing Lily or Stijn, perhaps I can persuade him to let me sit in.

'Please wait.' He gestures to the row of chairs.

I sit down and then stand up again. But I don't have to wait long.

'Pippa, what are you doing here?' Joe's face is stern.

For a moment I hesitate. 'I'm sorry, it's just I remembered some information that might be relevant.'

'You'd better come with me.'

He swivels around. I follow him, inhaling his musky scent as he holds doors open for me. He leads me to a small room with a light so bright I have to blink to stop my eyes from watering.

'What is it?'

Joe is making me feel nervous, insignificant.

'Annette's last words were "Coon, Coon".'

Joe frowns. 'I'm just about to start interviewing Lily.'

'Can I sit in?' I open my eyes wide. I know I'm flirting, but I can't help it.

Joe sighs and his features relax. 'All right, but no questions.'

I smile and nod.

. . .

LILY LOOKS TERRIBLE – washed-out skin, red eyes and crumpled clothes. I am struck by how young she seems, even though I know she's just turned thirty. I feel for her, having just lost her mother.

Joe and I sit down. He starts speaking.

'Lily, you are here as a voluntary attender under the provisions in Section 10 of the Police and Criminal Evidence Act Code C. You are not under arrest and may leave at any time. If you decide to remain here, you may obtain free and independent legal advice by phone.' Joe passes her a piece of paper. 'This sets out your rights as a voluntary attender. Please let us know if you need refreshments or need to use the facilities.'

'But why am I here?' she asks.

'Because you knew your mother the best. You lived with her, worked with her, and we need to find out who wanted to hurt her.'

She gulps and wipes her nose with a tissue. 'I'm not under suspicion?'

'We will be interviewing everyone to try and work out what happened.

'Please tell me, Lily, where were you between 7 p.m. on Sunday evening and 5 p.m. on Monday.'

'I was at home on Sunday evening with Stijn. Ollie stayed over too. I left for work at about 8 a.m. on Monday morning and was there all day. I got home about 5.30 p.m.'

'Who can provide alibis for you?'

Lily pales. Her fingers play with loose strands of her pale-auburn hair.

'Stijn. The staff at the garden centre. Why? I didn't have anything to do with this. I loved Mum.'

'We know you loved your mum, Lily,' Joe placates. 'These are routine questions.

'Lily, can you think of anyone who might have wanted to hurt your mother?'

Lily shakes her head, but I'm watching, and she is blinking rapidly, shifting in her seat. Now is the time to ask the crunch question. I know Joe told me not to say anything, but I can't hold back.

'Who or what is Coon?' I ask.

'Who?'

'Coon.'

She pauses, shaking her head. 'I'm not sure I can answer that. I can't recall ever having heard that name before.'

Bingo. It's all there. Lily is lying. There's the reluctance to answer the question, selective memory, the fact she identified the word *Coon* as being a name. Then there's the throat clearing and the licking of her pale lips. The micro-expressions of fear are all there too. Her inner brows rise whilst her eyelids tighten, and her mouth flattens out.

'What nationality is the name Coon?' Joe leans forwards.

Lily flinches. 'I don't know. Dutch, maybe?'

'Did your mother have many Dutch associates?' Joe asks.

'I don't know. A few, I suppose. We buy a lot of our plants from Holland.'

'Is that how you met your husband, Stijn?'

'No. Gerry introduced us. Stijn works for my brother-in-law.'

I clock that answer. She is being truthful.

'We believe your mother was poisoned, Lily,' Joe says quietly.

I fear that Lily might pass out. She goes so white, it looks as if all the blood has drained from her face. Her eyes glaze over and she grabs the side of the table. I push a glass of water towards her.

'Drink this,' I suggest.

She clasps her fingers around the glass, but her hand is shaking too much to get the water to her lips.

'Lily, would you like to take a break?' Joe asks.

She nods.

When she is out of the room, Joe turns to me.

'So?'

'She's lying. She knows who this Coon is. She knows much more than she's telling us. You need to press her on it.'

I feel uncomfortable as soon as I utter the words. Maybe I have been watching too many police procedurals on TV. I am a counselling psychologist, no longer a forensic psychologist, and I shouldn't be suggesting that Joe puts Lily under pressure.

'Go easy on her,' I add.

Joe looks at me askance.

When Lily returns, she looks ghostlike.

'You said this was voluntary,' she whispers.

'Yes,' Joe says.

'I'd like to leave please. I don't feel well. This is all too much.'

Joe is polite and arranges for a policewoman to drive Lily home. I feel cheated. I am sure we were onto something.

W hen Lily gets home, the police have left. Ollie is on the phone, pacing backwards and forwards. She goes straight to the living room and pulls out volume seven of the *Encyclopaedia Britannica*. Her breathing is fast and shallow as she pulls out volume eight, and before long the whole set is on the floor. The notebook is not there.

Lily collapses on to the faded carpet, hyperventilating.

'What's happened? Lily, what is it?' Ollie lowers himself onto the floor next to his sister. When Lily was sixteen and awaiting the results of her GCSEs, she had a full-blown panic attack. Annette had been so calm back then, producing a paper bag and getting her daughter to breathe into it until she calmed down.

Ollie holds Lily's hand and tries to remember what to do. 'Breathe in, one, two, three, four, and out, one, two, three, four. It's okay, Lily. Everything will be all right.'

'It's not,' Lily says, sobbing.

It takes a while, but eventually her breathing slows and becomes more under control.

'I know it's terrible about Mum. We're all in shock.'

'It's not just that. Now I've got to run the business.'

Ollie strokes her hair. 'You don't. We'll sell it, and then you'll have plenty of money to go and do whatever you like.'

Lily shakes her head. 'We can't,' she whispers. 'Stijn and I have great plans for it.'

Ollie looks at her askance. 'Stijn?'

'He hates working for Gerry. He's wanted to work at Rocks for ages.'

'Doing what?'

'He's really clever is Stijn.'

Ollie looks at her doubtfully. 'Now's not the time to make any decisions. Can you tell me why we're sitting in a sea of *Encyclopaedia Britannica*?'

'I was looking for something.'

'It's easier doing a Google search.'

Lily doesn't contradict him. She stands up, and together they put the books back on the shelf.

'Did they go through Mum's greenhouse?'

Ollie nods. 'But they didn't remove anything.'

'Did they take other stuff?' Something gets stuck in Lily's throat and she chokes.

'Yes. A few things,' Ollie says, slapping Lily on her back.

'What?' Lily can feel her breath quickening again. She digs her fingernails into the palms of her hands, but to little effect. She keeps them short to stop too much soil getting caked underneath them.

'There's a list on the kitchen table.'

Lily hurries to find it. She reads through it quickly, the piece of paper trembling in her hand. It isn't listed. She reads through the items again – vials in dark-brown glass, a diary, her car keys. No small notebook is listed. But if the police didn't remove it, who did?

There are only two possibilities, Stijn and Ollie, and Lily

doesn't want it to be either of them. She bursts into tears all over again.

By early evening Stijn has not returned, and Ollie wants to go home.

'Where is Stijn?'

Lily is back on her bed. 'Dunno,' she mumbles.

'Do you think you could call your husband and ask him to come and look after you? It's the least he can do, care for his grieving wife.'

Ollie doesn't mean to be blunt, but there's little he likes about Stijn. He sees the tears drip from Lily's closed eyes.

'Sorry, Lils. It's just I need to go home.'

He doesn't like to leave Lily alone, but he has problems of his own. Problems he needs to see to urgently.

Ollie senses something is wrong the moment he pulls up to the house in the Maserati. It drives him mad the way Fabian never switches lights off, so a house in darkness means Fabian isn't there. Since Fabian moved in, Ollie can't recall a single evening where he has returned home and Fabian wasn't in the hallway to greet him. And today of all days, Ollie needs his lover.

He wonders for a moment whether Fabian has cleared the house out. Although Fabian claims to be law-abiding, Ollie has never been sure he is telling the truth. Fabian knows too many people from the South East's criminal underbelly. But no, when he flicks the lights on, everything is where it should be. Pictures hanging on walls, trinkets on shelves and the flat-screen TV still on its stand.

He sends Fabian a text. *Where are u? I'm home. Hugs. Ox*

After grabbing a beer from the fridge, Ollie walks upstairs.

His neck aches, and his legs feel heavy. Perhaps he'll just get an early night. He looks around the bedroom, which is neat and tidy as always, the bed made, and drawers and wardrobes closed. But then he sees the note propped up on his pillow. He picks it up with a heavy heart.

Ollie, sorry about your mum. A bailiff turned up today. What the ??? I'm going away for a few days to make things better. Fx

Ollie sits down on the edge of the bed and rereads the note. He doesn't know what Fabian means, 'to make things better.' Can things get any worse? He has tried so hard to keep the dire financial situation away from Fabian. He kidded himself that it's because he doesn't want to worry Fabian, but the truth is, Ollie is scared Fabian won't stick around if the lavish lifestyle goes. And Ollie really wants Fabian to stick around. As he puts his head in his hands, he acknowledges to himself that he loves Fabian. Really loves Fabian. He's not sure he will cope if he loses Fabian too.

Ollie tries calling Fabian, but his call goes straight to voicemail. For a moment he hesitates, wondering if he should leave a message, but as he doesn't know what to say, he just ends the call. And then he calls his mate Dom, a wheeler-dealer broker with fancy offices near Victoria station.

'We're looking to sell the family business. Reckoned you'd be our man. It's one of the biggest garden centres in the south, fine piece of real estate, profitable but with plenty of potential. We're looking for a quick sale.'

Ollie expected Dom to salivate, but he sounds downbeat.

'It's not a good time to sell right now. The retail market is shambolic, and venture capitalists aren't taking any risks. Have you got an information memorandum and a list of potential buyers?'

'No, nothing. We're keen to get out as soon as possible, so it could be sold for land value if necessary.'

'Look, mate, I'm happy to have a look, but don't hold your breath. Times are tough.'

Ollie drops the phone and collapses on the bed. Too right times are tough. Ollie wonders how long probate will take and whether Annette has left him anything in her will, assuming she's even got a will. Laying his hands on his third of the business seemed such a good idea: plenty of cash and no headaches. And then it hits him: the answer to his immediate problems, at least. If Gerry wants the garden centre so badly, he can buy Ollie out; then, with Bella's share, Gerry will own the majority of the business.

He picks his phone up off the soft carpet and dials Gerry.

36

PIPPA

Joe and I are eating supper in his kitchen. Sleek white cupboards with hidden handles line the far wall. The worktops are white-and-grey-mottled marble, and he has a modern induction hob. It all looks very new. We are seated at a round glass table, eating Marks & Spencer shepherd's pie, accompanied by a bottle of Pinot Noir.

'The thing about poisoning is, it's unsubtle. Toxicology analyses are so sophisticated these days we can tell exactly what substance was used, exact concentrations, synergistic effects, and in some instances, we can even trace where the substance was acquired. It's not even a quick death, so there's a real risk the patient might be treated and recover. Good for the patient, not so good for the killer.'

'How long will it take for the full toxicology report to come through?' I ask.

'Can be up to six weeks,' Joe says, wiping his lips. 'According to the pathologist, local injecting of ricin toxin induces induration – swelling and hardening at the injection site, swelling of nearby lymph nodes, hypotension and then death. It's almost as if the killer wanted Annette to know she was dying, that she had been poisoned.'

'How horrible,' I say as I push the remaining morsels of my food to the side of the plate. I've lost my appetite.

'I can't work out why she didn't tell anyone what was happening. Ricin poisoning typically kills within thirty-six to seventy-two hours. She would have known she was severely ill or dying. Why didn't she call for an ambulance or ask for help?'

I grimace. 'I feel terrible. She came to see me and I did nothing. I thought she looked ill. I could have saved her if I'd called a doctor.'

'Pippa, that's nonsense. Even if you had called for medical help, there is no antidote. Annette would have died anyway. Our job is to work out who killed her and why.'

Joe takes our plates and places them into the dishwasher. He returns to the table with a large pad of paper and a pen.

'We're tracking down an independent horticulturalist to assist us with plant identification and, in particular, whether any castor plants are amongst those in Annette's greenhouses, both at home and at the garden centre.'

'Why?' I ask.

'Ricin is made from castor plants. Don't you remember your chemistry from your school days?' Joe says, grinning.

'I am quite sure that we were not taught about the components of poisons!' I say, laughing. 'On a serious note, it begs the question: was Annette poisoned because somehow or other she's involved with poisonous plants? But it doesn't explain why Scott McDermott was strangled. Do you think the two murders are related?'

'On the face of it, it doesn't seem as if they are, but it's too much of a coincidence. I don't like coincidences,' Joe says. 'And I forgot to tell you. I wrote the name Coon on the whiteboard in the office and one of my colleagues told me that it is spelled K-O-E-N. It's a reasonably common Dutch male first name.'

'Has your team found the name in any of Annette's possessions?'

'No. We haven't even found an address book, which is mighty odd. We've got her diary. One of my guys is working through it. She didn't appear to use a computer. We found her mobile phone on her person, but there are only four numbers on it – those of her children and deceased husband. Bella said she never used it. The woman who works in the office at the garden centre gave us access to their customer database and purchase ledger details. So far it hasn't thrown up anything out of the ordinary.'

'Talking about address books, I need to go home and get mine.'

'What do you mean?'

'In my hurry to leave, I didn't get the contact details of the clients I need to cancel this week. I'll have to go and get them.'

'I'll get someone to bring them over. Where are they?'

I shake my head. 'Firstly, they're in a locked cabinet, and secondly, client confidentiality is such that I can't possibly allow anyone else access.'

Joe sighs. 'In which case, I'll take you there first thing tomorrow morning.'

I SLEEP SURPRISINGLY WELL, considering I am just two thin walls away from Joe. He's right. I do feel safe here. Like me, he is an early riser.

We're both out taking Mungo for a stroll across the field at 6 a.m. There is a low mist hanging across the meandering stream. Weak sunlight makes dewdrops and cobwebs glisten. It's a beautiful morning.

By 7 a.m. we're parked up outside my house. I am surprised

no one is there. I had expected a policeman to be standing guard outside.

Joe laughs. 'We don't have the resources to work shifts. I have one team, and that team needs to go home and sleep. They'll be back here at 8 a.m.'

I get out of the car, walk up the garden path and put my key in the lock. As I open the front door, the door pushes against something. I walk into the hall, and lying on the floor is an A4 envelope about an inch thick. It's addressed to me, Dr P. Durrant, so I pick it up, place it on the hall table and hurry into my office. I am relieved that the house appears untouched. Even Mungo seems perfectly relaxed as he ambles through, at my heels. I unlock the cabinet, write down my client's details, lock the study door and walk back to the front door. I pick up the envelope on my way out, locking the door behind me.

I open it as I walk back to the car. Inside is a small book. Flicking through it, I realise exactly what it is. Annette Gower's address book. The names don't mean anything to me, until I flick through to the final page. I climb into the car and continue looking through it.

'Oh my goodness!' I exclaim, my finger pointing at the three names scrawled at the top of the page. Koen Smit, Janneke Visser and Scott McDermott.'

'Let me have a look!' Joe reaches over for the small book.

'Janneke Visser. She was Scott McDermott's ex-wife. They lost their daughter aged seventeen,' I say.

Joe glances at me, his eyebrows raised. 'This could be our lucky break,' he says, as he places the small book into an evidence bag.

'How curious that someone wanted you to have this,' Joe says. 'We'll need to fingerprint it, work out who pushed it through your door and why. But first I'm taking you back to my place,' Joe says.

'Can't I come into the station with you?'

'No,' Joe says. And this time I don't argue.

AFTER CANCELLING as many clients as I can get hold of, I spend the morning pottering. I do a telephone consultation with a client and make myself a sandwich for lunch. After taking Mungo for another walk, I'm ambling through the fields, nearly back at Joe's house, when I spot his car speeding down the lane.

'Come on, Mungo. We need to hurry.'

We jog back to the converted barn.

'Hello!' I call out.

Joe is in the kitchen, zipping up a small suitcase he has placed on the glass kitchen table.

'Who can look after the dog whilst you're away?'

'Sorry?'

'We're going to Holland.'

'What?'

'You and I are going to Holland. Have you got your passport here?'

'Yes.' I put my small collection of valuables, including the little box of Flo's memorabilia and my small jewellery pouch, into the suitcase when I left home. I never go anywhere without them.

'Harriet, my dog walker, will probably take Mungo. But why are we going to Holland?'

'I've tracked down Janneke Visser. I would like you with me when we interview her. I'm hoping she'll lead us to Koen Smit.'

'So Coon is Koen?' I ask.

'Yes. The Dutch pronounce the name more like "cone", but it's very likely a Brit would say "coon".'

'Won't the Dutch police track him down?'

'Possibly. Possibly not. Can you hurry, please? Our flight leaves at 6 p.m.'

Lovely Harriet couldn't be more helpful. When I explain

that I have to go away as a matter of great urgency, she offers to collect Mungo. Half an hour later, I have waved goodbye to my faithful dog, and Joe and I are on our way to Gatwick Airport.

'WE KNOW NOW without a shadow of doubt that Annette and Scott knew each other. Now we just have to work out where Koen fits in.'

'Could these murders be domestic, somehow or another?'

'Possibly, but there's only one way to find out. We need to talk to the individuals directly.'

'What if they don't speak English?'

Joe laughs. 'All Dutch speak English. But seriously, I doubt Annette spoke Dutch, so they must have been conversing in English.'

'Fair point.'

'We are off to a town in the east of Holland called Deventer.'

THE FLIGHT IS short and on time. The walk through Schiphol airport is long, and after the events of the past few days, I am tired.

With his long legs, Joe strides quickly, and it's hard for me to keep up. We pick up a couple of sandwiches.

Joe rents a car and then we're off. The traffic is bad, and before long I'm asleep.

'Wake up, sleepy head!'

I jerk awake, my heart hammering. When I see Joe's smile, I relax and look around me. It's dark outside. I've been asleep for over two hours.

'We'll have an early night and then get going first thing tomorrow. Sound okay?'

'Yes,' I reply, trying to suppress a yawn.

The air is fresh, and as I get out of the car, I realise we're adjacent to a wide river.

'The River Ijssel,' Joe says. 'There's no footbridge. The only way across is with that little ferry. It's an old historic town, rather lovely by all accounts.'

'Have you been here before?'

'No.'

'Is the area known for growing plants?'

'It's not, and that's what is rather strange. Annette wouldn't have bought any plants from here. The plant-growing area of Holland is in the Westland, between The Hague, Rotterdam and Amsterdam.'

The hotel is adjacent to the river, housed in an old building with a modern wing. I am both relieved and disappointed that we have separate rooms, next to each other, though. My bedroom is small and poorly laid out, with furniture too big for the room. For that reason, I'm glad I am sleeping there alone. Anyone on the left side of the bed would bash themselves on the way to the simple, functional bathroom. Nevertheless, the bed is comfortable, and I am excited to be somewhere I have never visited before.

'Sleep well, Pippa.' Joe is propping my bedroom door open. He leans forwards as if he is going to give me a kiss, but then he pulls away and disappears into the hotel corridor.

37

'I'm going out today,' Bella says as she peers into the bathroom mirror, rubbing Crème de la Mer face cream into her cheeks.

Gerry has stepped out of the shower. Bella doesn't like to look at him, with his fat, rubbery stomach, wobbling backside and moobs. She thanks her lucky stars he never reaches for her in bed these days.

'Oh yes,' Gerry says, rubbing himself dry.

'I'm going to Roedean to tell the girls their grandmother has died. I'll need to speak to their house mistress just in case it gets into the press. I don't want the girls finding out Annette was murdered. And then I'm going to the funeral home in Worthing to get things in motion.'

'It'll be weeks until they release her body, won't it?'

'Funerals should be planned as carefully as weddings. It'll just give us more time to give Mum a real send-off. I never understood why Dad's funeral was so low-key. It was wrong.'

Gerry leans over and gives Bella a quick peck on the cheek.

'I'm so proud of you, the way you're holding it all together. It's been a terrible shock and you're coping admirably.'

Bella harrumphs and wipes her cheek with her fingers.

An hour later and Bella has driven away. Gerry is in no hurry to go to work, but he does want to see Mae. She has become like a drug for him: addictive, all-consuming, the fire in his belly. The thought of seeing her every day when he owns Rocks Garden Centre is thrilling. He wonders for a moment whether this is love. When everything has been sorted out and he is Mr Kingpin in horticulture, he will divorce Bella and marry Mae. Mrs Isla-Mae Shelton. It works.

He can't believe he forgot about the little box in his jacket pocket. No time like the present, he thinks, as he picks up his mobile and rings Mae.

His second call is to his secretary, Kelly.

'I'm working from home this morning. I'll come into the office this afternoon. I don't want to be disturbed.'

Gerry spends the next couple of hours researching how best to raise money. He makes a list of who he needs to contact, and the information required to pull the funding together. He telephones his accountant and the bank manager. Neither are available to speak to him. He telephones a couple of leading estate agents, asking for someone to call him back with regard to carrying out valuations on a large retail property. And then the doorbell rings.

'I've parked my van down the road, just in case,' Mae says.

'Hello, gorgeous.' He pulls her towards him, but Mae struggles.

'Not here! What if any of your neighbours see?'

Gerry steps back, and Mae walks into the hall. She knows she should be impressed, but she's not. A little envious perhaps, but not impressed. It looks as if Bella and Gerry bought the show home and never bothered to add personal touches. She glances at herself in the large, fake silver-framed mirror in the hallway and licks her lips. Gerry leads her into the kitchen. It's black and white and sparkling. Mae thinks the house looks unlived in.

'Glass of vino?' Gerry asks.

'Just the one. It is my lunch hour and I've got to drive.'

'Of course, love.'

Gerry pours out two very large glasses of white wine and hands her one.

'How long have we got?'

'Fifty minutes,' Mae says.

'Do you want to see the bedroom?' Gerry leers.

'Honestly, Gerry, I'm not comfortable being in your home, and there is no way we are making love in the bedroom you share with your wife.'

'Of course not!' Gerry pretends to be shocked at the very idea. It hadn't crossed his mind that they should use one of the spare rooms. He wonders if the beds are made up. Perhaps he hasn't thought this through properly.

'Anyway, I've got something for you!'

Gerry strides over to the suit jacket hanging on the back of the chair and removes the little navy-blue box. He hands it to Mae. She hesitates for a moment before opening it.

'Oh, Gerry, it's beautiful!' She removes the ring from the box and peers at the tiny green stone set on a gold band with two even smaller diamonds each side.

'It's a sign of my commitment to you. I love you, Isla-Mae.'

'Gosh, thank you, Gerry.'

She tries to slip it onto her finger, but it's too small to fit even her little finger. Mae is relieved. She would never wear anything so insignificant, and besides, she doesn't like gold. If Gerry was observant, he would see that she only wears silver or platinum.

'It's an emerald. It's the birthstone for May.'

'But my birthday is in February!'

'And your name is Mae, and it's green because you work with plants.'

'Okay,' Mae says slowly.

'I'm gutted it doesn't fit.' Gerry moves closer to Mae. 'I'll get it made larger.'

'No, don't do that. I'll wear it on a necklace and then it will be closer to my heart.'

'And closer to those beautiful bosoms of yours.' Gerry makes a lunge for Mae's left breast.

The doorbell rings.

'Shit. I'm not expecting anyone. Let's ignore it.'

Mae feels uneasy and backs into the corner of the room, out of view from the windows.

'I think you should answer it just in case.'

The doorbell chimes again and a voice shouts, 'Gerry, are you there? Your secretary said you're working from home!'

Gerry paces towards the front door, glances outside and sees Ollie's Maserati.

'Shit!' he says again in a whisper. 'You'll need to hide, Mae darling. It's my bloody brother-in-law.'

Gerry swings open the door.

'What a surprise!' he exclaims, unsmiling.

'Your secretary said you're working from home, so I thought I'd pop by. She said you couldn't be disturbed, but I think you'll want to be disturbed by this.'

'Come in, come in!' Gerry beckons Ollie inside and walks towards the living room.

'Can I grab a glass of water? Ollie says, striding in the opposite direction, towards the kitchen.

'Um, hold on. I'll get it for you!'

Ollie turns around and frowns at Gerry, but doesn't stop walking. Gerry is right behind him, frantically thinking about how to introduce Mae without raising suspicions. But she's not there.

'Drinking alone at lunchtime?' Ollie smirks, pointing at Gerry's wine glass.

'Yes, well, just needed something to numb the pain. Awful business this. I'm very sorry about Annette. I'll miss her,' Gerry effuses. 'Bella is in a right mess. Understandably. Do the police have any idea as to what happened? I can't make head or tail of what Bella is telling me.'

Ollie thinks Gerry is a bumbling idiot. Where was he yesterday to support Bella? Besides, Bella was the most together of the three of them in front of the police. Annette and Bella never saw eye to eye.

'No further news yet. Look, Gerry, I've got an idea about Rocks Garden Centre. A proposition to put to you.'

'Oh yes?' Gerry says.

Ollie pulls out a chair at the kitchen table and sits down. Reluctantly Gerry does the same. He wonders where Mae is hiding. In the utility room, or the larder, perhaps?

'The thing is, I've been thinking,' Ollie says. 'I want to sell Rocks. You – and I assume Bella goes along with anything you want – want to buy it, but Lily doesn't want to sell. So how about you buy out my share? That way, you'll have the controlling interest, two-thirds of the business, and you can run it the way you see fit.'

Gerry lets out a whoosh of air. 'Well, that's an interesting proposal.' He leans back in his chair but then immediately sits forwards. His eyes are darting around the room. Ollie wonders what's up with Gerry. He seems unusually skittish.

There is a clatter, the sound of something being knocked over. They both jump.

'What's that?' Ollie asks. 'Is Bella here? I thought she was out, as her car is gone.'

'Yes, Bella's out. It's probably next door's cat or something falling over. The cleaner came this morning. She's useless.

Always leaving things lying around, knocking things over. She probably didn't put the polish away properly.'

Ollie frowns but lets it go. 'So, what do you think? Would you like to buy me out?'

Inside, Gerry is doing little cartwheels of joy, but he knows he needs to play it cool.

'I'll think about it, Ollie. I really wanted to own the whole thing, and I'm not sure what Lily will be like as the minority shareholder.'

'Oh, Lily will go along with anything you suggest. She's only interested in the plants, not the business side of things.'

'Leave it with me. We'll have to sort out an independent valuation.'

'Of course. In fact, I have someone who can do that,' Ollie says, smiling.

'Forward me his contact details.'

Ollie leans across the table, laying his palms face up. 'I'd like to get this sorted as quickly as possible. I've got another project I want to invest in so could do with freeing up some cash.'

'Fair enough, Ollie old man. I'll be in touch.'

Ollie stands up. 'And Gerry. Any chance you could keep this to yourself? I don't want Lily or her arsehole husband getting wind of this.'

'Quite understand. I won't mention it to Bella either. No need to rock the boat at such an emotional time.'

Gerry sees Ollie out, and only when the roar of the Maserati has faded into the distance does he let out his breath. Bloody hell, that was a close call.

He walks slowly back to the kitchen. It's true what he said to Ollie. He would prefer to be the sole owner, but this could work in the short-term. And it would mean he'd need to raise less money.

When he's back in the kitchen, Mae is sitting in the chair Ollie just vacated.

'Are you all right, my darling?' Gerry asks.

'Why shouldn't I be?' Mae flicks her jet-black, glossy bob.

'You nearly gave yourself away,' Gerry says, grinning. He moves towards Mae and unzips his trousers. 'Look what all this excitement has done to big boy!' He licks his lips while thrusting his groin forwards.

Mae stands up. 'I'm sorry, Gerry, but I can't. I've got a client visit this afternoon and I've got to go. You know how much I was looking forward to a repeat with big boy, but I can't afford to lose my job.'

'I can afford to pay your salary.' He lets his trousers fall to the ground. 'Soon I'll be your boss anyway. Please! Pretty please!' he simpers.

'Sorry, darling, but not today.' She leans over to give Gerry a quick peck on the lips, carefully angling her body away from his. When she's on the other side of the kitchen, she blows him a kiss, and then she's gone.

Gerry groans.

38

PIPPA

Joe is in the hotel restaurant, sipping a coffee and studying his laptop. He stands up as I approach.

'Did you sleep well?' He pulls out a chair for me.

'Yes, thank you, and you?'

I slept terribly, but I don't intend to tell Joe that. I feel awkward around him this morning, as if the easy familiarity of yesterday has been rubbed away and today we're just colleagues on a joint mission. After helping myself to a bowl of fruit salad, a pastry and some cheese and ham from the self-service buffet, I sit back down at the table.

'Aren't you eating?' I ask.

'No. I concentrate better on an empty stomach.'

He turns the laptop towards me. It shows a Facebook profile.

'We're going to visit Janneke Visser. She lives here in Deventer.'

'And Koen Smit? Did you find out where he lives?'

Joe sighs. 'No. It's a really common name, and so far we've

got no leads. I'm hoping Janneke can point us towards Koen, but other than the fact that both their telephone numbers are listed on the same page in Annette's address book, I don't know if there's any connection between them. I've already been in touch with the local police, but they can't help us without more information. They confirmed what I thought, though: the telephone number next to Koen's name is a mobile number from a pay-as-you-go phone. It's no longer in use, and there is no way to track the owner.'

Thirty minutes later and we're back in the hire car driving across the bridge into Deventer. There is a light drizzle, but it doesn't detract from the grandeur of the buildings adjacent to the River Ijssel, many shaped in the typical Dutch style, tall with pointed roofs in a mismatch of colours and styles.

'That is Saint Lebuïnuskerk, commonly known as the Grote Kerk, or "big church".' Joe points to the building that dominates the skyline with its imposing tower and Gothic features.

'How do you know that?' I ask.

'I'm a geek when it comes to visiting new places. I like to do my research,' he says, grinning.

I assume that is what makes him a good detective: an acute eye for detail.

Joe has a satnav system on his phone, which guides us. We turn left and follow the river for a while before veering towards the right and into a series of residential streets, at which point I totally lose my sense of direction.

'Here we are: 21 Twellohofweg.'

We are parked outside a row of semi-detached houses constructed from red brick with red tiles, boxy-looking with a 1970s feel to them. I am struck by how similar they all are, with the same pot plants on windowsills, white window frames and front doors painted in subdued colours. The key differentiating factors are the small front gardens. All are neat and cared for, but some are fenced with crisscross fencing, others are boxed in with hedging, and one house even has a modest display of topiary. Number 21 has a lavender-coloured door. Unlike those of its neighbours, the front garden is paved over. Two empty planters stand either side of the front door.

Joe rings the doorbell and we stand back. I glance around at the other houses, expecting net curtains to twitch, and I have to suppress a smile when I see an elderly woman poke her head around the curtains in the house opposite.

'What if Janneke isn't here?' I ask.

'I made an appointment with her,' Joe says.

I had expected we would be surprising her. I see the outline of a person behind the frosted glass of the front door, and then it is opened.

She is about my age, with ash-blond hair swept back severely from her face, exposing a large forehead and grey eyes.

'Please come in.'

Janneke has a strong Dutch accent. She is tall, only an inch or two shorter than Joe, but much taller than me. I notice her slightly bohemian clothes, the grey patterned tunic with orange patch pockets over black leggings. Her feet are bare, her toenails painted in bright-orange nail varnish.

'I am very sorry for your loss,' Joe says as we follow her into the small living room.

'Yes, I was astonished how much I was affected by Scott's death,' she says. 'We divorced more than fifteen years ago, but I wished him well. It is a horrible thing. He didn't deserve to die like that. No one does. Can I get you coffee or tea? I think I still have some of that builder's tea. Don't worry, it's not fifteen years old!'

We laugh. I am relieved that Janneke Visser is so open, surprisingly welcoming.

Whilst she is out of the room, we both look around. There are numerous pictures of a girl, taken from when she was a baby up until the age of seventeen. My heart sinks.

Janneke returns quickly holding a tray with three cups and a cafetière.

'Have you tried our stroopwafel?' She holds out a plate of waffle-like biscuits.

I accept one, even though I don't feel like eating any more. Joe declines.

'So, how can I help you?' She sits on an Ercol-style armchair with her feet tucked underneath her.

'When was the last time you saw your ex-husband?' Joe asks.

Her face clouds over. 'Seven years ago. At the funeral of our daughter.'

'I am very sorry,' I mutter. 'I understand your pain.'

'With respect, Doctor Durrant, I doubt you do.'

I shift awkwardly in my chair. I cannot believe I was about to turn the conversation towards me. I must be more tired than I thought.

'When was the last time you spoke to Mr McDermott?' Joe asks.

She sighs, and looks upwards to the left as she attempts to recall.

'Maybe eight months ago. He was planning a trip to the Netherlands. He wanted to know if we could meet for dinner. I said no. Scott and I had nothing left to say to each other.'

'Would you know who might have wished him harm?'

Janneke surprises us both by laughing. 'It's more like who wouldn't want to cause Scott harm!'

'Please expand,' Joe prompts.

'Scott was a very clever man, but he liked to – how do you say? – fly close to the sun. It wasn't enough for him to be the senior research chemist at Vingerhoedskruid Pharma and a professor at Wageningen University, he had to run an operation on the side. He worked day and night. We – my daughter, Mila, and I – we never saw him. When we split up, he moved back to

England. He set up his own business, researching *Aconitum*, *Ricinus communis* and one other. I forget its name.'

'*Ricinus*. Is that Ricin?' Joe asks, edging forwards on his seat.

'Yes.'

Joe glances at me. 'Does the name Annette Gower mean anything to you?' Joe asks Janneke.

She bursts out laughing. 'Of course! Despite their age difference, David Gower was Scott's best friend. Their families lived on the same street, and David became a role model, an older brother, to Scott. They spoke all the time on the telephone. I didn't know Annette well. Scott was quite a lot older than me, and Annette was his age, not mine, so we didn't have much in common. I haven't heard that name in a long time.'

'I'm afraid to tell you Annette is also dead. We believe she might have been killed by ricin.'

Janneke gasps, her hand rushing to cover her mouth. 'No! That is terrible, truly terrible!' I am sure her reactions are genuine.

She shakes her head. 'Poor Annette. I knew David died a few years ago. I understand that Scott was hit hard by his passing. It is very shocking. But it doesn't make sense that she died from ricin!'

'This research business that Scott was running: who were his customers?'

'Customers? He did research on behalf of big pharma companies. I don't think he had customers, as you call it. He got grant money. Look, this was a long time ago. I expect he retired, pottered about in the garden and read toxicology studies. We never talked about his work. I wasn't interested in it.'

'And what do you do, Ms Visser?'

'Please call me Janneke. I'm a Reiki practitioner. I work in an alternative health clinic near here. Scott never approved of my energy work. He said it wasn't scientifically proven. He was wrong.'

Joe pauses before asking the next question. I am well tuned in to him now, and I am ready for Janneke's response.

'Does the name Koen Smit mean anything to you?'

'No,' Janneke replies.

I don't detect any conflicting micro-expressions or involuntary body movements. She doesn't try to expand or deflect the question. The simple 'no' is attuned to her neutral mannerisms. She is telling the truth.

39

L ily is struggling. She can't stop crying, and Stijn is losing patience. Lily had expected that her husband would be there to comfort her, but it's as if the more emotional she becomes, the more he chooses to distance himself.

'I'm working late tonight, Lils.' He tries to keep his tone light. 'I'm sorry. I know it's bad timing. Blame that shit of your brother-in-law. He's sending me off to Newcastle.'

Lily bites her lip. Her voice quivers. 'I thought you didn't go farther north than the Midlands.'

'We've got a new customer. And if the traffic is bad, I'll have to stay overnight somewhere. You know I'm not allowed to drive for more than nine hours in a day.'

Stijn doesn't look at Lily. He's confounded by how much he is affected by her distress. The desire to fling his arms around her and tell her he'll protect her takes him by surprise. He's never felt like that towards anyone before.

'Why don't you ask Ollie to stay over. Or perhaps you could go to Bella's?'

'No.' Lily sniffs and dabs at her eyes with a sodden tissue.

'And Lily, you really must go into work tomorrow. We don't want Gerry getting his feet under the table. I know you're hurting, Lils, but we need to think about the big picture.'

She nods because she knows she should nod. But right now the very last thing Lily wants to do is go to work. How will she cope with the condolences and the sympathy? She tries to remember what her dad told her, what David would say if he was in the room with her now.

Stijn stands up. 'Be strong, darling.' He kisses the top of her head, her soft hair, which smells of rosemary and ylang-ylang, tickling his nose.

'Please don't go,' Lily whispers.

But Stijn has already left the room.

OLLIE LEFT Gerry's house in high spirits, hopeful that his dire financial woes might be rectified. Yes, he could go back to work, but he's been out of it for a few years now, and he doubts any of the banks would take him back. Besides, Ollie likes his lifestyle. It's just lousy luck that the investment fund he was convinced would give him the highest return bottomed out and collapsed. Lousy luck. He's living on borrowed time – or more accurately, borrowed money. And for Ollie, who was told by his father he'd achieve nothing in this world, it's about as shameful as it can get. Even worse than the prospect of his now-deceased mother finding out he is gay. Ollie was a millionaire by the age of thirty, and now it's all gone.

Ollie is sitting in his beautiful home in Hove staring at the pile of final demands and letters from bailiffs. Every credit card is maxed out, and he fears he will have to go to one of the loan sharks that demand 500 per cent APR. Yes, he could sell the car. Yes, he could sell the house, but he has no intention of doing either.

He has lost count of the number of messages and voicemails he's left for Fabian over the past couple of days. He misses him terribly. The loneliness is piercing.

The doorbell rings. Ollie ignores it. It rings again. He tiptoes into the corridor and peers around the side of the curtains in the living room. He's terrified it will be a bailiff.

The young olive-skinned man is wearing a Stone Roses T-shirt and jeans, and his white van is blocking the road, it's blinkers flashing. He is holding an electronic device in one hand, the little machine one signs when accepting a delivery, and a small brown package in the other.

Ollie exhales and opens the front door.

'Gotta delivery for you. Sign here.'

Ollie does as instructed, and accepts the parcel. His heart is pumping hard with relief. Bailiffs take things away. They don't send things.

He tears the package open and slides out a box wrapped in gold paper. There is a card attached to the front, typewritten.

Darling, sorry I've disappeared for a while. Enjoy these in my absence. Will be back soon, Fx

Ollie leans back and smiles. Fabian normally signs his name *Your Fab Fab*, but this looks as if it has been sent via a mail-order company, and there were probably limited letters available for the message. Eagerly he rips off the gold paper and opens up a little box of chocolates and a small bottle of pink gin. He grins. Fabian knows him well.

Although it's a bit early to start drinking, he finds a can of Fever-Tree tonic water and pours a couple of fingers of the pink gin into a fine crystal-cut glass. He carries the glass and chocolates back into the living room, puts his feet up and flicks between the television channels. There's nothing much on, but he doesn't care. The fact that Fabian hasn't totally disappeared out of his life makes all his other worries pale into insignificance.

He sends Fabian a text.

Thanks for the gin and chocs. I love you. Come home soon, Oxx

He wonders if he should call Lily. He knows she'll be a mess. The youngest of the family, he has always handled her with kid gloves. But before long he begins to feel drowsy and all thoughts of Lily dissipate.

Sometime later, Ollie awakes with a start, his stomach convulsing. He rushes to the bathroom, where he is violently sick. A layer of perspiration coats his body, his head is pounding and he can't stop shaking. He crawls upstairs, aiming to reach his bed, but he vomits on the beautiful silvery carpet.

Ollie has never felt this ill before. He pulls himself to the top of the stairs but then passes out.

FABIAN HAS HIS PHONE OFF, but he turns it on every hour or so to listen to Ollie's beseeching voicemails and read his texts. It feels good to be wanted. It's about 8 p.m. when he switches his phone on again and sees the message from Ollie thanking him for the gin and chocolates. Fabian frowns. He hasn't sent Ollie anything.

40

PIPPA

When we leave Janneke Visser's house, I am feeling dejected, so I am surprised Joe is upbeat.

'We had assumed Scott McDermott either broke into Rocks Garden Centre or was let in by someone who had the key. But if he was that close to David and Annette Gower, perhaps he had his own key,' Joe muses as we climb into the rental car.

'Did you find anything in his house about his research into poisons?' I ask. 'I remember the newsagent in Findon saying he regularly sent parcels all over the world. Was there anything to suggest he was running a business as well?'

Joe lays his hands on the steering wheel. 'Nothing. He had one filing cabinet where he stored personal information, bank statements and personal papers, but nothing to suggest he was running a business. Unless he was working out of another premises, which seems unlikely, as the neighbours described him as a bit of a recluse.'

Joe lifts his hands off the steering wheel, pulls the seat belt across him and starts the car engine. 'We are going to have a coffee, and then we're going to do a bit more research. Let's talk to people at Vingerhoedskruid Pharma and at Wageningen University.' Joe makes a hash of the pronunciation and we laugh.

We find a cute coffee shop tucked behind the main square on a narrow cobbled street. I decline my third coffee of the morning and settle for a glass of water. Joe has more coffee and a large bagel. He opens his laptop.

'Wageningen University is located about forty minutes from here, and the pharma company is on the outskirts of Amsterdam. I suggest we go to the university first and then head back to Amsterdam. There doesn't appear to be any reason to return to Deventer.'

Joe takes out his mobile and dials. 'Mia, any news?'

He is silent for a while, nodding his head.

'Can you ask the DI if we can have another look at the financial affairs of Scott McDermott, Annette Gower and Rocks Garden Centre? Employ the forensic accountant if needs be and get warrants. We think there might have been some dodgy commercial dealings going on. I'll let you know more later.'

I look at Joe quizzically, but he doesn't pass on any information. It reminds me that I am only peripheral to this investigation, and it annoys me.

He reads from a page on the internet. 'Wageningen University & Research specialises in economy and society, health, life sciences and technology, nature and environment, animals and plants. Their MSc programme is taught only in English, and they have a plant research institute. They teach and research in plant breeding, plant biotechnology and plant sciences.' He looks at me. 'It makes sense that Scott McDermott taught there. By the way, what did you think of Janneke Visser? Did you detect any lies or suchlike?'

'Nope. There was nothing evasive about her.'

The tiredness is catching up on me, and I struggle to stifle a yawn.

'Come on, let's go back to the car and you can have nap.'

I DOZE during the car journey, and when I open my eyes, we are entering a large campus, totally flat, with many vast geometric buildings. It is impressive.

Joe stops the car next to a big sign. 'I think Plant Research should be our first port of call,' he says.

We follow the signs to visitors' parking, where Joe parks the car. We get out and walk from the car park, following a path that leads towards a cluster of vast, squat buildings. There are plenty of people milling around, but it is difficult to tell who are faculty members and who are students. In the end, Joe stops a young man wearing a white coat, tall, lanky and with a serious expression.

'Excuse me. We are trying to track down information about a former professor, what his research projects were, who he worked with, etc. Could you tell us where to go?'

'The office,' he says, speaking in flawless English and pointing down a long corridor. 'The second door on your right.'

'Thank you.'

Joe knocks on the door, and I follow him in. It is a small office with a woman seated at a desk, thick-rimmed glasses sliding down her nose and an older man wearing a cabled bottle-green sweater rifling through a metal filing cabinet.

'Do you speak English?' Joe asks her.

'Of course.'

'Are we right in thinking Scott McDermott taught here?'

'The name doesn't mean anything to me, but I have only worked here for two years. I can ask my colleague. What is it in regard to?'

'We're from the UK police.' Joe shows her his badge. 'Unfortunately Scott McDermott died in suspicious circumstances, and we're investigating.'

She looks startled and pushes her glasses high up on her nose. She gets up, walks to the back of the room and whispers something incomprehensible in Dutch to the man. He puts down the files he is holding and strides towards us.

'I understand you are here about Professor McDermott. I didn't know he died.'

'Yes, I am sorry to be the bearer of bad news.'

The man's expression stays neutral.

'Could you tell us when he worked here and exactly what he did?' Joe asks.

'Yes. Have a seat and I will pull together some information for you.' He gestures towards two plastic chairs positioned against the wall.

Less than five minutes later and he is standing in front of us, reading from a file.

'Scott McDermott was a part-time professor for a long time. He left here seven years ago, and we have a forwarding address for him in England. He wrote a number of papers on the analysis of mycotoxins and plant toxins in food and feed. I can take copies of them if it would help you.'

'Yes, please,' Joe says. 'Do you have a list of his students or his associate researchers?'

The man shakes his head. 'No, it is too long ago.'

He walks over to a photocopying machine and copies many pages.

'Thank you very much for your help,' Joe says, standing up to accept the pages. 'If any of the current faculty remembers Professor McDermott, I would be most grateful if you could ask them to contact me.' Joe hands him a couple of business cards. 'Does the name Koen Smit mean anything to you?'

The man shakes his head. 'Sorry, no.'

. . .

'HE WAS INTO POISONS,' I say as we stride back towards the car.

'Yes, but he wasn't killed by poison, remember. He was strangled.'

I try to stop myself imagining what he would have looked like.

'Annette was poisoned, but Scott was already dead. So someone else was involved. We have to find this Koen Smit,' I mumble.

'Maybe we'll have better luck at the pharma company. Can you read through those research papers whilst I'm driving?'

'Okay.' I don't admit to Joe that I get car sick when I'm reading in the car, or that I am concerned I won't understand a word of the technical jargon in the papers.

I skim read, checking the names of authors of the papers, reading the abstracts at the beginning and the conclusions at the end. Mostly they mean absolutely nothing to me. Every couple of minutes I look out of the window to try to control the onset of motion sickness.

On the fifth paper I screech, 'Oh my God!'

Joe's hands tighten on the steering wheel and he takes his foot off the accelerator.

'What is it?'

'You will never believe who is one of the co-authors of this research paper!'

'Don't keep me in suspense.' A smile edges at Joe's lips.

'Stijn A. Eikenboom.'

'Our Stijn?' Joe asks, glancing at me with a look of astonishment.

'I don't know, but it could be. Do you think it's a common name?'

'Not sure, but it's easy enough to find out. Do a Google search.'

I put his name in inverted commas. 'Nothing.'

'That's very strange.'

Suddenly Joe steers the car off to the right. The car behind us hoots.

'What are you doing?' I ask.

'We're going back to the university.'

THE MAN in the office looks thoroughly unimpressed to see us again. He puts his right hand on his hip and raises his eyebrows.

'Yes?'

'We're sorry to bother you. However, in one of the research papers you gave us, the name Stijn A. Eikenboom was mentioned. He is another person of interest in our enquiry. Could you please tell us if he was on your faculty or a student here?'

'What year?' he asks without smiling.

I open the relevant paper and read out the date at the top. 'June 2011.'

'He was not a faculty member then. I started that year and would remember. Undergraduate, masters or PhD?' He sighs, as if this is a great inconvenience for him, which perhaps it is.

Joe and I look at each other.

'He's a lorry driver now. It must be undergraduate?' I suggest to Joe.

'But if he was an undergraduate, surely he wouldn't have had his name listed on a research paper?' Joe says.

'Not true,' I say. 'I used to list undergraduates who helped me with my research.'

'Indeed, the lady is correct.'

'Let's start with undergraduates then,' Joe says.

'Sit down,' the man instructs us. He walks to his desk and perches in front of his computer.

The minutes tick by. I look at my phone, checking for emails. Joe stands and ambles around the room, reading notices on the walls. The young woman at the desk follows him none too discretely with her eyes. Yes, he is handsome, I want to say to her.

Eventually the man with the green jumper wheels his chair around and gets up.

'Found him. He was a PhD student with the experimental plant sciences department. He studied the evolution of plant pathogens.'

'But Stijn doesn't even work for the Gowers. He works for Gerry Shelton as a lorry driver. It can't be our Stijn.' I frown at Joe.

'On the surface it does seem unlikely, but there are too many coincidences here.' He turns towards the man, who is fiddling with the unravelling cuff of his green jumper. 'Do you by any chance have photographs of alumni?'

'Yes, but—'

'Sir, this is a police matter. We would be very grateful for your assistance.'

He turns around and walks back to his computer. 'You'd better come here,' he says. After a few moments of flicking in and out of screens, he brings up a black-and-white photo.

'Well I'll be damned,' Joe mutters.

'It's our Stijn, isn't it? He's early twenties in this photo, or thereabouts.'

Just goes to show, you can't judge anyone on looks, I think to myself. These days he looks thuggish, filled out, somewhat unkempt. In the photograph he has short, cropped, blond hair, smiling blue eyes and a smooth face. He looks exactly how I imagine an eager, bright young man would appear at the start of a promising academic or research career. Stereotyping perhaps, but the face smiling at the camera fits the stereotype.

'Can you see if Scott McDermott was Stijn's supervisor for his research?' I ask.

He flicks through a few more screens. 'No, he wasn't. They would have known each other, but he wasn't Stijn's supervisor.'

'Who was?' Joe asks.

'Professor Kiet Woodsma.'

'Can we talk to him?' Joe says.

The man leans back in his chair. 'No, he died.'

I stifle a gasp, wondering if Stijn killed this man too. And then I have to check myself. We have no proof to suggest Stijn is a murderer.

'When?' Joe asks.

'Two years ago. Pancreatic cancer. It was quick.'

'I'm sorry to hear that,' Joe says. 'Thank you very much for all of your help, and once again, we apologise for interrupting your day.'

The man nods and we make to leave.

Just as Joe has his hand on the door, the man says, 'This Stijn Eikenboom. He didn't finish his PhD. Or if he did, he didn't complete it here.'

41

I t's contrary to what he planned to do, but Fabian calls Ollie. There is no answer. He tries Ollie's mobile and the home telephone. Both go to voicemail. He has a bad feeling. Fabian's intuition has never failed him. He checks the train times. If he leaves now and catches the 20.33 from Victoria, he will get into Brighton at 21.36. He'll get a cab and be home before 10 p.m.

Fabian picks up his small rucksack and runs to the entrance of the Tube station, cursing the crowds of people who are still out shopping on Oxford Street at 8 p.m., darting between tourists and shoppers and city workers, then sprinting nimbly down the escalators. He hops onto the Tube just as the doors are closing.

At Victoria station he pulls up his hoodie to partially cover his face and runs for the Brighton train. Waiting until the ticket collector is helping a group of Spanish tourists struggling with four oversized suitcases, he leaps over the ticket barriers and disappears just as a voice shouts, 'Hey, you! Stop!'

As normal, Fabian has timed it perfectly. He jumps up onto the Brighton train two seconds before the bleeping of the doors warns that they are about to close. He collapses on to one of the disabled seats, ignoring the scornful glance of a suited man opposite. Fabian isn't even out of breath.

He tries Ollie again. Both phones still go to voicemail. The unease makes Fabian shift in his seat. He wonders if his mad dash up to London was a mistake, whether he acted too rashly. His sponsor told him to think before acting, but he never does. Fabian was angry and terrified, and the two together forced him to run. And for once he wanted to do something for Ollie. Sort out the money problems Ollie had so selflessly been keeping from him.

Fabian sighs, plugs his headphones into his ears and turns up the music so loud the *thump-thump-thump* is audible throughout the carriage.

His estimates on timings are spot on. For once the train is on schedule, and there is a queue of taxis parked outside Brighton station. He is on the doorstep of Ollie's house at 21.48. Fabian's heart is pumping hard as he turns the key in the lock.

'Ollie babe, I'm home!' he shouts.

There is no answer.

He doesn't have to walk far into the house for the stench to hit him. He races up the stairs, hopping over the body waste and fluid, holding his nose.

'Ollie!' he screeches.

He finds him in the bathroom, collapsed on the floor. Ollie's eyes are closed; his face has a bluish tinge. A small puddle of blood and bile has formed by his mouth.

At first Fabian thinks Ollie is dead, but when he bends down and touches his heart, he can feel a weak pulse.

Fabain grabs his phone and dials 999.

'Ambulance now. My boyfriend is dying. Please come now!'

The ambulance dispatcher asks Fabian a number of questions and tells him how to position Ollie.

'He's been poisoned!' Fabian screeches.

'Has he taken drugs?'

'No! He's been poisoned!'

And then he hears the sirens and races down the stairs to let the paramedics in.

After assessing Ollie, they lift him carefully onto a stretcher. Fabian runs back downstairs. He sees the small empty bottle of gin and the beautifully packed box of chocolates – a miniature box with space for four little chocolates. One hasn't been eaten. He grabs the box and follows the paramedics out of the door.

'Is he going to live?' Tears are flowing down Fabian's cheeks.

'He's very poorly and unconscious, and he has tachycardia, which is symptomatic of severe food poisoning. We'll know more once we get him to hospital. Are you coming with us?'

Fabian leaves all the lights on in the house, locks the front door and jumps into the ambulance.

'Do you know what he has eaten to bring on this attack?' the paramedic asks as he attaches an oxygen mask to Ollie and hooks him up to a drip.

'These.' Ollie holds up the small box of chocolates.

'Chocolates?' The paramedic frowns.

'They are poisonous.'

TWO HOURS later and a doctor approaches Fabian. He is young, perhaps the same age as Fabian, and in other circumstances Fabian might have made big eyes and laid his hand gently on his forearm. Tonight, he doesn't even notice the doctor's chiselled jaw and tired green eyes.

'Are you Mr Gower's next of kin?'

'I'm his partner. We live together.'

He nods.

'I'm afraid he is very poorly. It might be appropriate for you to call his next of kin.'

Fabian's bottom lip quivers. 'To say goodbye?' He can't stop the tears from flowing.

The doctor nods sympathetically. 'We'll do everything we can, of course. The next six hours will be the most critical. He is in ICU and receiving the very best of care.'

'It was this that did it,' Fabian sobs, holding the small dark-brown box in front of him.

The doctor looks at it. 'What's that?'

'Chocolates. They're poisoned.'

'How do you know?'

Fabian shuffles uncomfortably. 'I just do.'

'In which case this is a police matter.'

Fabian grimaces. The last thing he wants is to be involved with the police again, but if it means Ollie might be cured and the poisoner brought to justice, then he'll do it.

When the doctor has walked away, Fabian crumples back onto the chair. He takes out his phone. He cloned Ollie's contacts a couple of months ago, so he's got all the Gowers' numbers. He'll call Lily. Ollie spoke about her more than any of the others, but she didn't react very well to him when he turned up at their house the other night. Then again, their mother had just died.

He hesitates for a moment and dials her number.

'Hello,' she says, her voice cracking.

'Is this Lily?'

'Yes.'

'It's Fabian. Ollie's...friend.'

'Hello, Fabian.'

'I'm sorry to tell you this, but Ollie is sick. He's in the hospital and...' Fabian starts crying.

'No!' Lily screams. 'That's not possible! How's that possible?'

'They don't know,' Fabian says, sobbing. 'But you'd best come to the hospital as soon as you can.'

· · ·

IT'S an hour later when Lily arrives, along with another woman, a taller, better-groomed version of Lily. Fabian is shocked at Lily's appearance: bedraggled hair; raw red eyes; sores around her lips; pale, waxy skin; and clothes that are creased and shapeless.

'I'm Bella,' the other woman says. 'The other sister.' She doesn't proffer her hand for shaking. 'What's the latest?'

'I don't know. I haven't heard anything for the last hour and a bit,' Fabian says, sniffing.

'Right. I'll go and find out what's going on.'

She marches out of the waiting room towards a cluster of nurses.

Lily drops down onto a chair at the end of the row next to Fabian and puts her hands over her face, her shoulders shaking up and down, her sobs too loud. Fabian wants to tell her to pull herself together, that Ollie's not dead yet. He leans away from Lily, placing the box of chocolates on the chair next to him. After a few moments, Bella returns.

'They're still carrying out tests. If he deteriorates, they'll call us in to see him, but for now we've just got to wait.' Bella sits down on the seat next to the small box. She picks it up and opens it.

'I'm bloody starving. Can I have one of these?' she asks.

'Drop it!' Fabian screams.

42

PIPPA

'We need to interview Stijn,' I say as we climb back into the rental car. 'Why would a scientist as bright as him be working as a lorry driver? It doesn't make sense.'

'He works for Gerry Shelton, Bella Gower's husband. I wonder whether they are running an illicit business together.'

'Rather harsh to have murdered their mother-in-law,' I say.

'Perhaps she found out what was going on,' Joe muses. 'But we still haven't worked out who Koen Smit is and how he fits into all of this. Everything is circumstantial at the moment. We need proof. Plan of action: firstly, we'll go to Vingerhoedskruid Pharma and see if anyone there knew Scott McDermott and whether Koen Smit works there. I will call my contact with the Dutch police to do a criminal records search on Stijn Eikenboom and to find out how often he visits Holland. Perhaps you could track down his family.'

'Okay,' I say weakly. I could do without having to look at my phone whilst we're driving.

About an hour later and we're on the outskirts of Amsterdam in an area called the Zuidas, the heart of the corporate centre, full of glass-fronted office blocks. Vingerhoedskruid Pharma is easy to find. Although the building is small in contrast to most of its neighbours, the name of the company is lit up proudly on a large green sign.

We park in a visitors' bay and stride up to the front door. The reception desk is straight in front of us, high-tech, glass with a pale-green tinge. Seated behind it are two girls, stereotypically Dutch-looking with fair, glossy hair swept back in high ponytails, blue-eyed and lightly tanned. They both wear starched white blouses and green scarves tied jauntily at their necks. If they are wellness advocates for the pharmaceutical company, then this firm must be doing a lot right.

'*Goede middag, hoe kan ik u helpen*?' the girl on the left asks.

'Do you speak English?' Joe asks.

'Of course, sir. How may I help you?'

'We are from the British police.' He shows his badge. 'We are tracking down three men who might have worked for this company. Who could help us with this?'

I expect the young woman to appear startled, but her face is open and warm, and she absorbs the request as if it is totally run-of-the-mill.

'Our head of personnel, Marije van Delden, should be able to help you. I will call her and see if she is free to meet with you. Please take a seat.' She gestures towards two designer-looking leather sofas with cushions made from fabric in the same pale-green shade as the company's logo.

About ten minutes later, a woman strides into the foyer. She is large-boned with masculine features, and hair that cascades to her shoulders in waves that stay rigid as she moves. Her face is caked in heavy foundation that splits when she smiles at us.

'Marije van Delden. How can I help you?' Her voice is deep.

Joe explains our quest, and she asks us to follow her. The meeting room is small and air-conditioned with no external windows. She gestures for us to sit down opposite her at the table.

'We take the security of our staff and our customers extremely seriously,' she says. 'Vingerhoedskruid Pharma works at the cutting edge of medical research, and what we discover can have great financial and commercial value. I am able to tell you if these people worked here, but I will not give you any more information.'

'I need you to understand the seriousness of our request,' Joe says, leaning forwards over the table.

'I do, but I will not compromise our security without the requisite warrants. Please write down the names of the people you are asking about.'

She pushes a notepad and pen towards Joe. He writes down Stijn's, Koen's and Scott's names, and passes the notepad back across the table. Momentarily her face darkens. I wonder which name caused that brief micro-expression.

'I will return when I have the information.'

The floor reverberates with her heavy footsteps.

We wait a long time. Joe checks his emails and makes a call to Mia Brevant to find out if they have discovered anything else relating to the case. I try to stay awake, drinking a glass of water, walking around and around the small room, swallowing my yawns.

After about twenty minutes, Joe says, 'Surely it can't take that long to check an employee database?'

Just as we're about to give up, the floor starts reverberating again. We sit down as Marije opens the door.

'Do you have a lot of employees?' Joe asks.

Marije narrows her eyes at him. 'Yes. I can confirm that all three of these men are known to this organisation.'

'In what capacity?' Joe asks.

'As I said to you earlier, I am unable to supply you with further information.'

'Then you are obstructing us in the investigation of two murders,' Joe spits.

Marije's over-plucked eyebrows dart up towards the widow's peak in her hairline. 'If you provide us with the appropriate paperwork, then we will do everything we can to help. Until then, I regret there is nothing I can do.'

She stands up. Our meeting is over.

'THAT IS SO FRUSTRATING,' I mutter as we walk out of the building. 'What are they trying to hide?'

Joe shrugs. We are just a few feet away from the car when he comes to an abrupt halt. I nearly walk straight into him.

'What is it?' I ask.

He doesn't answer me but strides towards the car. He takes a photograph of the windscreen with his phone, then opens his briefcase, pulls out a rubber glove and places it on his right hand. He reaches over the windscreen, lifts up the windscreen wiper and removes a single stem of thistle.

'What does a thistle mean?'

'I don't know,' I reply in a small voice. I take my phone out of my handbag and search for 'thistle' and 'floriography'.

'Austerity.' I read the further description out aloud. 'And the Victorian language of flowers says thistle signifies intrusion, specifically a warning against unwanted meddling.'

Joe and I freeze, our eyes locked.

'Someone here is watching us,' Joe says.

I give an involuntary shiver. He places the thistle in a clear plastic bag and throws it on the back seat of the car.

'We're going back in,' Joe says. He clocks my expression of fear and puts his hand on my arm. 'Don't worry, Pippa, I'll make sure you're safe.'

I smile weakly. We pace back to the glass-fronted building and up to the reception desk. The receptionist we spoke to earlier has gone. Her clone looks up, surprise on her face.

'Do you have security cameras overlooking the car park?' Joe asks.

'I'm sorry, I don't know. Is there a problem?'

'Yes. Someone has left something objectionable on our car.'

'I'm sorry, but—'

'Joe,' I say, touching his arm. I lean in to him and whisper, 'Look at the flower arrangement on the table over there.'

It is beautiful, organic, full of white and purple blooms chosen both for their colour as well as their form. Amongst the many stems I don't know the names of are thistles identical to the one we found on the car.

Joe swivels back to face the receptionist. 'Who took a sprig of thistle from the flower arrangement and placed it on our car?'

The girl's eyes widen and she frowns. 'I'm sorry, I don't understand.'

Joe types something into his phone. '*Distel.*' He strides over to the arrangement and extracts a stem of thistle. 'This is a *distel* in Dutch, a thistle in English. Someone placed one on our car.'

Her expression changes as if she is about to snigger.

'I'm sorry. I haven't seen anyone take a flower from the arrangement. I will ask my colleague when she returns from lunch.'

Joe's gaze sweeps the ceiling, the corners of the reception area and then along the walls.

'Who has access to the security cameras, in particular the one up there?' He points to a tiny camera which I would never have noticed if he hadn't pointed it out.

'Marije van Delden and Gustaaf Dieten.'

'Who is he?'

'Head of IT.'

'I would like to speak to him.'

'I'm sorry, sir, but he is not in the office today.'

'Then get me Marije van Delden again.'

The receptionist presses buttons on the phone and slips on her headphones.

'I am sorry, sir, but it goes to voicemail. She must be in a meeting.'

Joe produces a business card and slides it across the counter. 'Get Gustaaf Dieten or Marije van Delden to call me urgently. I will be notifying the Dutch police.'

He glares at the girl, and I watch her tremble under that stare. He then swivels around and strides out.

I have to run a little to keep up with him. He is silent as we get into the car. He starts it and reverses out quickly. I notice Joe looking in his rear mirror more frequently than before, and my stomach does a little lurch.

'Are we being followed?'

'Possibly,' he says. 'We're going to stay the night in Amsterdam so I can make contact with my Dutch counterparts.'

'Oh,' I say.

He glances at me. 'I would say go home, but I want you by my side, Pippa. I want to protect you, and I know you can help me. I hope you understand.'

I feel a little tingle in my abdomen. 'Where to now?'

'We'll find a hotel, have an early dinner and a good night's sleep. We've uncovered quite a bit today, and I don't know about you, but I'm tired.' We yawn in synchronicity and smile at each other. 'There's a particularly lovely hotel that I'd like to show you if I can find it.'

We drive along canals, over small bridges, passing the crooked, gabled canal houses, quirky and imposing and no doubt costing many millions to own.

'There!' he says, swinging the car into a parking space that has miraculously appeared alongside a canal.

I hold my breath as Joe reverses into it. One wheel too far over to the right and we would topple into the canal.

'Don't worry. I know how to park!' he says, laughing.

I blush.

'The hotel is there.' He points at a tall, narrow gabled house with four storeys.

'It doesn't look like a hotel,' I say.

'That's the beauty of it. Only those in the know!'

I follow him across the road, narrowly avoiding being mown down by several speeding cyclists.

The entrance lobby is dark. Joe rings a small bell, and in bustles a spindly woman holding a tea towel. Her face lights up when she sees Joe.

'My very favourite British detective! How are you?' She stands on tiptoes to give Joe a kiss on the cheek. 'You didn't tell me you were coming!'

'All rather last minute, I'm afraid. This is my colleague, Doctor Durrant.'

I put out my hand. She gives me a strong handshake, squeezing the bones of my fingers together.

'Do you have a couple of rooms for us?'

The woman's face clouds over. 'There is some big, big conference on at the moment. Computers, cyber, something I don't understand. Every hotel is booked. I have one room only because an American cancelled. My dear man, you won't find a room anywhere. It's good for business, not so good for you, I'm afraid.'

Joe looks at me and I feel my face warm up.

'You can have the bed. I'll sleep on the chair. Do you mind?' Joe asks.

I try to hide the embarrassment. 'I'm sure we'll manage.'

'We'll take the room,' Joe says.

. . .

THE STAIRS ARE VERY narrow and steep, and Joe has to duck as he walks through the doorway of our room. It has a delightful view onto the canal through two tall windows. The bed fills up most of the room. There is a narrow wardrobe painted with blue tulips and a small armchair totally unsuited to hold Joe's large frame for the night.

'Cosy but authentic,' he says, grinning. 'Would you like to use the bathroom?'

I feel awkward. I haven't shared a room with a man since Trevor and I divorced. I had a holiday fling, inconsequential and unsatisfying, two years ago, but that is it, and I didn't spend the night with him. I hurry into the bathroom and try to be as quiet as possible. I can hear Joe speaking on the phone.

'An early dinner?' he asks when I come back out.

I nod and follow him, walking gingerly down the stairs.

'How do you know Amsterdam?'

'I did a six-month exchange programme early on in my career and have been coming to Amsterdam regularly all my life. But things have got worse here. The stag parties, the pub crawls, it's becoming unpleasantly lawless. I have friends in the police. I will call them tomorrow.'

We walk alongside the canal and down various side streets until I am totally lost. And then he guides me up stone steps into a minuscule restaurant.

'Will we get a table if the place is so busy?'

'We should do, because we are early.'

We sit down at an intimate table for two near the back of the restaurant. The next two hours pass in a blur. The food is excellent and the wine even better. The alcohol goes to my head quickly, probably because I'm tired and we didn't eat any lunch. We talk about Joe's daughter. I tell him about George and my new grandson, Louis.

'You must go and see him,' Joe says, 'as soon as this mess is over.'

I blink to contain my tears. I wish I could see George tonight and hold his baby in my arms.

After a glass of grappa, which I really don't need, Joe insists on paying the bill. And then we're walking back to the hotel in the cold, damp, dark night, my arm looped through his, the whiff of cannabis mingling with indistinct spices and the sugary sweetness of waffles. Just as we're about to turn into the hotel, someone steps out in front of us. I scream as I take in the black balaclava, the black hoodie and jeans and the glint of a knife.

'No!'

43

B ella stares at Fabian as she puts the little box back on the hospital waiting-room chair.

'What's the matter with them?' she asks.

'The chocolates are poisoned. I think Ollie ate a couple.'

Lily shuts her eyes and leans her head downwards between her knees. She moans.

'How do you know?' Bella eyes Fabian suspiciously. Lily filled her in on the way here. She's finding it hard to believe that this waiflike youngster is her brother's lover.

Bella isn't the slightest bit surprised Ollie is gay. She's had her suspicions since Ollie was young, and who, at the age of thirty-seven, has never introduced a partner to their family? No, that's not at all surprising. Fabian, however, is a disappointment. She expected Ollie would be with someone like himself: attractive, intelligent. An older man perhaps, not a puny youngster.

'Ollie sent me a message thanking me for the gin and chocs. I didn't send him any.'

Bella frowns. 'How do you know they're poisoned?'

'I don't. Just putting two and two together.'

Bella stands up, deposits her Mulberry bag on the chair, leans over and takes out her brand-new iPhone. 'We need to call that policeman.'

Fabian sighs. There's no way around this.

When Joe's phone goes straight to voicemail, Bella leaves a message. 'Detective Sergeant Swain. You need to call me back extremely urgently. My brother, Ollie, has been poisoned. At least, that's what we think has happened. We're at the Royal Sussex County Hospital. Please call me.' As an afterthought she adds, 'This is Bella Shelton.'

'Lily, pull yourself together,' Bella snaps at her younger sister. 'We're all upset, but we need to stay level-headed.'

Lily looks away. Fabian feels sorry for her. They're the only people in the waiting room now. Bella's phone rings. She answers immediately, and then her shoulders sink.

'Yes, Gerry,' she says, as if she's exasperated by him. 'Of course I'll keep you posted. Yes.' And then she speaks more quietly and strides to the other side of the room. She lowers her voice to a whisper so Fabian has to strain to hear what she's saying. 'What do you mean Stijn isn't on a job tonight? He told Lily he was driving up north. Okay. Yup. Bye.'

Bella waits a few moments before turning around. She glances at Lily, who is still sobbing quietly, her head in her hands. Bella decides Lily has quite enough to deal with without adding to her miseries. She'll keep Stijn's deceit to herself for now.

And then the door swings open and the doctor walks in, the scent of disinfectant wafting through the air. Fabian feels as if his heart is going to stop. The man is expressionless.

'Are you Mr Gower's family?'

Bella nods. Lily looks up, her face stained with tears. Fabian stands up.

'We think Mr Gower has turned a corner. His gastrointestinal symptoms have eased. We are disturbed by the irritation to the mucosal membranes and the increased salivation. The mydriasis and confusion suggest toxicity to the central nervous system. The most serious are the tachyarrhythmias. We've carried out an ECG and he has been injected with anti-arrhythmic medication to control his heartbeat. We will have to assess whether he has permanent heart damage. Although we will be keeping him in ICU for the foreseeable future, I think you can go home. Unless there is an unexpected relapse, we believe Mr Gower will pull through.'

Fabian bursts into tears. Bella looks down her nose at him, whilst Lily's sobs become increasingly hysterical. Fabian throws his arms around Lily, and their tears mingle.

'Thank you, Doctor,' Bella says, handing him a gold-embossed business card with her name, home address and telephone numbers. 'Please call me if there are any changes.'

'Mister...' – the doctor points at Fabian – 'suggested that Mr Gower might have consumed something poisonous. This fits with his symptoms. Do you know what it was?'

Bella holds up the little box of chocolates. It looks so innocuous, as if it was purchased from an upmarket choco-latier. 'This and some gin apparently.'

'You suspect he was the victim of poisoning?' the doctor asks.

Bella nods. 'Our mother died of suspected poisoning a few days ago.'

The doctor pales. It's the first time he looks shocked. 'This will be a matter for the police. I will contact them at once.'

'Already done that,' Bella says. 'But they might act faster if it comes from you.'

'I would like to give the chocolates to the police for analysis, if I may.'

Bella hands him the box, briefly wondering how many fingerprints there must be on it now.

'Goodnight, Doctor. We'll be back tomorrow.'

He nods at them.

'Come on, children,' Bella snaps at Lily and Fabian, who are still in each other's arms.

They trot out of the hospital silently, until Bella says, 'Where do you live, Fabian? Do you want dropping off anywhere?'

'I live with Ollie.'

'Oh really. Ollie's never mentioned you.'

Bitch, Fabian thinks. He much prefers Lily.

Bella sighs. 'It's rather out of my way having to drive through Hove.'

No, it isn't, Fabian thinks, but he bites his tongue.

'Fabian can stay with me,' Lily sniffs. 'I don't want to be alone tonight.'

Bella raises her eyebrows but doesn't say anything.

GERRY HAS BEEN in a foul mood ever since Mae rejected his advances. He has tried ringing her numerous times, but to no avail. He has decided that tomorrow morning he will go to the garden centre and make her an offer she can't refuse.

He's on his fifth whisky of the evening when Bella walks through the door a little after midnight smelling of hospitals and with lines etched into her face that he could have sworn weren't there earlier in the day.

'How is he?'

'He'll live,' Bella says, pouring herself a very large glass of red wine.

'Two deaths by poisoning in the same family within a week would be very dodgy indeed,' Gerry says, taking a sip of whisky. 'Bloody hell! Do you think you and Lily are at risk too?'

Bella leans against the island unit, the cool granite welcome against her back as heat runs through her body. Did she tell Gerry Ollie had been poisoned? She can't remember. What did she say when she rang him in a panic to say that Ollie had been rushed to hospital? When did she know about the poisoning? Was it before or after they got to the hospital? Bella shuts her eyes and tries to still her mind. The stress of the past week is too much. She can't think.

'I'm going to bed,' Bella says, scooping up her handbag and holding the large glass of wine out in front of her.

When she's in the bedroom, she swallows a sleeping pill with most of the red wine, wipes her face with a ninety-pound bottle of make-up remover, does a cursory brushing of her teeth, drops her clothes onto the bathroom floor and slides into bed. After turning her phone up to maximum volume to ensure she will be awakened if it rings, she switches off the light and waits for sleep to claim her.

44

PIPPA

It happens so quickly. A blur of dark bodies, the flash of a blade, grunts, kicking, yells and then a splash. I hear a scream, but it's only afterwards that I realise it was me. And then arms are holding me tightly and I am engulfed by Joe's musky scent.

I bury my face into his chest. 'Are you hurt?' I whisper, not wanting to look up. I can hear his heart pounding in his solid chest.

'No.' His lips are pressed onto the top of my head. His breathing is slowing. 'Are you?'

'No,' I whisper.

'*Gaat het wel goed?*'

The man makes me jump. Joe is still holding the tops of my arms, but he steps backwards slightly.

'Is everything okay?' The stranger has a heavy, guttural Dutch accent.

'Thank you, yes. Someone tried to mug us,' Joe says.

'You can call 112 for the police,' he says.

Joe smiles and the man walks away.

'What fell in the canal?' I ask. My body is trembling.

'The knife. Our attacker got away.'

I shudder.

'We're safe now, Pippa.'

'Was it a random attack?'

Joe hesitates. 'I'm not sure. Let's go in.'

He takes my hand and leads me to the entrance of the hotel. He uses a key to let us in, and the door latches closed behind us.

'I'll get you a brandy.'

'I've drunk enough,' I say, my teeth rattling.

'A hot shower then.' He holds my hand as we walk up the stairs.

Joe uses the key to open the room. He walks inside and immediately puts the 'Do Not Disturb' sign on our door. He then throws his arms around me. I am facing into the room and I see it first.

I gasp.

'What is it?'

'The flowers!'

Joe releases me and turns around. 'Oh shit,' he says, striding over to the bouquet.

There are five black roses held together with raffia and wrapped in florist's transparent plastic in a bucket of water. A small white envelope protrudes from the flowers. Joe puts on a pair of latex gloves and opens the envelope. He peers at the note.

'It says, *Stay away. You're next.* It's typewritten. It's not clear if it's addressed to you or me,' Joe says, dropping it into a small clear plastic bag he extracts from his briefcase.

'Me, I assume.' The shivering is making my teeth rattle.

'Pippa. I promise I will not let you come to any harm.' He holds my shoulders and peers into my eyes.

I nod, wondering how he can really make such a promise.

'I'm going to run you a hot shower, and whilst you're in it, I'm going to call a colleague based here with the Amsterdam police. Okay?'

I nod. He walks into the bathroom and turns on the shower. He hands me a fluffy white dressing gown from the wardrobe, and I do as he tells me. I go into the bathroom, shed my clothes and step into the steaming-hot jet of water. I lose track of how long I am there. Five minutes, ten or even fifteen minutes perhaps. By the time I emerge, I am warmed up, my skin is tingling, and the terror has eased. I brush my teeth, rub my hair dry and put on the dressing gown, which swamps me.

Joe is seated in the small chair, his laptop on his knees. 'Feeling better?' he says, smiling at me.

I nod.

'I've spoken to Henk. I'm not doing anything tonight. We'll go and see him tomorrow morning. Get into bed, Pippa.'

I climb in coyly, but I needn't worry. Joe has his back to me, switching off his computer. I listen as he uses the bathroom. He emerges wearing the twin white dressing gown, which looks too small on him. I try not to look, but my eyes are drawn towards him. He sits down in the chair, stretching his legs out.

'You'll never get any sleep there,' I say quietly.

'I'll try.'

'I don't mind if you'd like to sleep in the bed.'

'Really?' he says, grinning.

He doesn't wait for an answer. As Joe slips into the bed next to me, I lean over and switch off the lights. He puts his arms around me, and I feel myself falling into him, my insides thawing, my heart pumping faster and faster. As he kisses me, I melt into his body, the firm but tender touches, the newness of him, turning all fears into excitement. And then as he runs his fingers gently across my stomach and farther down, exploring and searching, I lose myself totally in the sensations and we make love, exactly the way it should be.

MUCH LATER I am dragged from a deep sleep by the sound of a phone ringing. Slowly my eyes adjust to the darkness. Joe is sitting up in bed, his solid torso shimmering dark against the white pillows. He is speaking quietly on the phone.

'What's happened?' I ask as he finishes the call and places the mobile on his bedside table.

He gives a little sigh before speaking. 'We have to return to the UK first thing tomorrow morning. Ollie Gower has been admitted to hospital. He is in intensive care, although they expect him to pull through. They believe he was poisoned.'

'What!'

'Initial tests suggest that he was poisoned by ingesting oleander.'

'Oleander? But that's his name!'

'Exactly. And *Nerium oleander* is a highly toxic plant. It's found as a small tree or bush and has attractive clusters of little white or pink sweet-smelling flowers with thick dark-green leaves. The leaves, flowers, stems and twigs all produce severe gastric, neurological and cardiac symptoms. It has been known to kill.'

I am wide awake now and my brain is processing fast.

'And Bella, otherwise known as belladonna or deadly nightshade, is equally poisonous. And lilies too. A friend's cat died after eating lily pollen. All three Gowers are named after poisons!'

'And quite possibly all three are at risk of death from poisoning.'

'Why would anyone name their children after poisons?' I muse.

'Could be a coincidence,' Joe says, his fingers gently trailing over my stomach.

'Unlikely, though.'

'I agree. I'm sending Mia a message to bring both Stijn and Gerry in for questioning.'

'Why Gerry?'

'He's in a financial mess and I want to find out more.' He wriggles back down under the covers and lays a heavy leg over mine. 'Let's not think about it for a few hours. There are more important things to do right now.'

Gerry falls asleep in the living room and awakes at 5 a.m. with a pounding headache and a sore back. By the time he has used the guest bathroom, he is wide awake. He tiptoes into the master bedroom, where Bella is asleep, snoring quietly, and removes some fresh clothes from his wardrobe.

He is glad the Lexus is such a quiet, smooth motor. He starts the engine, opens the electric gates and glides out. He puts his foot down on the dual carriageway and turns the music up loud. Verdi's 'Anvil Chorus' is suitably rousing, and he grins to himself as the darkness of the night slowly begins to lift.

He has never been to Mae's flat before. In fact, he shouldn't even know where she lives, but he followed her home one evening. After she entered the communal door, he waited ten minutes and then walked over to look at the list of names against the door buzzers. Flat Number 5 read 'I-M. Carruthers'.

He stops off at Tesco, grateful for the store's twenty-four-hour opening times, and nips in to buy a bouquet of flowers. There isn't much choice this early in the morning. He picks up a big bouquet. They're rather garish, but cheerful. He also buys a box of croissants and some fresh orange juice. And then he's on his way.

Gerry notices Mae's small van parked on the opposite side of the road. Clutching the flowers with one hand and the bag of breakfast items with the other, he strides across the road and presses the buzzer to Flat 5. There is no answer. He's not surprised. Poor thing, she'll probably be in a deep sleep. He presses it again. And again. He wonders whether he should call her. Perhaps she's in the shower. And then suddenly the intercom crackles into life.

'Who is it?' Mae asks. Her voice is heavy with sleep.

'It's your lover come to bring you breakfast.'

'What?'

'It's me. Gerry.'

'What the hell are you doing here?' Mae snaps, all vestiges of sleep quickly banished.

'I've come to bring you flowers and breakfast,' Gerry says. He shifts from foot to foot. Perhaps this wasn't such a good idea after all.

'It's six o'clock in the morning!'

'I thought I'd cheer up the start of your day.'

'Well, you haven't.'

Gerry waits for the door to buzz open. He puts his ear up to the intercom but can't hear anything. The crackling noise has stopped, and the door remains firmly closed. He puts his finger on the buzzer again. Nothing. He tries again. Still nothing. He swears profusely under his breath. He tries calling her, but Mae's phone goes straight to voicemail.

'Little bitch,' he mutters, eventually walking back to the car.

He glances up at the block of flats, wondering if she's watching him, laughing at his retreating back, but he doesn't know which floor she's on, whether her flat faces the road or is at the rear of the block.

He sits in the car for several long minutes, deciding what to do, and then he starts up the engine, slowly drives away and parks up on the next street. He gets out of the car to check he has a good view. Satisfied that he'll be able to see Mae when she exits her building and walks towards her van, he settles back into the driver's seat and eats his way through the bag of croissants.

A little over an hour later the sun has risen, and Mae appears. Gerry wipes the croissant crumbs from his mouth and jumps out of the car, clutching the bouquet of flowers.

'Mae, baby, wait!' he shouts as she approaches her van.

She turns around and stares at him, her eyes narrowed and cold, a thick black puffer jacket making her look much larger than she is.

'What are you doing?'

'I wanted to cheer up your morning. Can't you let me?'

'You can't turn up here!' Mae hisses.

'Why not? Will your boyfriend get pissed off?' He laughs.

Mae puts her hands on her hips. 'Actually, yes.' She doesn't smile.

'What?' Gerry gasps. 'You've been bloody two-timing me?'

'You're married, Gerry. In case you forgot!'

'I never pretended I wasn't, whereas you…You never said anything about having a boyfriend.'

'This is ridiculous, Gerry. Stop behaving like a jealous teenager.'

'I love you, Isla-Mae!'

'No, you don't. Can you move? I need to go to work.'

Gerry drops the bouquet of flowers and grabs her wrists. 'No, you do not! You're with me, and soon I'm going to be your boss and we'll be together day and night!'

'Let go of me, Gerry, otherwise I'll scream!'

He releases his grip from her wrists immediately. She clicks open the van doors and slides into the driver's seat. Before shutting the door, she pokes her head back out.

'We're over, Gerry. It was fun whilst it lasted, but we're done. See you around.'

GERRY IS SO ANGRY, he doesn't know what to do with himself. He kicks the pavement, strides back to the Lexus, and slams the door as hard as he can. He pulls out of the parking space, not looking where he's going, his tyres screeching. He misses a car coming the other way by millimetres, and screams as the other motorist sounds his horn.

Gerry's eyes are smarting so much he has no idea where he is or where he is going. When he finds himself on the seafront in Worthing, he pulls up and gets out. A brisk walk along the coast might clear his head, although it won't mend his heart. He can't decide what to do: beg Mae to return to him or play hardball. Perhaps that's what bitches like her prefer.

When it starts raining, Gerry makes his way back to the car and is surprised that it's nearly 9 a.m. Calmer now, he drives to the office. As he walks in, Kelly comes out to greet him. He senses there's something off about her, a nervousness. *Shit*, he thinks to himself. He hopes Ollie hasn't died.

'Spit it out,' he says.

'There's some people waiting for you in the boardroom.'

'I'm not expecting anyone.'

'No,' she says, blustering. 'Um, it's the police.'

Gerry stops walking. Should he turn around, get back into his car and do a runner, or face the music? But he doesn't have time. The young policewoman with the short hair and sexy eyelashes has stepped out into the corridor. She's in uniform today.

'Mr Shelton, we would be grateful if you could come with us to the station. We have some questions we'd like to put to you.'

'Is everything all right with Ollie? Bella was asleep when I left this morning. We are so worried.' He glances around, trying to see which of his staff are in already.

'As far as we are aware, he had a comfortable night.'

'And Lily? Is she okay?'

Mia Brevant narrows her eyes. 'Why shouldn't she be?'

'She's fragile is our Lily. The death of her mum has hit her hard.'

As they are walking to the car park, Gerry makes as if to get into his car.

'No, Mr Shelton,' Mia says. 'We would like you to come with us.'

'Am I under arrest?' He stands still, his knees quivering.

'No. But we would like to interview you under caution.'

'But I haven't done anything!' Gerry moans.

'You'll have the chance to tell us everything. Please get in the car.'

46

PIPPA

What Joe didn't tell me was the time of our flight. I have barely been asleep an hour when his alarm clock awakes me. I lean over towards Joe, but the bed is empty. And then I hear the sound of water cascading from the shower.

'Wakey-wakey!'

He strides out of the bathroom with a towel around his waist. I try hard not to swoon.

'It's 4 a.m.!'

'And our flight leaves at 7 a.m. We have two murder suspects to interview.'

Groaning, I roll out of bed and grab my clothes. After a cursory shower and a quick dab of make-up on my face, we're ready to go. I feel a wonderful post-coital glow and can't stop smiling. Joe notices and leans over to give me a peck on the cheek.

· · ·

I SLEEP on the short flight, and before I know it, we are gliding to a halt on British soil.

'Don't you get special privileges through customs?' I ask as we join the queue.

'Alas, no. Just an ordinary Joe!'

'Hardly!'

When we're in the car, Joe rings Mia Brevant. 'What's the latest?'

'We're at Gerry Shelton's place of work and waiting for him to arrive. Stijn Eikenboom is at the station waiting for you to arrive.'

TWENTY MINUTES later and we're at Crawley police station. After two cups of coffee so strong a spoon could stand up in them, and a couple of pieces of toast, I am feeling ready for the day. I follow Joe into a windowless room, where Stijn is already seated with his arms crossed over his chest and his eyes narrowed at us. Mia Brevant sits to one side.

Joe goes through all the formalities, explaining that this is an interview under caution, it will be recorded and that Stijn is able to be accompanied by a lawyer.

'I don't need a bloody lawyer,' he snaps. 'I've done nothing wrong.'

I am surprised he is rejecting the offer of a solicitor. Perhaps he is a brilliant chemist with limited common sense.

'How do you know Koen Smit?' Joe asks.

'Don't know who you're talking about.' Stijn's Dutch accent is increasingly pronounced. I look for those fleeting micro-expressions. He is lying.

'Please explain why a man with your qualifications, a chemist who was studying for a PhD, is now working as a lorry driver.'

Stijn shrugs his shoulders. 'Too much pressure. I had a breakdown.'

Joe leans forwards. 'You don't look like the type of man who would have a breakdown.'

I swallow, uncomfortable with Joe's statement. How can he judge someone's mental health?

'Did you kill Annette Gower?'

'No!' Stijn leans back in his chair. 'Annette is my mother-in-law. I loved her.'

'We visited Wageningen University and Vingerhoedskruid Pharma. Both organisations have been very helpful to us.'

Stijn's eyes narrow. I glimpse fear.

'Did you kill Scott McDermott?' Joe asks quietly.

'No.' Stijn swallows. 'I am free to go whenever I want, aren't I?'

'Yes,' Joe says.

Stijn stands up. 'You might like to investigate Gerry Shelton. He has secrets to hide, a business to front other activities. He's greedy. Look into Shelton.'

He nods at me and walks out of the room.

'Stijn Eikenboom has left the room. This interview has ended at 10.14 a.m. and I am now switching off the recorder.' Joe sighs.

'What next?' I ask.

'We interview Gerry Shelton, and then I suggest we bring in Lily Gower. We need more evidence. Everything is circumstantial right now.'

Joe stands up and stretches. I want to throw him a conspiratorial glance, an acknowledgement that we are lovers as well as colleagues, but his gaze is fixed across the room. I sense that he has totally forgotten I am there. After a few moments he picks up the phone.

'Mia. Is Gerry Shelton here yet?' There is a pause. 'Right. Bring him in.'

.   .   .

Two men enter the small room.

'Arthur Quigley. I'm Mr Shelton's solicitor.'

I assume he's close to retirement age, with a reddened nose, indicative perhaps of a proclivity for drink, and a stoop to his shoulders. He shakes Joe's hand, but when I move to put out mine, he ignores it, inclines his head towards me and tells Gerry to sit down.

Gerry rakes his fingers through his thinning hair and tugs at his dark-green tie. His eyes are bloodshot. Even when seated, he is fidgety, his knee shaking up and down, his fingers tapping on his leg, tugging his earlobe and adjusting his glasses.

Joe goes through all the formalities, reciting the scripts that I am becoming increasingly familiar with.

'Thank you, Mr Shelton, for attending this interview. Did you know Scott McDermott?'

'No, and I don't know—'

His solicitor interrupts him. 'You don't need to answer, Gerry.'

'I want to. I didn't have anything to do with the murders of McDermott or Annette. I don't know why I'm here. And no, I didn't know the man.'

'How do you know Stijn Eikenboom?'

'He works for me. He's my brother-in-law. If anyone has done anything, it'll be him. Shifty bastard.'

'You might be surprised to learn that he says the same thing about you!'

Gerry explodes. His cheeks turn puce. He stands up, leans on the table, blusters and fails to form a coherent sentence.

'Sit down, Gerry,' his solicitor urges.

Gerry does as he's told.

'I sense antipathy between the two of you,' Joe says. 'I understand Stijn works for you. In what role?'

'Lorry driver.' Gerry's lower lip extends like a belligerent toddler's.

'Why are you employing a highly qualified chemist in the capacity of a lorry driver?'

'What?' Gerry sneers.

'Did you do any background checks on Stijn Eikenboom before employing him?'

'I knew he was a lying bastard!' Gerry erupts.

'Please, Mr Shelton, answer the question,' Joe says.

'I assume so. I don't know. That's something my HR woman would do. Anyway, he came to me as a recommendation.'

'Via whom?' Joe asks.

'My mother-in-law, Annette Gower. I was looking for more drivers, and she said she knew someone. I was hardly going to question my mother-in-law!'

'Was this before or after Stijn met Lily Gower?'

'Before. Stijn Eikenboom has been on my books for nearly three years. He started courting Lily about six months later. And then they got married. Terrible taste my sister-in-law's got.'

Joe and I glance at each other. This must be significant. Annette knew Stijn first. She introduced him to Gerry and to Lily.

'I assume Stijn's done it. Killed them?'

'Why do you say that, Mr Shelton?'

'He's shifty. Too big for his own boots.'

'What is your interest in Rocks Garden Centre?'

'Well, they're a customer. The place is owned by my wife's family, and... It's confidential obviously... I'm going to buy the place.'

'Is there anything else?' Joe sits forwards.

Gerry wriggles. 'Um.'

His solicitor interrupts again. 'You don't need to answer any question you don't want to.'

Gerry's eyes slide everywhere except towards Joe and me. But he is a lousy liar, and Joe isn't in the mood for standing any nonsense.

'Mr Shelton, we are investigating two murders, both of which appear to be related to Rocks Garden Centre. Please answer my question.'

'Um...'

Joe inhales loudly. 'Mr Shelton, we know you are lying to us. Kindly answer my question.'

'I'm not lying. There's nothing else!' He runs his fingers through his hair again and glances towards his solicitor, whose face remains impassive. Gerry fidgets, shifting in the chair, tugging at his ear.

His solicitor reiterates, 'You do not need to say anything.'

'Mr Shelton, can you tell us what you import?' Joe asks.

'Plants, pots, garden sundries, many of the things you'd find in a garden centre.'

'And cut flowers?'

He shakes his head. 'No, very rarely. They're brought over from Holland in specialist refrigerated lorries. I've only got one of those. It's not economical.'

Joe opens the file on the table in front of him and slips out a photograph.

'For the record, DS Swain is showing Gerry Shelton a photograph of a black rose.'

Gerry pales.

'Mr Shelton. Have you ever imported these roses?'

'No, I don't think so. But honestly, I don't get involved in the detail. Anyway, it's a rose. Could have been bought anywhere. What's so special about it?'

'Did you kill Annette Gower and place this rose on her body?'

'No, I bloody well did not! How dare you accuse me of such an atrocity!'

'They're not accusing you. Please sit down!' Gerry's solicitor puts his hand on Gerry's arm.

But Gerry doesn't sit down. He picks up his jacket and

strides towards the door.

47

L ily has been staring at the sealed envelope ever since Annette died. If she opens it, then she knows all the horrors will be real, but if she doesn't open it, she's not fulfilling her mother's wishes. And Lily has always done what both her parents told her to do – well, what her father told her to do, at least. Why should things be any different from beyond the grave?

She is sitting on the side of her bed, shivering. She has sent Stijn five texts and left three voice messages. He has never ignored her for this long before, and tonight of all nights, when she is oscillating between sorrow, self-pity and fury, she needs him. Although she thinks he's a bit strange, she is glad Fabian is sleeping on the sofa downstairs. At least she's not alone in the house, and if Ollie loves him, then he must be all right.

She picks up the envelope and toys with it; then, taking a big gulp of air, she carefully breaks the seal. Her hands are shaking so much she drops the piece of paper as she removes it from the envelope. She sobs as she sees her mother's flowery writing.

.   .   .

DEAREST LILY,

If you're reading this, it means I'm dead. Know that I love you and will always do so. Of the three of you, you, my darling Lily, are the most similar to me. That is why I have chosen you to be my successor. Of course you love plants and flowers as much as I do, and I know you will make a better horticulturalist than either your father or myself. But Lily, you must believe in yourself now.

Be strong, my sweetest. There are people around you who will make themselves known to you in the coming days and weeks, some of whom you are very close to already. Do as you are instructed to do, be bold and never be fearful.

This may not be the path you would have chosen for yourself, and indeed it wasn't mine, but when your father died, I had no choice but to follow in his footsteps. And now it is your turn.

I tried to get out, my sweetheart, and that is most probably why I am dead. Go with the flow, Lily, and you will have a good life.

Goodbye, my darling girl,

Your mum, Annette xxx

LILY'S TEARS drip on to the paper. She lays it on the bed next to her, not wanting the ink to smudge from her tears. None of the words are a surprise to her, other than the fact that Annette professed to love her the most. But reading them makes everything so real.

The house is empty without Annette. The old floorboards moan and sigh as the night gets colder. Lily wraps a blanket around her shoulders and, taking her torch, she walks to her parents' bedroom. After switching on the bedside lamp, she pulls back the eiderdown and slides in between the sheet and blankets, trying to inhale the fading scent of her mother. But all she hears is her father's voice, angry and disappointed.

A packet of sleeping pills lies next to the silver gilt clock. She picks up the strip. Eight pills remain. Is that enough to send her into permanent oblivion? Then she thinks of Ollie and Stijn and how much she loves them, and how she hopes one day she and Stijn will have children of their own. She pops out two pills, swallows them without water, switches off the bedside light and waits for sleep to arrive.

'LILY, LILY. WAKE UP!' Stijn's voice curls into the fog of her head.

'What is it?' Her body feels heavy, and her tongue is rough against the top of her mouth.

'We need to talk.'

Stijn is pacing up and down the room. Annette's room.

Lily remembers then. Her mother is dead. She is lying in her mother's bed. And Ollie...She sits up suddenly.

'Ollie! Is Ollie all right?'

'Yes, fine.' Stijn waves his hand dismissively. 'Have you read your mother's letter?'

Lily opens and closes her mouth. How does Stijn know about it? She can see the impatience in his eyes, the way his fingers are clawing at the fabric of his jeans. Lily nods.

'Right. We need to plan. The police suspect us.'

'Suspect us of what?'

Stijn sighs and sits down on the edge of the bed, almost crushing Lily's leg.

'The poison business.'

Lily's eyes widen. 'Poison?'

Stijn puts his head in his hands and with his head still bowed says, 'I thought you said you'd read your mother's letter.'

'Yes.' Lily turns away from Stijn. 'But she didn't say anything about a poison business.'

'Typical bloody Annette. Always in denial. Never getting to the point.'

'I don't understand!' Lily's chest constricts. 'What have you got to do with it?' she says in a whisper.

Stijn stands up.

'I am Scott McDermott's successor. You are Annette's. Come on, Lily, darling. Don't be naïve.'

'No!' Lily shakes her head and doesn't stop shaking it. The room blurs around her.

'What do you know about preparing poisons?' Lily whispers. 'You're just a lorry driver!'

He bends into his knees and lays his hands on Lily's shoulders. 'Come on, Lils. You don't really believe that, do you? This has been planned for years.'

'But we've only known each other for two years!'

Stijn slants his head to one side. The look of pity scores Lily's heart.

'You mean you used me? You didn't marry me for love?'

The hesitation in his voice, the shameful glance away, says it all. Lily rips back the bedcovers and leaps out of bed.

'No, Lily! I love you now. I really love you! You are my everything!'

But Lily isn't listening. She pushes past him, tearing out of the room, into the hallway, into the bathroom, where she jams the lock in the door and slumps to the ground.

Stijn raps on the door.

'Lily, you've got to hold it together. I can't believe this was truly a shock to you. And I do love you. I didn't realise that I would fall so passionately in love with you. I might not have done at the start, but now I really do. Please, Lily. Let me in.'

Lily runs her fingers over the threadbare carpet in the bathroom, thinking of all the dead cells that must be stuck in the fibres. Hers, Bella's and Ollie's, all mingled together from when they were babies. And now Stijn's will be there too.

She runs a fingernail over the cork of the bathroom seat, gouging out a little piece, then crumbles it between her fingers, letting the little grains of cork flutter to the ground. How well does she know Stijn? How well did she know Annette?

'Lily, let me in!' Stijn raps on the door. 'The police are suspicious of me. They interviewed me again this morning. But you know I'd never hurt your mum, don't you? I love you all. Come on, Lils!'

She sits there for a long time, shivering, waiting. Eventually she hears footsteps receding. She pulls a towel off the rail and wraps herself in it. The old towel rail used to pump out so much heat that she burned her fingers on it when she was little. But now it gurgles and hiccups, and however much they let the air out, it only ever becomes tepid. That's what Lily feels. As if all the joy and heat have oozed out of her life.

There is a knock on the bathroom door, so light and feathery Lily wonders whether she is imagining it. It comes again. A tapping. Nothing like Stijn's forceful rap.

'Lily, it's me, Fabian. Are you all right?'

Lily stares at the closed door, startled. She has totally forgotten that Fabian stayed the night. She stands up, letting the towel fall to the ground.

'Ollie. Is Ollie okay?'

'Yes, he's doing fine. He's out of ICU and on the ward. We can go and see him later. What about you?'

Lily undoes the bolt on the door and opens it. Fabian takes a step backwards when he sees her. Her face is the colour of alabaster, but her eyes are red and sore. Her hair is messy and tangled, and she's wearing a thin cotton nightdress, her bare arms lined with goosebumps.

'Is everything all right with you and Stijn?' he asks.

Lily shakes her head. 'Has he gone?'

'Yes. He left about ten minutes ago. He took your car. I've boiled the kettle. You look like you could do with a cuppa.' Fabian's grin is crooked.

Lily sniffs.

Five minutes later Lily is dressed and she and Fabian are sitting at the kitchen table, nursing cups of tea. Lily sniffs and sniffs. It's annoying Fabian, but he stills his mind and tries to let it gloss over him.

'I think my husband killed my mother.' Lily's voice is so quiet, Fabian isn't sure he heard her correctly.

'You what?'

'Nothing. It's nothing!'

Lily bursts into tears, knocks the cup of tea over and rushes out of the room.

48

PIPPA

We are still in the police interview room.

'Gerry was lying.' Joe yawns and doesn't make any attempt to cover it up.

'Yes, but there were plenty of truths in there too. Can you give me some time to study the video, and I'll prepare a quick report for you?' I suggest.

'Why don't you go back to my place, have a sleep, write the report and I'll see you later?'

'I'd like to go home. Have they finished searching my garden?'

'Let me check.'

Joe stands up and pokes his head out of the corridor.

'Mia, just the person I want to see. Is it all right for Doctor Durrant to return home?'

'Yes. We're all done there.'

Joe comes back into the room and leans against the closed door.

'The thing is, Pippa, I don't want you to be at home alone.

We've been warned with those flowers; we were attacked in Amsterdam. It may all be circumstantial, but I don't believe in coincidences. I'd rather you stayed with me for a few days until we've completed our investigations.'

I am conflicted. I want to be with Joe, but I'm missing my home. And I'm missing Mungo.

'How about I go home and collect some stuff, and return to yours later?'

He thinks for a moment and then nods.

'I'll organise a taxi to take you back to my place so you can collect your car. But be careful, Pippa.'

I want Joe to clutch me to him, to kiss me, to feel his strength and inhale his scent, but he stays on the other side of the room and then simply opens the door, waiting for me to walk out in front of him.

IT IS a joy to be home. The police have tried to put the garden back together again, but the flowerbeds are ruined. I really do need the services of Isla-Mae, I think. How ironic.

Harriet brings Mungo back, and he greets me with unbridled joy, pulling his upper lip back in a smile, then bringing me his favourite soft toy – a rather mangled, dirty duck. I throw my arms around him, burying my face in his soft fur, and thank Harriet for caring for him at short notice.

After I have put a load of washing into the machine and made myself a sandwich, my mobile phone rings. I don't recognise the number.

'Is this Doctor Durrant?' He has a strong South London accent.

'Yes,' I say cautiously.

'You don't know me. My name's Fabian Sherman. I'm Ollie Gower's partner.'

My heart misses a beat and I envision the worst.

'Is he okay?'

'Yes, doing fine. I need to see you. I've got some information. It's really important.'

'But it's DS Swain you should be giving information to, not me.'

'Nah. Don't want to get involved with the police, even if he's lush.'

I can't stop the smile edging my lips. I quite agree with Fabian's description of my new lover.

'I'm a psychologist, not a policewoman.'

'I know that,' Fabian says impatiently. 'Ollie says I should talk to you.'

'I'm listening,' I say.

'Nah. This isn't a conversation for the phone. I'll meet you.'

I hesitate. How do I know Fabian isn't the killer?

'Can you get to Rocks Garden Centre? I'll meet you in the coffee shop in an hour.'

He doesn't give me the chance to reply but hangs up. On the one hand, I am relieved he wants to meet me in a familiar public place. On the other hand, I can hear Joe's voice in my head: *Do not get involved. It isn't safe.*

I decide to compromise. I call Joe. His phone rings out. I don't leave a message.

THE GARDEN CENTRE is the quietest I've seen it during the past fortnight, and I find a parking space just beyond the disabled bays.

'I won't be long,' I promise Mungo.

It is as if the energy has been sucked from the shop. The staff walk around slowly, their faces long, their eyes glancing around shiftily. I notice a few plants with dead leaves and drooping flowers in the houseplants section and litter dropped on the concrete floor. Then I realise: there's no music. Normally it's piped through the tannoy system, but now the incessant Christmas carols have been silenced. The restaurant is a little busier and considerably noisier, with the rattling of cutlery and crockery and the whooshing and grinding of the coffee machines. I wonder what Fabian looks like, whether we will recognise each other.

I glance around, and immediately it's obvious. He looks totally out of place: a young man, skinny and small, wearing a black leather biker's jacket and tight black drainpipe trousers.

'Fabian?' I ask.

He jumps up but doesn't put his hand out. 'Yeah. Mrs Durrant?'

I nod and don't correct him. The table he is sitting at is empty.

'Would you like a drink and something to eat?' I suggest.

He nods eagerly. 'A Coke and a slice of that chocolate cake would be great. Ta.'

I leave him and join the queue, glancing over to him from time to time. He is sitting quite still, almost as if he is in a trance. How very different he is to Gerry Shelton, who was restless and agitated.

When I place the drink and plate in front of Fabian, he dives in.

'Thanks for meeting me,' he says, his mouth full of cake. The tension I was feeling eases. There is nothing threatening about this young man.

'I feel bad for Lily. And bad for snitching on her, but she said something, and what with Ollie being poisoned I can't keep it to myself.'

I lean forwards, using my body language to encourage him to keep talking.

'Her husband, Stijn – whatever he's called – he did it.' Fabian takes a large slug of Coke, finishing off half the pint glass in one mouthful.

'He did what?'

'Killed them. That man Ollie knew and his mum.'

I am speechless. This information should not be landing in my lap.

'He's here, by the way. That Stijn bloke. I saw him a few minutes ago. He didn't see me.'

I shiver. I can't help it. 'How do you know?' I ask.

'Lily let slip. Said her husband is a murderer. She's really upset. I didn't want to leave her, but my priority's got to be Ollie and looking out for him. We're going to get married.' Fabian's smile lights up his face. It makes him look even younger.

'Will you tell DS Swain everything you know?'

Fabian shakes his head; the smile vanishes. 'Nope. I don't like the police. That's why I'm telling you.' He wipes his hands over the plate, tips the final droplets of Coke into his mouth and stands up. 'Ta for this.'

And then he's gone.

I stay sitting for a few long minutes, finishing off my coffee, wondering what I should do. I need to speak to Joe.

Wandering back through the garden centre, I see Isla-Mae's landscape design table. It is empty and she's not there. I feel a curious sense of relief.

I pick up a chewy bone for Mungo and wait my turn in the queue. Just as I have paid and the cashier puts the bone in a brown paper bag, I catch sight of Stijn. He is walking briskly, eyes straight ahead. He passes just a couple of feet from me, and I shiver and hurry out after him. He presses a key fob and climbs into a bright-blue Mini Countryman parked just two spaces away from me. He pauses for a moment. I think I see him looking at a phone, but it gives me just enough time to hop into my car and start the engine.

I follow him out of the garden centre.

The traffic is light as he weaves along minor roads, turning onto the A27. He drives quickly, faster than I am comfortable with, but as he comes off the dual carriageway on to the Arundel bypass, he has to slow down to a crawl. The traffic is always bad there as it weaves around the outskirts of Arundel, the majestic restored medieval castle perched on the hillside, rising ghostlike above the town, bare trees cloaking its feet. With just one vehicle between us, I follow the bright-blue car on to the A29. He is slowed again by a large articulated lorry that chugs up the hill, and then once we are up and over the other side of the South Downs, he overtakes the lorry.

My heart is in my mouth as I follow suit, only just weaving back in time as another vehicle screeches past in the opposite direction. I normally love this road, with its sweeping vista of the South Downs, where the hills roll down towards the flat plain of fields and the River Arun snakes into the distance. But today my fingers are white as I grip my steering wheel, my eyes never veering from the road in front. I follow him, staying two cars behind, as we pass through Bury and slow down through Coldwaltham before winding through Hardham. As we go over the little bridge into Pulborough, where the river always used to burst its banks, he indicates to the left. And then, just before the station, he turns. I hesitate, wondering if I should follow him, and in that moment of vacillating, the blue car disappears. I pull up on the side of the road and thump my fist on the dashboard. I have followed him for thirty minutes, and now I have lost him.

But then Stijn appears, walking rapidly, almost running, a set of keys in his hand at the ready. He slides a key into the door of a block of flats and vanishes inside.

49

PIPPA

'I need to speak to DS Swain.'

'He's in a meeting. Can I take a message?'

'No! It's urgent.' I have slid down the driver's seat, desperate not to be seen. I am trembling. Ridiculous really, as Stijn doesn't know I'm here. Perhaps it's the tiredness, the overwhelming events catching up on me. I remember how I told Joe that I am fearless. It's laughable to think I felt that. Right now I am terrified, and happy to admit it.

'Pippa, what's up?' Joe sounds frustrated, and for a second, I hesitate.

'I'm outside a building where Stijn is. Fabian, Ollie's partner, says Lily told him Stijn is the murderer.'

'Slow down and repeat that.'

I explain what Fabian told me. I admit to following Stijn. I hear Joe sucking his teeth.

'Where are you?'

I give him the street name.

'I'll be there as soon as possible.'

'Shall I wait?'

'I don't want you to be a position of danger. Did he see you?'

'No, I don't think so.'

'If you can stay out of the way, or at least call me if he leaves, that would be very helpful. Keep in touch, Pippa, but mostly stay safe.'

He hangs up on me.

'Oh, Mungo, what shall we do?'

The dog lifts his nose up from the seat, lets out a sigh and collapses back down again. I can't even take him for a walk for fear of missing Stijn should he leave. I start the engine and edge the car forwards, trying to find a less conspicuous parking space but one that still affords me a view of the front of the building.

There is a small trading estate with boxlike buildings and a couple of lorries parked in front. I notice, then, the bright-blue car tucked behind a large truck. As I'm turning my car, I see the wording on the side: 'Shelton Bros'.

Gulping, I drive slowly out of the estate and park my car behind a small silver van, the wheels on the passenger side of my car up on the pavement. From here, I have a good view of the building and will see if Stijn leaves in either the lorry or the Mini. I turn on the radio, but it's frustrating, as the car switches it off after three minutes. Eventually I give up, lean back in my chair and try very hard not to let my eyes close.

I am startled by the ringing of my phone.

'Pippa, we're on our way. My team ran a search on the owners of the block of flats where Stijn Eikenboom is. You won't believe it! Flat Five is owned by an organisation called KIM Smit BV.'

'Koen Smit?' I gasp.

'We don't know for sure, but I would hazard a guess that is correct.'

'So Stijn does know Koen.'

'It would appear that way. We're getting a warrant to search the premises. It'll take a little longer, but please hold on there. We'll be as quick as we can.'

My heart starts pounding. I pray Stijn doesn't come out before Joe and his team arrive. I do not want to give chase in my car. I let Mungo slide onto the front passenger seat and stroke his ears over and over, until he shifts away from me.

I lose track of time but eventually two marked police squad cars turn into the road, followed by Joe in his car. Six uniformed police jump out.

I open my door.

'No, Pippa, you're staying here!' Joe says.

'I am not! It's thanks to me that you're here, that we know who killed Scott McDermott and Annette Gower.'

'We think we might know,' Joe corrects me. I bite my bottom lip. 'I'll call you if it's safe to do so.'

Joe marches over to the communal front door and presses something on an intercom. I can see him talking but, frustratingly, can't hear anything. I am desperate to go in, to listen to what Stijn has to say. I consider ignoring Joe, as I have done before, but this time there is a whole team of policemen, and I don't want to get in their way. I pace up and down the pavement and then see Mungo eyeing me. I unlock the car, attach his lead to his collar, and out he jumps. We walk backwards and forwards, never too far away, as I need to keep my eyes peeled, not wanting to miss out on anything. And then I stop.

Stijn is being marched out of the building in handcuffs, flanked by two uniformed officers. Joe is a few paces behind.

As he is climbing into the rear of the police car, Stijn looks up and catches me staring at him. He narrows his eyes at me and mouths something. I can't make out what he's saying, but it sends a shiver down my spine.

Someone places a hand on my shoulder, and I jump.

'It's okay, Pippa,' Joe says softly. 'You came up trumps. We've just arrested Stijn on suspicion of the two murders. Would you like to come and have a look at what we found?'

I put Mungo back in the car and follow Joe up a flight of steps. The door to Flat 5 is wide open. On first glance, there is nothing out of the ordinary. A small entrance hall with scuffed paint on the walls leads into a living room with a tattered beige sofa and a television. There is a tiny kitchen, and I can see through into a bedroom with a small double bed, unmade. The place looks barely lived in. There are no pictures or personal items to lend it warmth or individuality.

'In here,' Joe says, pushing open a door.

'A laboratory?' I gasp.

'Yup. He has quite the little factory here, and behind that door is a staircase. Do you want to see?'

'But what is all of this?' I circle around, staring at the stainless-steel counters and racks of test tubes and pieces of machinery and equipment, all of which are alien to me.

'We have centrifuges, vortex mixers, refrigerator and freezer, spectrophotometers, microscopes, spectrometers and, to be blunt, I haven't got a clue what most of this stuff is or what it does. Actually, that's not true. I think I do know what it does. I think Stijn Eikenboom is running a very sophisticated poison factory. Follow me.'

Without Joe pointing out the door, I would never have noticed one was there. It is hidden behind racks and opens with a lever; nothing as obvious as a door handle.

'Watch your steps.'

The stairs are concrete, and the air is heavy with damp and bone-chillingly cold. The stairwell is lit by a glaring fluorescent light, a jarring contrast to the atmosphere. As Joe opens the steel door facing the bottom of the stairs, a pinkish-purple glow seeps out.

The room is about ten metres square. In here the air smells damp and warm, almost jungle-like. Plants are growing on tiered metal shelving, with the strangest pink glowing lighting attached both to the ceiling and on the underside of shelves. There is a large box on the wall, lit up with blue and red lights, and a computer on a table to the right of the door.

'What is this?' I ask in amazement.

'An LED plant factory, super-high-tech. These little plants are supported with whitening light mixed by red and white LED lights to enhance photosynthesis. These ones over here, the ones that are a bit sturdier, are illuminated by red light mixed by red and blue LED light, which promotes the growth of the leaves and roots. Everything is computer-controlled. The lighting, the heat and the water. It's a perfect plant-growing factory.'

'What is he growing?' I sniff the air. 'Cannabis?'

'A few plants, but nothing much. I think this is much more sinister. I am no horticulturalist, but I would bet a lot of money on many of these plants being toxic in one form or another.'

'How do you know all this?'

Joe grins. 'I am a font of what is normally useless knowledge. Just occasionally it comes in handy. But the truth is, I saw a documentary on LED growing a few months back. The Dutch are growing lettuces and tomatoes in great big warehouses, all computer controlled.'

'I wonder where Stijn got the money to set this all up. It doesn't look cheap.'

'That we don't know. Koen Smit perhaps. We have a great deal to find out. Is this a small business or part of a much larger international poison ring? Is Stijn working alone, or is he part of a large crime organisation?'

'Do you think Lily is part of this?'

Joe shrugs. 'We need to find that out too.'

'I still don't understand why Stijn killed Scott McDermott and Annette Gower. What was his motivation?'

Joe holds the door open for me, and I step into the corridor.

'Let's go and find out. Are you too tired to join me?'

50

Gerry cannot get out of the police station fast enough.

'You didn't need to—' Arthur Quigley says as they emerge into daylight from the bowels of the building.

'Don't bloody tell me what I should or shouldn't do.'

'Indeed,' Quigley says. 'If you need anything further from me, you know where I am.'

'I need a bloody lift back to the office. The bastards made me come here in their squad car. Can't imagine what all the staff are saying.'

'I'm not sure that it is financially sensible for me to give you a lift. My office is in Croydon, and yours is on the South Coast. My hourly rate is such that it makes much more sense for you to get a taxi.'

'Off you go then!' Gerry says, flapping his hand at his solicitor and striding off down the street.

He has no idea where he is or where he's going. He just needs to get out. The bloody police! How dare they accuse him. He needs to speak to Mae, give her the heads-up that the police know about their affair. He calls her, but the phone goes straight to voicemail. Instead he calls Bella.

'Can you give me a lift? I'm in Crawley.'

'What the hell are you doing there?'

'Never mind. Just get over here.'

'I can't, Gerry. I'm in Brighton at the hospital with Ollie. He's awake and feeling the worse for wear. Get a cab.'

Gerry hangs up on Bella. His fury erupts. He kicks the kerb and lets out a blood-curdling scream. A woman pushing a pram stares at him from the other side of the road and then rushes away.

Eventually Gerry hails a taxi. The driver grins at the prospect of a nice, long, expensive fare down to Arundel. He tries to make small talk, asking Gerry how his day is going, where he lives.

'Can you just bloody well belt up,' Gerry snaps. 'I'm having a crap day and need to think.'

The driver turns on Radio 2.

Gerry calls Rocks Garden Centre.

'Can I speak to Isla-Mae Carruthers?'

'Who's calling please?'

'A client.'

'Your name, sir?'

'She doesn't know me.' Gerry assumes that Mae won't speak to him if he gives his name. The receptionist puts him through.

'How can I help?' Mae's voice is breathy.

'Mae?' he says.

There is silence, then a click and nothing. Mae has hung up on him.

Gerry doesn't go into the office. He can't bear the thought of Kelly looking at him with pity or Pete eyeing him with curiosity. It isn't every day that your boss gets taken away by the police.

He gets the taxi driver to drop him next to the Lexus, and he just hops from one car to the other. He needs to see Mae. To tell her he loves her and that he is sorry for his behaviour this morning, that his intentions were good. Of course, it is hypocritical of him to think she can't have a boyfriend when he's married. He'll pledge himself to her, get down on one knee and promise that the moment his divorce to Bella comes through, he'll make an honest woman of Mae. He has the whole conversation planned out in his head. He'll make her general manager of the garden centre and ply her with jewellery and as many holidays as she wants.

He parks up in the disabled bay at the garden centre. Buoyed up with how the conversation is going to play out, he strides through the place, his chest all puffed up, smirking. But Mae isn't there. Instead, he sees a little notice on her table: *Back at 2 pm*.

He stops a member of staff.

'Where's Isla-Mae?'

'She's literally just left for her lunch. Can anyone else help?'

'Is she on the premises or out out?'

'I'm sorry, sir. I'm not sure.'

Gerry feels the rage inching up through his chest. He knows where she parks her van – in the staff car park tucked around the back of the main car park. He races to his car, reverses the Lexus and, with stones flying up under the wheels, drives too fast over the potholes towards the staff car park. He is just in time to see Mae's van edging out, turning left on to the main road. He spins his car around and follows her.

Mae doesn't go far. Just to the local Harvester pub and restaurant a few hundred metres down the road.

'Who's the bitch going to meet? Her boyfriend probably!' Gerry mutters under his breath.

Gerry hangs back, not wanting Mae to see him. He gasps as a much older man opens her van door. He bends towards Mae and gives her a kiss on the cheek. Gerry assumed Mae's lover was someone of her own age, or a toy boy perhaps. Not a man older than Gerry.

He is tall, with a slight stoop to his back, his dark-grey hair combed over the top of his head.

As they walk towards the entrance of the restaurant, he keeps his hand in the small of Mae's back. Gerry waits. He's not sure how Mae will react. The last thing he wants is an explosion like this morning, in public as well. And then he decides. He is not going to confront her. No. He is going to be much cleverer than that.

GERRY NIPS into Worthing and goes shopping. When he returns to his car, he is laden with goodies, including a bouquet of flowers, a bottle of champagne, a silver necklace with a heart pendant and some sexy black lingerie in what he hopes is Mae's size. He then heads towards Lancing. He'll be contrite this time, apologetic, gentle. And he'll proffer the bottle of Moët and the gifts.

He parks up and waits, listening to his favourite opera tracks and singing along. His confidence soars. If that old man is her boyfriend, then he'll be no match for Gerry.

And then he sees Mae's van pull up and park on the side of the road. She climbs out of the driver's side, but that old man gets out of the passenger's door. Mae goes around to help him.

Despite Gerry's resolution to be calm, he sees red. He can't help himself. He jumps out of the Lexus and runs heavily up behind the couple. They stop a mere six feet in front of him.

'*Goedenavond. Spreek morgen*?' The man leans towards Mae and kisses her cheek.

Gerry stands there motionless. Has he got it all wrong? Has he got absolutely everything wrong?

51

PIPPA

'Who is Koen Smit?' Joe asks.

We are in a different interview room this time. It is more formal, with cameras in the corner of the ceiling and what could quite possibly be a one-way mirror on a wall. Stijn is accompanied by the duty solicitor. Joe and Mia sit opposite them. I am in a chair positioned farther back from the table, allowing me a clear view of Stijn.

'A Dutchman.'

'With a name like Koen Smit, we have worked that one out. Kindly tell us: what is your relationship with him?'

'I used to work with him.'

'At Vingerhoedskruid Pharma?'

'Yes.'

'And what is your relationship with him now?'

'I don't have a relationship with him.' Stijn crosses his arms.

'It is in your interest to cooperate with this line of questioning,' Joe says, frowning.

Stijn glances at his solicitor, who nods.

'Koen is the big boss. You'll never find him. It's his fault we're all in this mess.'

'What mess?'

'The business. The facilities you saw in my flat. The Gowers.'

'For the record, I assume you are referring to the laboratory set up in your flat.'

Stijn nods and uncrosses his arms.

'Are you running a poison business?' Joe asks.

Stijn's solicitor swallows loudly.

'Yes. I'm a chemist. I didn't want to get involved in this, but it just happened.'

'And how does the Gower family fit in?'

'Annette grows the plants and develops the genetics.' Stijn buries his face in his hands.

'Why did you kill Annette?'

His hands fall away from his face, and he slams his palms on the table. 'I didn't kill Annette! I would never harm my family!'

'From what you are saying, it would seem that Annette was your boss, not just your mother-in-law.'

Stijn lowers his voice and sinks into his chair. 'No, Annette was not my boss. I cared for her. I would do anything to protect Lily and her family. Annette had no choice.'

'What do you mean, Annette had no choice?'

'After her husband, David, died, Annette had to take over.'

'The running of the garden centre *and* the illegal poison business?'

'Yes.'

'Everyone has a choice in life,' Joe says.

'She didn't,' Stijn says in a whisper.

'And Scott McDermott. How did he fit into this set-up?'

Stijn looks up at the ceiling. There is a long silence.

'Please answer the question,' Mia urges.

'He was in charge of logistics, the admin, all sorts of stuff I don't know about. I didn't know him well.'

'Did you kill Scott McDermott?' Joe asks calmly.

'No. Why are you asking me? I would never do anything like that.' He bunches up his hands and his eyes are unblinking. 'I want to protect Lily.'

Stijn is lying. It is obvious both from his body language and his phraseology.

'We will be bringing in Lily for further questioning,' Joe says.

'Why? Lily hasn't done anything!'

There is a long pause. Joe stares at Stijn, who shifts uncomfortably in his chair.

'Look,' Stijn says eventually. 'I'll tell you everything, but here is the deal.' He thumps his fist on the table. 'You need to protect my Lily. She is innocent of all of this and she could be in danger.' Stijn is leaning so far across the table his solicitor puts a hand on Scott's arm to encourage him to sit back. 'Is that a deal?'

'We will do our best to protect Lily,' Joe says.

Stijn shakes his head. 'I need more than your best. I'll come clean if you promise to protect Lily? If you don't, I'm staying schtum.' He crosses his arms in front of his chest.

'Okay,' Joe nods.

Stijn sighs. 'Scott McDermott was about to put Annette and Lily in an untenable position; their lives were in danger. I couldn't allow that to happen.'

'And...' Joe says, with raised eyebrows.

Stijn moans. 'I didn't mean to. He attacked me, came for me out of nowhere.'

'What were you doing at Rocks Garden Centre on the evening of Scott McDermott's death?'

'Koen asked me to meet Scott. He was angry that Annette wanted to get out of the business. He and Koen needed

Annette. She had the big successful business, the infrastructure with the greenhouses, the in-depth plant knowledge. He wanted me to persuade Annette to train up Lily, to keep the business in the family. But when he told me that it was my job to rope Lily in, things got heated. Annette never knew the truth about me. She didn't know who I was or who I really worked for.'

'You attacked him?' Joe suggests.

'He attacked me first,' Stijn says.

'Scott McDermott was more than thirty years older than you. He was overweight and arthritic. You are young, fit and strong. How can you claim you killed him in self-defence?'

'Well I did.' Stijn crosses his arms again.

'Scott McDermott was strangled with a piece of twine.'

'It was impulsive. I grabbed some string that was hanging on the end of a bench of plants. He made me do it.'

It feels as if the air has been sucked out of the room. Stijn has admitted murdering Scott McDermott, and it is quite clear from his words that no jury would consider his actions to be in self-defence.

'So, if you killed Scott McDermott, then we must assume that your life is in danger too.'

Stijn shakes his head. 'I'm too valuable to them. A joke, isn't it?'

'Why did you kill Annette?'

'I didn't.' The anger has dissipated, and Stijn sinks down in his chair.

'How long has this poison business been operating?'

Stijn shrugs. 'Twenty, thirty years. I don't know. Long before my time.'

'And it operates where?'

'Headquarters in Holland, here in England, and I assume all over the world. I don't know. It's not good to ask questions.'

'And who recruited you?'

'Scott and Koen. I'm a good chemist. They called me brilliant at the university. And now look at me! I never wanted this life, but once you're in, you're in for life. If you try to leave, you're dead.'

'Why did you poison Oleander Gower?'

'You're not listening to me!' Stijn shouts. 'I didn't poison him, and I didn't poison Annette.'

'We don't believe you,' Joe says, leaning forwards. 'You have the means and the motivation. Why won't you admit it?'

'You've got to protect Lily,' Stijn says, tears smarting his eyes.

'Are you suggesting that Lily is unaware of this illicit operation?'

'Yes. Lily knows nothing. That's why I gave Doctor Durrant Annette's address book. You need to protect her.'

'And the other members of the Gower family?'

'It's like the mafia. David Gower, Scott McDermott and Koen Smit, they go back years and years. Their tentacles spread deep. They made all sorts of promises: money, career prospects, cutting-edge technologies.'

'Are you saying that the drugs or poisons you were making were to be put to positive use?'

'I'm not saying anything. I don't know who they sold to, what they were used for. It was done on the Dark Web. I was just a small cog in a big wheel.'

'You must lead us to Koen Smit.'

'No. No!' Stijn shakes his head vigorously. 'I don't know how to find him, and you won't either. No one is allowed to walk away. You've got to protect Lily. Please!'

'Annette Gower was murdered by ricin poisoning. I have no doubt that we will find ricin in your personal laboratory. Are you expecting us to believe that you made the substance but you had nothing to do with administering it? Let me remind you that we found intravenous needles in your laboratory.'

'I didn't touch Annette. You've got to believe me!'

Joe and Mia look at each other with raised eyebrows. It is quite apparent they don't believe a word Stijn is saying. They appear to have some silent means of communicating. Mia gives a slight nod. Joe sits up straight.

'Stijn Eikenboom, I would like you to come with me to the custody suite, where you will be officially charged for the murders of Scott McDermott and Annette Gower and the attempted murder of Oleander Gower.'

'No! It's not right. You're not listening to me!' Stijn yells.

'Mr Eikenboom, calm down,' his solicitor urges.

'I admit to killing Scott, but I didn't kill Annette! It'll be Koen. The poisoning of Ollie, it'll be Koen. He'll be going for Lily next, and if she doesn't do what he tells her to do, she'll be dead. You've got to believe me. If Koen wants to kill someone, they're dead. He doesn't make mistakes. We're all just pawns in his big game. You've got to believe me!'

'This interview is now terminated.' Joe leans over and switches off the recording equipment.

Mia walks out with Stijn and his solicitor. We follow behind them. Stijn turns around to look at me and his stare sends shivers down my spine.

'Where are we going?' I ask Joe.

'To the bridge. It's where Stijn will be charged.'

The custody suite, or custody bridge as it is colloquially called, is in fact a space-age-looking area where three custody sergeants sit on a raised podium.

'Wait here,' Joe whispers to me as he steps forwards to stand next to Stijn and his solicitor. To his right there is a large screen. CCTV cameras point towards Stijn and Joe. As the investigating officer, Joe reads the charges that appear on the screen.

'You do not have to say anything. But, it may harm your defence if you don't mention now something which you later rely on in Court. And anything you do say may be given in evidence.'

Mia steps over and whispers in my ear. 'Do you want a coffee? This will take a little bit of time.'

I nod and follow her back to the reception area where she gets me a coffee from the vending machine. I sit on a chair and let my eyes close.

'Wakey, wakey!' Joe says as he places a warm hand on my arm. 'I'm exhausted and I assume you are too,' he says.

'Yes.' I smother a yawn.

Joe winks at me. 'Come back to mine,' he suggests, 'and let's talk about the interview. I can't begin to tell you how relieved I am this is all over.' He stretches and rolls his neck in circles.

I bite the corner of my lip. I need to play this carefully.

'I would really like to go back to my house,' I say. 'I've got loads to catch up on.'

Joe's mouth turns down in disappointment. It's almost comical to see.

'Why don't you come back to mine? I'll make us an omelette and we can have a drink,' I say.

He doesn't hesitate to accept.

I LET Joe do all the talking, quietly making us an omelette from the few ingredients I have in my fridge. Exhaustion is making my bones feel heavy, and I go carefully on the wine. I have no doubt that a glass of the fruity red wine we are drinking will put me into an immediate slumber.

'I'm so relieved this one is over. Thank you for supporting me,' Joe says as we tuck into the food.

'I think he was telling the truth,' I say.

Joe's fork hovers mid-air. 'What?'

'Stijn. He didn't kill Annette.'

'Oh come on, Pippa. The evidence is all there. Are you also going to say that he killed Scott in self-defence?'

'No. I think he murdered Scott, but he didn't kill Annette. It was in his body language, the micro-expressions, the phraseology. He was being truthful at that point.'

'And here we go again.' Joe's eyes narrow. 'As much as I respect your work, Pippa, we cannot build a case on a psychologist's hunch. Look, I don't mean to be rude, but we know he was making poisons, and I believe we will be able to pull together sufficient evidence to prove that he did it. Let's just enjoy the food and the wine and each other,' he suggests, grinning at me and holding my eyes with an expression of adoration.

But I can't. I can't accept Joe's view, and I can't separate my feelings for Joe from his dismissal of my professional opinion. We finish eating in silence.

'Would you like a coffee?' I ask.

'No, thanks.'

He stands up and takes his plate to the sink, and I can sense him coming towards me, reaching out to take me in his arms. I step backwards. His eyebrows shoot up his forehead.

'I'm really tired, Joe. Do you mind if we postpone for a couple of days just so I can recharge and catch up on sleep?'

His face falls.

'This isn't me shoving you away,' I say hurriedly. 'I am genuinely exhausted. I'm not used to all of this detective work and travel and threats with flowers!'

'At least you don't have to be scared any more,' Joe says. This time I let him scoop me into his arms. He hugs me tightly and places gentle kisses on the top of my head. 'Sleep tight, and call me in the morning.'

Mungo lifts his head, eyes Joe and collapses into his basket. I make myself a herbal tea and go to bed. But despite my exhaustion and aching limbs, I can't sleep.

And when the phone rings at 1.36 a.m., I answer it immediately.

52

PIPPA

I hold the phone to my ear as I lie in bed.

'You might have been right,' Joe says.

'What?'

I may be awake, but it doesn't mean my brain is functioning at full speed.

'Bella has been rushed to hospital with suspected poisoning. Stijn is in custody, so it can't have been him. Unless she has been poisoned with a substance that incubates over a long period, in which case he could have poisoned her yesterday.'

I am sitting up in bed now.

'I assume you've told the hospital that she might have been poisoned with deadly nightshade.'

'Yes,' Joe says. 'Belladonna. At least, that's what I suggested it might be. We won't know for sure for some time.'

'If she has been poisoned by belladonna, she can't have been poisoned by Stijn. The effects come on quickly and are particularly potent in the first three to four hours. Confusion, terrifying hallucinations—'

'A rash and convulsions,' Joe interrupts. 'You've been doing your research. According to the doctor I've just spoken to, she's presented with all of those.'

'How horrible,' I mutter. 'Is she going to be all right?'

'I don't know. We'll find out more in the morning.'

I hear what sounds like the clutter of trolleys in the background.

'Where are you?'

'At the hospital,' Joe says.

'Do you want me to join you?' I suggest.

'No. There's nothing we can do right now. Bella is in the best place. Gerry is with her. I'm going home to get some sleep, and I suggest you do too. Let's touch base in the morning. Sleep tight, darling.'

My stomach warms with his words.

'Good night.'

But he has already hung up.

I WAKE up with a start at 6 a.m. If Stijn didn't poison Bella, then who did? Belladonna is a strange substance to use because, whilst it makes someone extremely ill, unless large quantities of the root are somehow injected or ingested, it is unlikely to kill an adult. I researched the effects of Olean-der, Belladonna and Lilies whilst we were waiting at the airport.

And then it hits me.

Whoever poisoned Ollie, whoever poisoned Bella, doesn't want to kill them. If what Stijn says is correct, it is a warning. But a warning of what? Just as Stijn said, Lily must be next. Lily must be in danger.

I jump out of bed.

After a quick shower and hastily eaten breakfast, I call Joe. He speaks before I can voice my concern.

'I'm going to the hospital to talk to Gerry. I still wonder if he's got something to do with all of this.'

'You don't think it's this Koen bloke?'

'No. I reckon Koen is a red herring. Besides, the big boss of a major crime ring is not going to do anything as trivial as poison people to scare them off. If he even exists, he'll have henchmen do his dirty work for him. I am sure it's someone closely connected to the Gowers. Possibly even Lily herself.'

I am silent. Once again, I don't agree with Joe, but he is the esteemed detective, and I'm just a novice at this.

'Would you like to join me at the hospital?' he asks.

WE ARE in a small room tucked away behind the ward. It crosses my mind that this might be the room where medical staff give relatives bad news. A room with no windows; a room with soft, low seating.

Gerry is pacing backwards and forwards, his face creased with anguish.

'I love Bella. Truly love Bella. She's the mother of my children, and she can't die!' His hands are restless, in and out of his pockets, fingers raking his thinning hair. Then he blows his nose on a sodden cotton handkerchief.

'The doctors are hopeful that Bella will be fine, with no lasting effects,' Joe reassures. 'Please sit down, Mr Shelton.'

Gerry does as he is told, but he finds it difficult to remain static.

'And I so nearly destroyed my marriage with that woman,' he cries.

'What woman?' Joe says.

'It doesn't matter!'

'It certainly does,' Joe insists. 'We are dealing with a double murder and the suspected murder of your wife and brother-in-law. I suggest you tell us everything unless you want me to arrest you!'

'Oh please, no! I'll tell you, but you must never tell my Bella! Please never tell her!'

Gerry buries his face in his hands. 'I had a stupid affair with a woman called Isla-Mae Carruthers.'

'The Isla-Mae who works at Rocks Garden Centre as a garden designer? Joe asks.

'Yes. And she was stringing me along anyway. What a joke to think that I nearly tore my family in half over her!'

There is a knock on the door, and a nurse pokes her head around. Gerry jumps up.

'I've got a couple of people who would like to talk to you,' she says.

'Bella? Any news on Bella?'

The nurse smiles patiently. 'She's doing just fine, Mr Shelton. You really need to stop worrying.'

She opens the door wider, and in shuffles Ollie, wearing pyjamas and a thick, burgundy dressing gown, which could well be made from pure cashmere. He is supported by Fabian.

'Quite the little family gathering we've got here!' Ollie says sarcastically. 'I hear Bella has been subjected to the same treatment as I have. I suppose Lily is next.'

I glance at Joe in alarm. Ollie is probably right, and Lily hasn't got anyone to look after her now Stijn is in custody.

'Has anyone spoken to Lily this morning?' I ask.

'Yes. Mia Brevant has spoken to her. She said she would be at the garden centre all day, never alone.'

'I can't believe Stijn poisoned Bella too. And straight after killing Annette. What the hell does he want?' Fabian says, holding onto Ollie's arm with a firm grip.

I can see a nerve pulsate in Joe's jaw. He stands up.

'Mr Sherman, Fabian, I would like to have a discussion with you in private please.'

I frown. Why does Joe want to talk to Fabian?

'Before you do that, please can I have a word?' I say quietly to Joe.

We step outside into the corridor.

'What is it?' Joe asks hurriedly.

'Why are you talking to Fabian?'

'We have run some more background checks on Fabian. He has been involved in a lot of petty crimes and I suspect he is in a relationship with Ollie for the money and the status. On top of that, he has been very vocal in laying the blame at Stijn's door for both murders as well as the poisoning. I've come around to your way of thinking. It's unlikely Stijn did the poisoning, and I'm more of the opinion that you might be right, that he didn't kill Annette.'

'If Stijn didn't kill Annette, it must have been this Koen Smit. What are you doing about finding him?' I ask.

'I have a team looking for him, but I'm not even sure he exists. My bet is that Fabian is involved with this somehow. He is too eager to accuse Stijn.' Joe strokes my hand. 'I'll catch up with you later,' he whispers before returning back to the room.

I am sure Joe is wrong.

Fabian scowls as he follows Joe out of the room, with Ollie shuffling behind them in his old man slippers and nightwear.

I am left alone with Gerry.

'You know the bitch Mae has got a Dutch lover!' Gerry blubbers.

'Dutch?' I ask.

'And I didn't even know she spoke the language. All that time we spent together, and I had no idea! Now I just feel so stupid. We travelled abroad a few times. The first time she used a passport in her married name, Isla-Mae Carruthers. She's divorced, in case you were wondering. The second time she used a passport in her maiden name. I asked her about it.

Didn't think it was legal and all that, but she assured me it is. And now I don't trust a word she ever told me.'

'What was her maiden name?' I ask Gerry.

'Smith or something. I thought it was the German way of spelling it, but you know Mae never liked to talk about herself. It was all about sex for Mae. And bloody hell, she was good in bed—'

'Did you say Smit?'

'Yes, possibly. Maybe. What a bloody mess!'

Gerry has told me quite enough. I race out of the door.

'DS Swain. Do you know where he is?' I ask a nurse breathlessly.

She looks at me blankly. I hurry away, dialling his mobile. It goes straight to voicemail.

'Joe, call me as soon as you get this message. Isla-Mae, she's got something to do with this. Her surname is Smit. I'm going to the garden centre. I'm really worried about Lily.'

53

PIPPA

I drive so fast, I am surprised I'm not stopped by the police. All I can think about is Lily. If she isn't about to be poisoned, then perhaps an even worse fate awaits her. I try not to think about it. I try not to think about what I am doing. Putting myself in the eye of danger. Again.

I suppose it's a typical day at Rocks Garden Centre. The car park is half full; most of the shoppers are retirees or young mothers with babies and toddlers. The place looks a little more swept and cared for than it did earlier in the week, but the shock death of their owner must still be reverberating through the employees.

I stop the first member of staff I see.

'Excuse me, I'm looking for Lily Eikenboom. Where can I find her?'

The young woman appears startled. 'Do you have a scheduled meeting?'

'No, but it's urgent.'

'I'm not even sure if she's in today, but I can find out for you.'

'Is Isla-Mae in?'

'Yes, I think I saw her earlier. I'll call through to Lily's office.'

She saunters away. *Go faster*, I want to screech at her. I wait thirty seconds, a minute, and then I go, hurrying through the houseplants into the garden sundries section. I hang back for a moment, glancing over towards Isla-Mae's table, relieved she isn't there. I hurry forwards, weaving in and out of ambling shoppers, only noticing 'Jingle Bells' has been playing through the tannoy system when I am outside in the shrubs area.

The main door to the office block is open, so I ignore the 'Private. Staff Only' sign and dash through, keeping my eyes to the ground to avoid being stopped by anyone who might catch me trespassing.

The door to Annette's office is open, as is the door to Lily's. Although her coat is hanging on the back of the door and a handbag is dumped on an office chair, there is no sign of Lily. I sigh.

'Excuse me. What are you doing in here?'

'I'm Doctor Durrant, consultant with the police. I'm looking for Lily Gower.'

The man hesitates. I wonder if I am allowed to pull rank.

'I haven't seen Lily for a while. I think she was going out the back, into the private greenhouse.'

'Could you point me in the right direction?'

'Um, no. None of us are allowed to go there.'

'It's extremely urgent. Possibly a matter of life or death.'

He pales and takes a step away from me. I wonder if I've said too much.

'I'll point you in the right direction,' he says, stuttering. 'But I can't go in. None of us have the keys.'

'Thank you.'

I follow him around the side of the office block. I will him to walk faster, but he strolls along, unaware of my pounding heart and the feeling I have of imminent doom. He unlocks the padlock to a gate that leads into a back yard and a loading bay. There is a vast warehouse to the left and further glasshouses on the other side of the road.

'It's over there,' he says, pointing to a high fence. 'Knock on the door. She might hear you.'

And then he scuttles away. I wonder why he seems so nervous to be going anywhere near the family's private greenhouse. What do and don't the staff know? Joe will have to investigate.

Feeling emboldened now, I walk to the wooden fence, which must be about seven foot high. There is a gate in it. I expect it to be locked, so am surprised when, with a gentle push, it swings open easily. I see a padlock hanging loose from the rear of the gate. I stride up a short path towards the greenhouse, which to me looks like any other commercial glasshouse, with opaque glass walls and a clear glass pitched roof held up with metal framework. As I approach, I go forwards on tiptoes. I hold my breath whilst I decide whether to knock, to call out Lily's name or just to go in.

And then I hear a voice.

The sliding door has a metal frame with opaque glass. I wonder if whoever is inside can see me, or at least see my silhouette. I step closer and, with one hand on the door handle, put my ear up against the door.

'Give it to me!'

I hear a whimper and something crashing to the ground, splintering. I ease the door open as quietly as I can.

'Everything. I want everything. Annette's notes, the recipes, the growing schedules, all contact names and addresses. I know Annette had a notebook. I saw it, so don't try and pretend you don't have it.'

'I don't!' Lily sobs. 'I hid it and it's gone.'

There's a scream, and my heart feels as if it's going to burst out of my chest. Blood is pumping in my ears.

Isla-Mae has her back to me. She is holding a handgun to the rear of Lily's head.

'I can read you the list Pa gave me, and you know what it says at the bottom? If Lily refuses to hand over anything, dispose of her.'

Lily sobs.

Isla-Mae shoves Lily forwards with the gun. 'Your beloved Stijn will never disclose our secrets to the police. He knows all about the people we have got rid of in the past, the people who refused to follow orders. Even in prison, your husband won't be safe. Our spies are everywhere. If you value your life and the lives of your husband and your siblings, you will do what we tell you to do. Your stupid mother wanted to get out. She didn't want you to be involved in the business. But we like to keep things in the family. We didn't want Gerry Shelton, your idiot brother-in-law, getting his filthy paws on the business. How I degraded myself by my liaison with him.' Isla-Mae shakes her head. 'So, Lily Gower Eikenboom, or whatever you call yourself, now is your time. Give me everything or I shoot.'

'No! You've got it all wrong! That's why I—'

I hear Isla-Mae release the safety catch; her finger tightens on the trigger.

'No!' I scream, launching myself forwards.

Isla-Mae swings around, the gun pointing at me. She loosens her grip on Lily, who pulls away, her hands grabbing a terracotta pot on the bench. Isla-Mae turns back towards Lily, her eyes darting manically around the greenhouse.

'What are you doing here?' Isla-Mae yells at me.

But she is too late. With a strength that astounds me, Lily hurls the terracotta pot at Isla-Mae. It hits her on the head, and as Isla-Mae crumples to the floor the gun fires, a shot ringing out loudly, followed by the splintering of glass. Shards of gleaming glass rain downwards, cracking, tinkling. I cover my head with my arms, expecting the daggers of glass to splice, cut, embed into flesh. The screams are ear-piercing.

'Lily!' I screech. 'Lily!'

When all is silent, I know I need to look up, but I am terrified by what I might see. A large pool of blood seeping across the concrete floor, a scarlet river surrounding pale, ethereal Lily?

'Police! Police! Stand back.'

I look. There is no blood, just thousands of pieces of blunt glass scattered on top of everything like leaves that have rained down after a strong gust of wind. Lily is crouching underneath a bench of plants, shivering, shaking. She is alive. Isla-Mae is on the floor, face downwards, unmoving.

Strong arms grab me. 'Pippa, you're safe.'

54

PIPPA

'I still don't understand how it all fits together.'

It is the first time I have seen Joe since Isla-Mae was carted away in the back of an ambulance under police guard. We are out walking Mungo on the Parham estate, one of my favourite places, where Mungo can run for miles underneath the ancient oak trees and alongside the lake, eyeing the resident herd of deer with wariness. Autumn has turned the leaves shades of amber and sienna, and with every gust of wind they swirl downwards onto the sodden grass. It is cold and damp, but I don't care. It's a privilege to be able to get out into nature, to walk through this glorious historical land.

'It was certainly a complicated case. People often view garden centres as boring or staid, certainly not hotbeds of intrigue and illegal activities.'

'I read some old marketing material, and someone wrote a rhyme about Rocks Garden Centre. *It was heralded by word of mouth to be the garden centre of the South!*'

'And indeed it is! Just a shame about what was going on behind the scenes.'

'Tell me exactly how it fits together.'

Joe stuffs his hands in his pockets and gazes into the distance, where we can just about make out the roofline of Parham House.

'Isla-Mae is Koen's daughter, and she was his eyes on the ground. He planted Isla-Mae in the garden centre to keep an eye on things. No one, including Annette, Stijn or Gerry, realised who she was. It seems that ever since David died, Annette has been difficult. She was looking for any means to get out of the illegal poison business. Stijn was to become Scott's successor, Lily would be Annette's successor and Isla-Mae was to step into her father's shoes. When Stijn found out that Scott wanted to involve Lily, Stijn went ballistic and killed Scott. I don't think it was part of the game plan for Lily and Stijn to fall in love; it complicated things. It was vital that Rocks Garden Centre stayed in the Gowers' ownership, with Lily and Stijn heading it up. They could not let Ollie sell out or Gerry buy in. Due diligence would have thrown up too many unanswerable questions, too much poking around. It seems that death is the only way one gets out of that business. Isla-Mae killed Annette, probably on her father's orders, and we assume she poisoned Ollie and Bella to warn them off, but she isn't as clever as her father, because no one realised what she was warning them about.'

'What now?'

'We will investigate the poison business, find the key players and hopefully bring them to justice. There is an international arrest warrant out for Koen Smit.'

'And what about the flowers? The black roses?'

'Isla-Mae has a penchant for flowers and an interesting library of books on floriography and poisons. You might like to have a look at them sometime.'

I shake my head vehemently. 'And Fabian?'

'An innocent party. I thought he was with Ollie for the money, but I admit I got that one wrong. Ollie is broke, although perhaps for not much longer. The Gowers are free to sell up now.'

'And Gerry Shelton?'

'Another bit player. Bumbling, greedy, and also living beyond his means.'

'How is Lily doing?'

Joe sighs. 'She has disappeared. Gone travelling, apparently. She wrote her siblings a note.'

I gulp. Joe ferrets in the pocket of his waterproof jacket and produces a piece of paper.

'This is a copy of the original,' he says as he hands it to me.

I read it out aloud.

Dearest Bella and Ollie, Someone took mum's notebook. I hid it behind the Encyclopaedia Britannica and then it disappeared. At the time, I didn't know what it was, but now I suppose it was her recipe book. If you find it, please destroy it. I don't want anything to do with Rocks Garden Centre. You can sell the business, do whatever you want with it and spend my share, I don't want the money. Whatever he has done, I love Stijn and when he is released from prison, be that in five years or twenty-five years, I will be there waiting for him. Until then, please don't come looking for me. I want to be free. Your loving sister, Lily x

'Do you think Lily is still in danger?'

Joe shakes his head. 'No. She is of no use to Koen Smit now.'

'Poor Lily,' I say. 'But why did Isla-Mae want to kill Lily?'

'She needed Lily to be compliant, to either step into her mother's shoes or to hand over all Annette's knowledge. But not only did Lily not have the recipe book, it appears she is stronger minded than anyone thought.'

'And have you found the recipe book?'

'Yes, it was in Stijn's laboratory. He must have found where Lily hid it.'

'And Isla-Mae?'

'She's still in a coma. There's talk about switching off her life-support machine, but they are waiting for a next of kin to step forwards and that hasn't happened.'

'Perhaps Stijn will talk,' I suggest.

'Maybe he will when his case is up for trial, but for now Stijn isn't saying a word. There is still a lot that we don't know.'

I sigh and then I let the piece of paper fall from my fingers. The wind sweeps it up and lifts it high into the air before swirling it away from us towards a cluster of bushes and trees to our left. I am surprised to see a tree covered with sweet little white flowers tinged with pink clustering on the branches, even though the leaves are turning to ochre. So unusual for this time of year. With his long legs, Joe reaches the tree before me.

'What tree has the letter landed on?' I ask.

Joe raises one eyebrow.

'It looks a bit like a cherry tree,' he says, peering up at it.

I take out my phone and do a search for winter-blossoming cherry trees.

'*Prunus x subhirtella 'Autumnalis*', and do you know what the winter cherry tree means in floriography?'

Joe shakes his head as he picks up the letter, folds it neatly and places it back into his jacket pocket.

'It means deception.'

I think of the Gower family as we walk in silence back to the car. I think of how difficult and complicated families can become. And I think of my own, George in particular.

'Would you like to come back to my house?' Joe asks.

'I would love to,' I say. 'But can I put the offer on hold for a week or so? I need to go home and book a flight. Geneva and my new grandson are calling.'

FROM MIRANDA

Dear Reader,

Thank you very much for reading Fatal Flowers. This book is dedicated to my dad. I promised my parents I would set a novel in a garden centre, but I promise you that every element of this book comes from my imagination!

My dad has been an extraordinary innovator in the UK horticultural industry, changing the way we shop and eat. He brought us mustard and cress in a punnet, potted chrysanthemums and edible flowers, to name just a few. His was the first garden centre to have a coffee shop and led the way in transforming a garden centre into a leisure and retail destination.

As with all my thrillers, this book was set in Sussex, England. However this time, Pippa and Joe visited Holland. They went to the lovely town of Deventer, near where my husband was brought up and where his parents still live. It's well worth a visit!

Special thanks to Becca McCauley and Adriana Galimberti-Rennie for answering my questions. All mistakes are mine alone. And thank you to Emily Tamayo Maher for her support during the last couple of years, and to Brian Lynch and Garret Ryan of Inkubator Books who work their magic on my novels, bringing them to life.

If you could spend a moment writing an honest review, no matter how short, I would be extremely grateful. They really do help other people discover my books.

Leave a Review

With warmest wishes,

Miranda

www.mirandarijks.com

ALSO BY MIRANDA RIJKS

FATAL FORTUNE

(Book I in the Dr Pippa Durrant Mystery Series)

I WANT YOU GONE

(A Psychological Thriller)

Published by Inkubator Books
www.inkubatorbooks.com

Made in the USA
Lexington, KY
07 June 2019